D1498174

The Courage of Girls

The
COURAGE
of
GIRLS

JEAN McGARRY

RUTGERS UNIVERSITY PRESS
New Brunswick, New Jersey

Library of Congress Cataloging-in-Publication Data

McGarry, Jean.
    The courage of girls / Jean McGarry.
      p.   cm. — (Rutgers Press fiction)
    ISBN 0-8135-1771-0
    I. Title.   II. Series.
    PS3563.C3636C68   1992
    813'.54—dc20   91–23149
                                              CIP

British Cataloging-in-Publication information available

for Mark Crispin Miller

Contents

The Courage of Girls

Days of the Red Turk

■ ■ ■

B ALANCING on the bars of the fire escape, a blue cat peered in through the French window. For the few minutes it took the sun to sink below the skyline, the cat could see nothing but molten light reflected on glass. Once the glass had cooled, the cat saw what it had come to see, what it had seen once before and wanted to see again. The blue cat studied the yellow cat on the bed, then fixed its eyes on the girl. It scanned the one-room apartment: a clutter of scavenged or hand-made furniture, light bulbs hanging naked from the ceiling, a rough table with paints and paper, rickety easel, another rough table with a manual typewriter, and every square inch of wall lined with worn hard-cover and tattered paperback books—the walls were not plumb, so the books tilted on their metal shelves, or flung themselves on the floor, black with age and built-up wax, warped and creaky.

The Burmese let out a thin rattle: the girl and the yellow cat both looked up. With two pairs of eyes now fixed on it, the blue cat pushed open the French door and leapt into the room. The yellow cat, still limp with sleep, dragged itself to the bed's edge to watch the invader glide across the floor, watched while the blue animal stepped into the yellow cat's own litterbox, watched the vandal deliberately squeeze out a green and pungent shitball, kept watching as the thief then made over to the patch of kitchen to ram its blue head into the small plastic dish and eat the brown pellets of cat chow, eat and eat until there was not a pellet left to rattle in the dish. Then the blue cat turned and glared up at the cat on the bed—electrified, paralyzed—and then tore across the rugless floor, slid on a drop-cloth, leapt to the windowsill and licked its flank.

The cat on the bed cried, but the girl laughed until a man came crawling up to the window and grabbed the blue cat, and began to talk, crouching in the window, about his kitty, "Cantilever Roof," about the restorations being done to his apartment, about the kitty's neurotic hatred of the new decorator and the ways it had chosen to show its rage. The man, Jerry he said his name was, stayed there in the window for fifteen minutes—Loretta asked him in, but no, he had to get back—with the heavy cat perched on his knee, while he patted it and reasoned with it. Loretta asked him twice what the cat's name was; when she finally got it, the man said sometimes they just called him "Cant." Loretta's cat (still whimpering) was named Peewee, but she hesitated to tell this to the man in the window. Luckily he wasn't that interested. Come over some day, he said, his friend was an excellent cook: they made theatrical costumes, he and Larry, they worked at home and they loved to entertain.

When Cant and Jerry finally left, Loretta closed the window and locked it, then poured chow pellets into Peewee's empty bowl. The poor yellow cat had slunk under the bed and was shivering there. It refused, all that afternoon, to use its box or to eat from the bowl. It kept its eyes on the window where the foreign cat had staged its spectacular entrance, but Peewee was doomed to disappointment because Roof didn't come back that day.

Loretta relished the thought of telling Daniel, her boyfriend, about the wonderful arrogance of the pedigreed cat. It was the kind of story Daniel liked to hear because it reminded him that he and his girlfriend still had something in common. He loved Loretta more than anything: she was big and sexy, mysterious and cat-like herself, but he tired of people quickly and he had known her for two and a half years already. He had perceived the many contradictions in her thought, bruised himself on her attitude of calm and indifference and studied to his fill the coil of problems she had inherited or made up, as people so often did, to make their lives exciting. She didn't bore him so much as remind him of the fact that so much of one's life is spent on psychic upkeep. The cat story was a counter-example, an instance of the eyes looking outward at the world, so asinine, instead of looking inward. This is why he would enjoy the story, she thought, and she was right.

When Daniel came home that night, tired from teaching the philosophy survey to the jocks and frat boys at Apostles and Martyrs' College, sick and fed up with colleagues who were in philosophy just to pontificate and suck on their pipes, he was glad to hear a story about cats. It was rare that Loretta was willing to tell any story. Usually she conserved her energy and her words, and if she had a thought, she kept it to herself, or waited until she heard it expressed in someone else's words. It was just as well because Daniel loved to talk—to observe and report, analyze and interpret: he was a Freudian, a Hegelian, a Marxist, an existentialist, an ironist, an absurdist, a pragmatist and a Pataphysician, so he had many schemas to draw on and could easily convert one set of terms into another, then back again, or into a third set of terms. This was the dialectic, he had often explained to Loretta, and it was inevitable; it wasn't as slippery as it sounded.

But that night, after a day of teaching, reading and groping toward the heart of his dissertation—the 2nd-and-a-half, a bridge between Kant's Critiques of Judgment and Practical Reason, the work that would fuse Mind to Art, and both to Plato—he was ready for a joke, and the thought of *their* ("Are they gay?" "What do *you* think?") cat streaking through the window like Superman and muscling his way to Peewee's shitbox and his pellets, while fat Peewee lay prostrate with rage and impotence up on the bed, made Daniel laugh.

"So what did *you* do?" he asked, when he'd stopped laughing.

Loretta said she did nothing, but eventually, the owner came to the window and introduced himself and Cantilever.

"Who?"

"Cantilever Roof."

"You're making that up."

"You know what they call him for short?" she said, but he didn't seem to hear it.

"The cat's name is Cantilever *Roof?*"

"Yes."

"What does that mean?"

"It's a kind of roof," Loretta said, "that juts—"

"I know what it *is,*" Daniel said. "What does it mean to call a cat Cantilever Roof?"

"I don't know. What *does* it mean?"

"I'm asking you. You understand this kind of thing."

Loretta laughed, but Daniel didn't wait to hear the answer to his question. He arranged the neat stacks of books and papers on his table, and lit a cigarette. He liked to use the "good hours" of the day for his own work. A metal drafting lamp burned over his beautiful, sleek head. He could concentrate at a moment's notice and in any surroundings, and his concentration was absolute. Loretta watched him: she had known a lot of irritable people (and Daniel was very irritable), but never anyone capable of such stillness and attention, so tireless and disciplined. She liked to think of his mind as a scene out of *Metropolis*—he went down the hole and he was gone, working, till he came up again.

While he read his two Kants in four books—English and German—and made notes, she scoured the newspapers, the *News* and the *Post* mainly. For such a homebody, such a timid soul as everyone thought she was, Loretta loved the tabloids, the cheaper and more violent, the better. Every squalid word of these stories was a treat—the clichés, the stomach-turning descriptions, the outraged innocence of the reporters, the absurd but grim logic of the thieves and murderers. She didn't understand why Daniel didn't like the tabs better. According to him, the Department of Philosophy at A & M was a sinkhole of banality, an island of small souls preoccupied with their mortgage payments and patio furniture, yet *here* was a world free of middle-class pieties, a world swollen up with a certain kind of magnanimity—crimes of all levels, of all species, and for any reason. To be a thinker in this sewer, this hellhole of crime, wasn't this more Nietzschean? "Don't impute your voyeuristic tendencies to me," he said once, when she'd suggested he start reading the papers. That was before she realized that Daniel hated suggestions. She remembered the look he gave her, fragile glasses sliding down his nose, fierce furrow running from brow to hairline. "You can afford to wallow in crap like that," he'd said when she had snatched back the papers. "You have no vices," he added sourly. She laughed at the way he put it, but it was true, he said, it wasn't meant to be funny.

Daniel hadn't always been so testy. Once, on a five dollar bet that he could score, he hitchhiked to the sleepy suburb where the class of '72 at St. Mark's College on the Lake was holding a dance, and Loretta was dancing among the other juniors, the boys from St. Jude's College and the girls from St. Mark's, and three nuns stationed here and there as chaperones.

Daniel, up at Harvard, had been lonely for a girlfriend—his suitemates had kicked him out that night after making the bet, and after days of cracking jokes about a poster in their hallway: "Spring Hop at St. Mark's, Tues., 8 to 11 p.m., Rte. 12 A, Wesley, Mass."

They had made fun, mocked, but they had also mooned over the prospects of those juicy Catholic chicks, dim bulbs, liquored up and hot to trot, so they sent their emissary, Daniel. "And instead, you met me," Loretta said, interrupting the story the first time she heard it, during their first slow dance. They had also told him to use a fake name. "What is it?" she asked, but he wouldn't say.

"I've offended you," he said, when the dance was over, but neither of them moved away. "Yes, I can see that I've offended you," he repeated, as they started the next dance.

"Oh," she said, "not really. It's hard to offend me." They were dancing closer and she was enjoying it more than she had ever enjoyed dancing with the boys from St. Jude's, or the boys from St. Xavier's, the boys from Boston College, or Holy Cross, or Villanova, Providence College, Canisius College. . . .

"Stop," he said. "I don't want to hear about all those boys just so you can make up for the bet. Forget the bet."

And dancing the whole night under the discreet gazes of Sisters Martina, Fidelis, and Assumption, and the other, more astute probes of the roommates and the hallmates, they forgot about the bet. Later, these girls were anxious to know his type, a Harvard boy, and over the weeks, she told them: Mensa, the Beatles playing live in London, a motorcycle, played guitar, wrote songs and poems and had burnt his draftcard. First in his class in high school, but refused to give the valedictory speech until they let him wear a black band representing his views on Tricky Dick's criminal war.

And, unlike most boys she knew, he liked to talk. He even liked listening to a girl's talk, and not just as a ruse to get the girl out of her clothes and settled in a convenient position for the boy to relieve his aching desire. (The girls at St. M's had discussed these tricks and their own ways of teasing out the flattering talk before they relieved their own desires.) Daniel listened, and he understood what he heard. Every time they got together, they made a plan to do something, but would spend the time talking instead. She remembered telling him how she had changed her major from hospitals to art. "I walked out of my lab on inorganic bottled chemicals with Sister Francesca. It was a beautiful day. Cars were streaming up College Drive, boys coming to pick up St. Mark's girls and take them away. I went and sat down under a tree. The ground was covered in apple blossoms, and I wondered why I'd wasted the day cooking water and powder over a Bunsen burner, when I could have been doing nothing." She waited for a response. "Haha," Daniel said, "that's good. That's a beginning." "Next day," she went on, "I was in my drawing class. This class had always bored me—it bored me even more than bottled chemicals. Make marks on a page—we were drawing from life—erase, make more marks. I used to wonder what was the point of it?"

Daniel listened to this riff lying on the floor in the dorm lobby; Loretta was sitting beside him. They were waiting for the curfew buzzer to sound and the lobby to be swept clear of boys, as it was every night. His eyes were closed, he was smoking a French cigarette and listening to the story in a blue cloud. "I used to hate drawing," she continued, "but that day I loved it. We drew for four hours. Torture. The time dragged on. There was a big clock on the wall so you could see it drag." "Yeah?" "I had the abyssal feeling, just as you said, like going down a drain. And I also read that book you gave me—'Rilk,' is that how you say his name? You know, about the man who decided to stay home the rest of his life and mark time? And the one who covered his walls with confetti? I liked both of them. Do you remember?" "Yes," he said. She asked: "Am I on the right track?" He didn't answer. She explained to him that she realized now what a mistake it was to try and kill time, or to use it up doing "interesting" things: you should save it, *experience* your time, she said, so she had decided to take more of those long afternoon classes, with no distracting formulas or cooking, no memorizing or bridge games. "Just ennui," she said, "like in Baudelaire." He laughed. "Baudelaire was a fraud," he said.

Eventually, the buzzer rang and the housemother marched into the lobby with her keys. Daniel ignored her. "So," he said, "you've broken with the ordinary. It's good, but it's hard to sustain. Now you need to read Beckett and Hamsun. When you've really gotten a handle on the mind, the soul, Kierkegaard is next"—the housemother was bearing down on them, and Loretta made Daniel sit up—"then, you can read Goffman and Marcuse on the social order. That's just kindergarten, but you can start there."

After the housemother left to drive out the other boys hidden in the parlor, Daniel pulled Loretta over to sit—no, to lie on top of him. He held her head in his two hands: "Stop brooding for a minute," he said in a husky voice, "and concentrate on me." Then he kissed her, softly, yet so thoroughly that she had to steady herself on the handrail as she mounted the dormitory steps to where her friends were waiting to find out what he had done and the latest thing he had said, because he was always saying something that made them scream with shock and pleasure.

To this day, she still liked to regale her one friend Margaret—they had met in a summer school course at Columbia, "Art and Psychopathology"—with the style and substance of her very original boyfriend's remarks, lectures, outbursts and manifestos. This was part of the fun of knowing someone so smart. The two summer students met after class at a cafe in

Greenwich Village—the Red Turk, a dark, moody place that reeked of coffee, clove and reefer. A rusty red statuette bathed in the light of vigil candles was one relic among many that connected the Turk to a more romantic past, a time when Villagers had met to read poetry or listen to jazz or to a folksinger accompanied by just one guitar. Margaret sought out these places, aiming to instruct Loretta, who had spent her entire life in Catholic schools, in how to appreciate the various Bohemian modes. Some of Loretta's ignorance seemed put on. She still, for instance, called their favorite brew "not-Ex," after Margaret had hissed into the smoky room: "*Esss*-presso, Loretta. Not *Ex*."

Margaret Hopkins, a stylish girl, liked to drape herself in dead black, many layers of different fabrics: suede, silk, crepe, black denim, velveteen and leather. In the darkened Turk her pale face and moon-like eyes seemed to float above the shadowy garments. Margaret wore black, she said, because it was her aim in life to obscure the body she hated—and, it was true, you couldn't get a sense of that body's size or borders, so distracting were the wraps. In spite of the shapeless clothes, Margaret had her beauties: smooth, ivory skin and hair so black and glossy, it glinted in the cafe's low lights. Margaret didn't seem to be aware of any beauty, though, referring only to the constant and nerve-wracking difficulties of shaping and shading, with fine skins and drapes, the treacherous body.

Margaret and Loretta happened to be sitting in the Turk the day after Cantilever Roof's invasion, and Loretta was telling the story again. Margaret was only mildly interested. She'd much rather use the time to discuss her favorite subject: the other women in their class, how homely they were, how cheap and hideous their clothes and make-up, and how they were little better than glorified sluts, which was the only reason why their teacher, a sex-starved Freudian, paid any attention to them. "These Freudians, take my word for it," she told Loretta, "are insatiable. I know! I've been in analysis for years." Loretta tried to explain that Daniel, much more of a Freudian than their teacher, was not like that at all, but Margaret hadn't yet met Daniel, so she couldn't judge. Margaret was anxious to meet this man she'd heard so much about, and although she had criticized everything she heard, she still wanted to see how he could be so different from the types she knew. Just as she finished saying this, Daniel walked by the window with Peewee in his arms. Margaret said, "Hey, look at that cute guy with the cat!" Loretta looked, then flew out the door.

Peewee, still crazed by the visit of the foreign cat, had found and swallowed something bad; the floor was striped with cat diarrhea, Daniel said. Margaret had followed Loretta out the door and up the street. "Is that your cat?" she said. "It looks like it's dead."

But Peewee lived. He spent the night at the dog and cat hospital, and Loretta, Daniel and Margaret (Margaret had sat in the waiting room while the cat doctor pumped Peewee's stomach, and she stayed until they knew Peewee was safe) went to get something to eat. At first, Margaret and Daniel had nothing to say to each other. Margaret, in addition to catching Daniel being sentimental about a cat, stood for everything Daniel hated, and Daniel could see this before the girl had said a word. Loretta mentioned how they were both from Chicago and had both gone to school in Boston. "Sarah Lawrence," Margaret said, "unless you know something I don't, is *not* in Boston, Loretta. But I did go to high school in Boston—is that what you meant?"

Margaret did not wait for an answer, but asked Daniel where *he* had gone. He said it didn't matter. "Tell me," she said. "I went to school in Boston," he said. "Where in Boston?" "Harvard College," Daniel said. "Really? I thought you went to a Catholic school." "I was in the seminary for one year, if it's any of your business," Daniel said, "and I studied"—looking not at Margaret, but at Loretta, who wasn't supposed to relay personal

information about him, especially not *this* thing—"in Rome."
Margaret said nothing; she expelled some air and drank half her
glass of wine, then some water. Daniel hardly looked at her the
entire evening, but that didn't mean, Loretta explained when
Daniel had gotten up and gone to the bathroom, that he didn't
like her. "He despises me," Margaret said. "He never looks at
anyone when he talks," Loretta said. "No matter who he's talking to, he always looks at me." "Why it that?" Margaret asked
blandly.

When Daniel returned to the table, Margaret patted her
lips with the cloth napkin, and gave Daniel a smile, first finding
his face and then smiling into it. "What class were you in? My
brother went to Harvard and so did most of my friends, and all
of my brother's friends. My parents graduated from Harvard."
She gave Daniel no chance to respond. "One of the buildings,"
she went on, "is named after my grandfather. Almost all my
ancestors were Harvard graduates, some of them were enrolled
at birth. I didn't go," she said quietly. "I couldn't get in," talking directly to Daniel's face, less chilly, but still expressionless.
"Even though a building," she started up again and louder, "is
named after my grandfather, who designed it, they wouldn't let
me in."

Daniel must have guessed that some of this was made up,
because he didn't pay the kind of close attention that Loretta had
told Margaret he could pay, so Margaret went on: "Do you see
what I mean?" "It's not that complicated," Daniel said. They
were eating lemon ices and plain white cookies, drinking white
wine and soda water (Margaret had ordered). "You're saying
your whole family went to Harvard and even donated a building, but that didn't get you in. And you're anxious to tell me
why, so go ahead." Margaret chose a cookie. "No," she said, "I
didn't get in—that's right—but not because of my family. It
was because," she paused, "of what happened in high school."
Daniel lit a cigarette and sat back in his chair: "So what did you

do in high school? Were you expelled? No, they like that kind of thing—they encourage criminality in their students. It's useful in later life." Margaret had bitten all around the edge of the cookie, and put it down. "They like a certain kind of imbecile, too," Daniel went on. "Did you burn down your high school? Were you in a mental hospital? Did you shave your head and join the Krishnas? They can't get enough of that stuff." Daniel was still not looking at Margaret, but she was looking at him. "So what did you do?" he said in a voice so loud, the couple at the next table turned to look. "You must have bored them. They hate bores."

Loretta was surprised at the tone—Daniel was famous for saying nasty things just for the fun of it, but this was different. It must have been the strain of waiting to see if Peewee was going to pull through. But Margaret—and this was even more surprising—seemed to be pleased; she liked the attention, and didn't seem to mind its quality. Loretta waited to see if there would be more; there wasn't, so she got up and went to the ladies' room. When she got there, she sat on a spindly chair in front of the sink—it was a filthy bathroom, small, and all the walls were covered with mirrors. There was one stall and someone was in it, and whoever it was stayed in there.

After sitting a while, Loretta stood up and tried to calm her hair, very spiky looking from the twirling and twisting she'd been doing at the table. It was light colored hair, curved around the head in a staticky fringe. The face was pale and soft with large, sleepy eyes. People said—they *used* to say—it was a pretty face, but to her it always seemed like a stranger's face. Her cousin Gloria had a theory about this; Loretta had grown up with Gloria and Gloria's parents after the accident. The cousins were looking in the bathroom mirror, as they often did—Loretta was a few inches taller, so Gloria stood on the bathroom scale. They had just tried the same purple lipstick that Loretta had brought home from the 5 & 10. At first, it looked beautiful, then Gloria announced: "It's looks crummy on you, and it looks lousy on me." How can you tell? Loretta asked her. Gloria didn't understand: "Can't you see what you look like?" she asked back, pointing to the image in the mirror. Loretta said she could see the different features but couldn't put them all together into a face that she could remember. Gloria found this puzzling, but soon hit on what she thought was a satisfactory explanation: "It's because you can't see *her* face. That's why you can't see your own!" she said. Whose face? Loretta had said, but she knew who Gloria meant.

The woman in the stall finally came out and glanced quickly into the mirror, saw both herself and Loretta, who *could* imagine her own face in that woman's critical eyes. She could always see herself through another set of eyes and Daniel had worked that one out: "The looking-glass self," he had said. That meant her self-image was a product of whatever criticism was flickering on other people's faces.

Now another woman had pushed into the small bathroom, and Loretta squeezed past her, returning to the table where Margaret and Daniel were staring in different directions. She couldn't read their mood. Margaret looked up and said she had to go: her father would be calling and she had to be home. She said goodbye to Daniel. "I never found out," she said, "what you did in the cemetery—I mean seminary." Daniel laughed. "You know what I mean," Margaret went on. "I did most of the talking."

On the way home, Loretta was wondering what Daniel thought of Margaret, but didn't think it wise to ask directly, in case it was bad or he didn't want to talk about it yet. They were walking in a strangely quiet 8th Street, west of Broadway. Where was everybody? Lights were on in every block: felafel counter, boot shop, movie theater, deli, guitar store, but there

were no people on the street. Loretta could hear the clunk of
Daniel's boots. It had been a tiring day and poor Peewee, hurt
and afraid, was in the hospital with all those strange cats. They
reached their street and turned into it: still quiet, and their
building, all four floors, was entirely dark. Daniel nudged
Loretta through the doorway, and they filed up the stairs.
Peewee was not scratching at their door. Peewee did not try to
make a run for it when they entered, but lying on the floor just
inside was a note: Sorry about your cat, Jerry S. "How does he
know what happened to Peewee?" asked Loretta.

"They know everything," Daniel said, then added: "They
must have heard him puking."

"Oh."

In the course of the evening, Loretta offered Daniel a few
facts about Margaret. He said he wasn't the least bit interested.
But long after the conversation was over and forgotten, he sat up
from where he was lying on the bed. "With a shark like that," he
said, "you're in way over your head."

"What shark?"

He flopped back down. "You know what I mean."

Loretta considered: she called up an image of Margaret,
lurching as she did through the rubble of her studio, but she
could see no shark. Margaret was an artist, a materialist, and her
life was tied up with things and battles with things, a life Daniel
would never understand. Margaret battled on two fronts. There
was the studio that her mother had rented for the year and
Margaret had crammed with so much stuff that there wasn't
room for an easel. When she painted, Margaret had to tack papers onto the wall or hold them on her lap. She tried to be
careful, but there were always accidents. Margaret tripped on an
open jug of turps and knocked it over, stuck her feet into open
paint cans, dropped envelopes of glitter, spilled boats of glue,
and once sat on a stack of wet pallets. She broke two clay busts
borrowed from the school when she was interested in sculpture,
had been poisoned, punctured and clunked in the head. The

little room was a junkyard and Margaret kept dragging in more things: things she had taken from the supply room, or bought with her credit card at the art stores in the Village. Her apartment was the same—jammed and crushed with supplies and appliances: two exercise machines, a stereo and six speakers, a tape player, two air conditioners, a humidifier, white-noise machine, odds and ends of furniture, unopened boxes of clothes, two trunks and hundreds of small statues made of glass, porcelain, stone, marble, papier-mâché, plush, wood, straw, brass, ivory, jade, soapstone, leather, crystal and shell. The statues were mostly human figures, but there were a few animals, some Buddhas, abstracts and a collection of hands, feet, heads and genitals. None taller than three inches, these statues stood on every free surface, including the bedboard, the rim of the sink, in bowls and ashtrays, on top of the records, along the windowsills, on the arms of chairs, on the stereo dustcover, as well as massed in a big clutter in each corner of the room and marching forward. Margaret tried to buy one of these every day; some were cheap, some weren't. She felt that they organized a chaotic life: "I'm not centered like you," she explained to Loretta, "and I have no boyfriend, so I need things."

Loretta admired Margaret for the humor (if it was humor) she could inject into a hobby that might otherwise seem greedy. She could breathe in Margaret's easy, crowded rooms—but was it breathing, or just a cheap way of scoring off Margaret's foibles? The sin of pride—did she still believe in it? Or did belief even matter, if the sin of pride could operate without it?

Loretta decided—while she and Daniel were lying there relaxing—to go ahead and tell him about Margaret's collections. He listened, but said nothing. Suddenly, through the thin wall behind them, came a series of knocks and thuds (fighting?), then a burst of glassy arpeggios (dancing?). Loretta looked for Daniel's reaction, but there was none. "You don't care about things," she said carefully, "I know."

"I'm not interested in the shit people own and I'm less

interested in their personal lives. In fact—" Daniel sounded like
he was just warming up, but he didn't say any more. He seemed
caught in an atmosphere like glue or honey: every time he lifted
his head out, or an arm, it was sucked back in. "I don't need to
be reminded how trite life is. The futile things people do to
make themselves seem interesting." He paused, and said in a
different tone: "Who cares how many little Buddhas she has!
Only you."

Loretta, who had been hugging Daniel's slim, well-shaped
chest, unclasped her arms and moved away from him. "Why are
you so hard on people?" she asked him.

"Why shouldn't I be hard on people when they're so easy
on themselves? You don't understand this, Loretta, because
nothing ever bothers you. That's your problem."

When she didn't answer, he turned to look her in the eye:
"Admit it."

"I do," she said serenely.

The apartment next door was perfectly quiet. "That means
nothing," he concluded, "because you'd admit anything." He
went on: "Margaret is a simp and a fool, but she needs an audience to function. That's where you come in."

Loretta was silent.

"It's your code," Daniel went on, "speaking through you.
Your code that says: shrink the self and pump up the jerks. It
works," he said. "The jerks always fall for it, and why wouldn't
they? They don't know it's insincere. They don't know it's a leftover from the nuns."

"A leftover?"

"You know what I mean."

Loretta considered. "Maybe," she said.

"*Maybe!*" Daniel shouted. "Either I'm right or you just let
me throw up all over you!"

Loretta laughed.

"It's not that funny," he said, but he, too, was smiling.

But it was turning into a serious conversation, and Daniel

noted the number of times he had observed the code in action, how it functioned, its relation to present life and past. It was flattering to hear how each quirk could be translated into a mechanism of the greatest complexity. Daniel treated her psyche with the utmost respect. Maybe he overdid it sometimes, but people had always shown too much interest in her—pushing and probing with the kind of curiosity a child feels for an odd piece of sluggish life, a caterpillar or guppy.

"That's how you protect yourself," he was saying. "It's understandable, given all you've been through. I just think it's wasted effort, that's all."

She was silent, so he fell silent too. "It's so hard to have a conversation with you," he said glumly. She nodded. "Can't you see that things have changed?" he went on. "You're with me and I love you. Why doesn't that make a difference?" She said it did, but he insisted it didn't. It was his fault, he said: he was a second-rate thinker, emotionally compromised. He had nothing to offer. "Yes," he went on, "you're just too beaten down to admit it. You don't feel any safer with me than you did with them. Otherwise, you wouldn't pick a friend like Margaret."

Loretta closed her eyes. She was going to ask what else was wrong with Margaret, but she should know the answer (Everything!) already. The harsh light from the naked lightbulb made her eyes tear and the water was squeezing through the crack between her eyelids. And slowly I turn, she whispered, step by step, inch by inch. . . . And she laughed.

Daniel heard the laugh; he studied her face. "You're happy in some way and it's not me who makes you happy. That's true, isn't it?"

What was the answer to this question? While she was thinking, Daniel kissed her in a way that meant more was coming. But now she was entering the void he had just left, sinking into it, the wind of thoughts he had set in motion whirling around her. Like a corpse she received his attentions, his embraces, his tender words. He continued to give them, then leapt from the bed and cried out: "You say you love me—yet I never feel it! Why *is* that?"

"What are you brooding about?" Margaret said the next day, when Loretta found her in the studio. Margaret had pinned a sheet of rice paper to the wall and was smoothing it with her fingers. Loretta found a nail barrel to sit on and was squeezing an old tube of paint until the very last bit of chrome yellow had rolled up to the mouth. "Nothing." Margaret turned back to the rice paper: she rolled her shoulders and did a little war dance, but then she blocked the paper with her body so that Loretta couldn't see what she was doing. Margaret never read philosophy, or anything hard, so Loretta wondered if they had any common ground for discussing problems. When she had suggested a couple of titles to Margaret, the girl replied that she was an artist and didn't need to read. "Do you think I'm one?" Loretta had asked her. "One what?" Margaret said. "An artist." "I don't know." In college at St. Mark's on the Lake, one of her teachers had said: "You're an artist, or rather" (he was cute, all the students liked him, but he was married, with two babies, to a doctoral student in Cambridge) "you could be, Miss Costello. You have the talent." They were in his office. No one had ever said a thing like that to her before, but as soon as she heard it, she thought there might be something else involved. "But you have to let people help you," he went on, "and from what I've noticed, you don't let people get very close, do you?" Loretta couldn't quite believe what she was hearing, but he said it again in a different way, and it had nothing to do with art.

Margaret turned around and stepped gingerly between several stacks of paint-encrusted pallet boards, and Loretta saw on the rice paper a beautiful calligraphic *L,* in blue. "This isn't *L* for you," Margaret explained, "although you can think of it that way if you want. An artist's work is open to any interpretation, but it's really an *L* for love. It's my birthday present to Mr.

Aschenbach—his middle name is Louis. I'm going to stick it in the portfolio my mother bought me from Abercrombie. You should see it. It's not really a portfolio, it's a big suitcase, big enough to put everything in."

Margaret said she was bushed. She had been absorbed for twelve full minutes in the *L,* and enough was enough, so they made their way to the cafeteria for lunch, and Margaret spent the time looking for Mr. Aschenbach, talking about the *L* and the suitcase it would come in. Loretta ate half of the tuna sandwich that Daniel had made: How could anyone not like Margaret, she thought—Margaret was the life force.

That night, Daniel and Loretta went to pick up Peewee at the dog and cat hospital. Daniel carried him home in a blanket. Peewee looked thinner and his fur was greasy and matted. When they got home, Peewee jumped up to the windowsill and whimpered. Loretta lifted up the cat, and they both stuck their heads out the window, looking long and steadily to the left, but there was no one on the fire escape and the Roof window was closed.

"What are you doing?" Daniel asked, but before she could answer, he had arranged his books and resumed his work. It had been a nice, peaceful day. Loretta carried Peewee to the bed and went back to pull the window closed. Later, Daniel made a simple dinner, then worked under his lamp while Loretta sat on the bed, sketching necks and heads. A moon had risen to the fire escape and now peered in the window. Even with the lamps blazing in the room, the moon dropped its own greenish light on the uneven boards of the floor. The evening was perfectly quiet—Daniel had unplugged the telephone and would read silent and immobile at the plank table until long after Loretta was asleep. He was getting closer to the heart of the problem—he said this emphatically—or was he?—he also said this. Loretta drew one more stumpy muscular neck: Daniel had a long thin neck with a prominent bump of vertebra visible through the

back of his shirt. There were a few versions of this neck on the
page, too, but there wasn't much to draw, a simple column with
a node; everything was in the face, but the face was turned away.
He had books stacked upon books, he had made several pages of
notes, he had drunk two cups of coffee, a coke, and smoked half
a pack of cigarettes; the floor was covered with a light and uneven snow of balled-up white sheets, but there was also a small
stack of unrejected sheets on the right-hand corner of his desk.

When Loretta awoke some hours later and saw Peewee in
the sunken pool of the other pillow, she looked over that pool to
see Daniel asleep at the desk, his face on the table resting on an
arm and the room cloudy and acrid with smoke. Turning to the
window, she saw that the green moon had drifted up beyond the
fire escape and now was nested in the branches of the two courtyard trees, spiky and leafless. These trees shared a grassless bed.
They were very old and they looked old; they had had their
summers and springs, they had grown up in a field with other
trees, grasses, with small sleek animals like you, she said to
Peewee, and big ones. Pastures, meadows, streams, hillocks and
the salt breeze blowing on the island, and the trees—were they
that old?—with a clear view to the harbor, and of both rivers.
Now, in their oldness and feebleness, they were penned in by a
blacktop border and by brick walls on all sides. Their conditions
were degraded—even the rain from heaven was poison—but
still they tolerated life. Was it toleration, or simple renuncia-
tion? Let this be your model, she whispered to the cat, who,
hearing one of its favorite voices, moved from the pillow pool to
the smooth neck, to enjoy the warmth there and to cover the
exposed skin with a yellow fur. With this comfort, and the sentimental thought that went with it, she fell back to sleep,
ignoring the scene of frustrated industry at the table, labors
discontinued, talents bullied and cursed, and the industry of
frustration also building inside her.

And they all slept until a different ball rose up the window and pierced Peewee's green and sparkly eye, and lit the sleeping scholar, making of his reddish black hair a fiery net, and seeding his brain with the day's thoughts and doubts. Loretta had a doubt, waking and seeing him radiant in a solar halo: How much life, in a poisoned condition, could they tolerate together? Daniel didn't have much tolerance for conditions. He wasn't a type like Kant, happy to be a stunted tree in a tenement courtyard. Daniel would be better off planted in a glass box, a corporate atrium in midtown, fanned by precision winds. He could see out, but nothing could get in, not the weather, not the cars in the street, wailing, screeching and crunching. He should be some kind of shiny-leaved mock-tree, and fill the glass space with the air of philosophy, hanging a green inedible ball on each branch. This was good: too bad he wasn't awake to enjoy it. Each of the trees in his artifical garden could be different so the place wouldn't get too boring. The trees wouldn't touch, but each rootball could twist unmolested in its own barrel.

When she woke again, she was facing in and he was working; she could hear the steady beat of a foot against the table leg, and saw fresh smoke billowing into the room. Without having to look, Loretta could tell that the thoughts were now falling thick on the page. There would be more white balls on the floor, but the stack of paper on the desk would be tucked under his elbow, anchored there until he could type it and then put it in the freezer where he kept his best sheets of the growing 2nd-and-a-half. She tried to go back to sleep. How many nights would he need? Every night of his life, maybe. And it would help, she said to Peewee, if you were less of a big, fat slug. She smiled. And, she went on, I don't see why you can't shape up. But Peewee was studying the window. Even so sluggish a being had a life, and into that life there had bounded a magnificent blue thing to keep this languid animal on the sharpest pins and needles.

Three Ventures

■ ■ ■

I T was a beautiful February night: freezing, clear, the sky pricked with stars, when you could see the stars. Sometimes all you could see were lights: orange neon, blue neon, glaring pink sodium lamps, thousands of incandescent bulbs on theater marquees, a stream of car headlights, floodlights, spotlights, laser lights, fluorescent bars around the store windows and the subtle fan of light spreading under the heated awning of the hotel. Even when you couldn't see a single star for the lights, the sky was a high, black bowl. It was the real winter, Mrs. Eikenberg said when they piled out of the cab and into the lobby of the Carlyle Hotel, bringing the cold in with them and dispersing it as they shed coats, scarves, gloves, capes and Mrs. Eikenberg's fur-cuffed, high-heeled boots.

They were having a night on the town. Mrs. Eikenberg (Lila Adele James Hopkins Eikenberg) was free; she had left Mr. Eikenberg in Chicago, where he always stayed when she came to visit her daughter, Margaret, a painter in New York, a bitter, unhappy girl, according to him, and a steady drain on her mother's pocketbook. "But he doesn't hate you," Mrs. Eikenberg said, "as you always say."

"I never say that," Margaret said. "What I say is that I hate *him*."

Mrs. Eikenberg smiled at Daniel, as if he understood about stepdaughters and stepfathers. She had talked to Daniel most of the night, directing her rapid, breathless comments to that fragile skull with its tense-looking face; his lips were dry and chapped, a bad sign. She was explaining how she came to marry Mr. Eikenberg—they had all had martinis, and now they were drinking the first bottle of wine, as Mrs. Eikenberg ordered courses of appetizers and fish, veal coins and then the sweet, air-filled dessert. "He's a homely man, I don't deny it," she said. (She couldn't see, Loretta guessed, how uninterested Daniel was in this kind of topic.) "That's why Margaret never liked him. *Her* father—I don't like to say his name, Daniel. When I think how nasty he was in every—"

"He was not," Margaret said.

"But he was a handsome man," Mrs. Eikenberg continued. "At least my daughter thinks so."

"Oh, please," said Margaret.

"If it wasn't for this homely man, whom she despises," Mrs. Eikenberg went on quietly, "we wouldn't *be* a family. And she knows that."

"Can we change the subject, please?"

But Margaret didn't change the subject. For fifteen minutes more, she monopolized the conversation with funny stories about Dad and how cool he still was. He was staying at the Hounds Club ("Harvard Club," Margaret explained to Daniel) for good now, although he also had a little place in Westport. He was busy spending the rest of the family money—what he hadn't already spent—as fast as he could, drinking day and night to do it. Margaret and her mother never saw one cent of this money, she went on, because it was locked in an uncrackable trust with not a drop of liquid that Mr. Hopkins hadn't already sucked up in his earlier days.

"Mr. Hopkins?" Loretta said.

"Sometimes Margaret likes to call her father 'Mr. Hopkins,'" Mrs. Eikenberg explained to Daniel. "That way she can enjoy his immaturity without being hurt by it."

Margaret talked right over her mother. Dad was still the coolest guy. Daniel, who hadn't spoken for a while, said he'd rather hear about the homely man.

"Who?" Margaret and her mother said in unison.

"Mr. Eikenberg. What's his first name?"

"Herbert," said the mother, and then she excused herself to visit "the powder room."

"His name is Her-bert," Margaret said, "and don't call him Herb. He *luhves* Mummy. When she leaves him, he's so sad, sometimes she has to plug him into the wall to keep his lights on. Imagine going to bed with a man like that?" she said to Loretta.

Here was Mrs. Eikenberg, her face pale from a layer of powder and by contrast to the liver-colored lipstick. Loretta thought she was pretty good-looking for fifty; a terrible color lipstick, though. Daniel was studying his menu, so as not to have to honor Margaret and her puerile remarks with his attention. He'd held a chair for Mrs. Eikenberg, and she sat in it, knocking over the two umbrellas she'd hooked to the back of it—the only proof so far, Loretta thought, that she was related to Margaret. Mrs. Eikenberg had bought three not-tennis umbrellas ("Not tennis, Loretta," Margaret had already said. "*Golf*"), one for herself and one for each of the girls, and presented them in her hotel room when Loretta, Daniel and Margaret came to call that afternoon. The mother was sorry she hadn't brought something for Daniel. "All I hear," she said to him, "is 'Loretta this, Loretta that,' but Margaret has never said a word about you."

"Not true," Margaret said, but her mother paid no attention.

They had looked at the umbrellas, and Loretta had opened hers; then they lay them side by side across the starchy white bed, huge, and there was an Oriental rug, four handsome, uncomfortable chairs, floor ashtrays and brass lamps. Mrs. Eikenberg's beautiful supply of perfumes and cosmetics—gold and crystal flagons—was arranged on the dark wood of the bureau. Mrs. Eikenberg sat down on the bed beside her daughter. The couple perched on the divan. Loretta could see the mother's eyes fixed on Daniel, so tall and dark-haired, a slim column in his dark suit and narrow English shoes. Daniel rose and circled the room, coming to rest at the window and turning his back to them.

"It's too early for dinner, isn't it?" Mrs. Eikenberg said. "So what shall we do, children?" She got up and circled the room, landing next to Daniel and putting a broad, flat hand across his back. Margaret pointed to the big glassy-looking ring on her finger and mouthed the word 'vulgar.' Daniel must have felt the ring through the suit, tapping with its silver band against his thin back. They were looking out at a church, all pink and rosy in the twilight.

"Why don't we visit the cathedral," Mrs. Eikenberg said briskly, patting the back and pointing out the window with the other hand. "I've never seen the inside. There might be an afternoon mass. I've never been to a mass, and neither has Margaret, I'm sure. Could you take us there, Daniel? There's a lot we don't know that you could explain." She turned to include Loretta, solitary on the divan and changed her tone slightly: "Now you'll tell us you don't go anymore."

There was a ripple of anxiety in the warm hotel air. Loretta could see it stiffen Daniel's already stiff back. The sun had dropped to the level of the green building across the way and was piercing their window and putting a fire to the mirror "You want us," Loretta said, attempting a tone of her own, "to take you and Margaret, a pair of infidels, to mass—which we don't go to anymore, just so we can explain what you don't know?" Daniel laughed. Loretta's face flushed red. Then Mrs. Eikenberg laughed and gave Daniel's back a hug.

"Forget the mass," Margaret said.

Her mother moved to the mirror to apply a tissue to the edges of her dark red lips. "I didn't mean anything by it, I'm sure," she said.

"Yes, you did," said Margaret. "I'll tell you what you want to do, Mummy. You want to get into a cab, drive uptown, get out—" "Don't be rude, Margaret," the mother said, putting an extra tissue in her purse.

"—so we can walk around for a while, then take us to wherever you're taking us, Mother."

No one liked this tone. To make up for her outburst, Loretta started telling a story Daniel had told about how F. Scott Fitzgerald and Hemingway were in a hotel room one day and—

"You're getting it wrong," Daniel interrupted.

"—a fight broke out," she went on, borrowing something from Margaret's tone, "over even less than this."

"Less!" shrilled Margaret.

"Are you ready?" Mrs. Eikenberg said, and Loretta got right up.

When they got to the restaurant, Mrs. Eikenberg sat next to Daniel. They had eaten their first course, a jellied soup, when she suddenly stood to allow a cracker crumb to slide off her shiny blue dress—or was it to show Daniel her lap with its delicate nest of sharp wrinkles and shadows? They had discussed the homely man and now Mrs. Eikenberg was asking after Dad. "How is that man? Tell me how he really is."

"Daddy's fine," said Margaret with her mouth full. "I see him all the time and he's fine." Margaret looked at Daniel when she said this, and Mrs. Eikenberg looked at Loretta. Loretta was the one who knew that Margaret never saw Daddy, although sometimes she talked to him on the phone, if she thought to call him.

No one had seen him, Margaret explained to Loretta the first time they had had this conversation, in ages. The last time he'd visited home was five years ago, on his fiftieth birthday. Before that, he had come home that one time at Christmas to break Mrs. Hopkins's neck. Margaret blamed her mother for everything. "She was different then," she told Loretta. "She's mellowed out a lot. In fact, since she's married Ugly, she has no nerves at all." Margaret told this story a long time ago at the Turk, after Loretta had told a story of her own. "Your mother and father are both dead," Margaret said, in response to the story of the accident, a story that wasn't very practiced and was hard to tell, but Margaret had listened patiently and didn't ask any unnecessary questions. "So you think that's the worst that can happen? I'm not saying it isn't. I'm just saying that other things can be just as bad."

Mrs. Hopkins hadn't gotten a Christmas present in ten years, maybe longer, and that very Christmas, Mr. Hopkins took the train up from the city in a suit he'd worn for a week, without changing his underwear, Margaret said, *or* his socks, carrying a Christmas present. There was nothing for Margaret and nothing for little Sam, only the small, gift-wrapped box for Mummy. "It was a Tiffany's box," Margaret said, "even *I* knew that." "How?" Loretta asked, but Margaret was still talking.

"Mummy was excited. Daddy took the box out of a little shopping bag and threw it on the dining room table. I grabbed it, but she ripped it out of my hands. I thought she was going to hit me—and she never hits me. If she hit me, I'd hit her right back. Daddy said, 'No, Mags, you let Mummy open her Christmas box.' Sam was there too and he said it wasn't Christmas yet. Daddy said it didn't matter. He had the Christmas spirit, that's what mattered. He could see we all had it too. 'Don't you have the Christmas spirit?' he said, and we all screamed, 'Yes!' 'Good,' he said, because he had the Christmas spirit too and he had had it for a long time, only we didn't know because we hadn't seen him in a coon's age."

"Did he say that?" Loretta asked. Margaret gave her a look, so Loretta urged her to return to the moment when the box was flung on the table.

"She opened the box," Margaret said, "and in the box were earrings." Loretta said that was nice: earrings from Tiffany's. "No, it wasn't nice," Margaret snapped, "because they were the cheapest earrings on earth. They were diamonds, or they were supposed to be diamonds, but they were just chips, just specks—I used to lie awake in a rage thinking about those earrings. And they weren't from Tiffany's either. They were from some cheap junk store."

"Why did he do it?" asked Loretta.

Margaret glared at her. "Don't you understand anything?"

Loretta understood that the cheap earrings were an insult, and coming in the Tiffany's box made it worse, but why did her father go to the trouble of doing it if he hated her that much?

"I don't know," Margaret said. "He's a bastard," but she seemed annoyed by the question. "Should I go on?" she asked. "Should I tell the rest of the story, or are we going to stop here?"

"Go on."

"My mother spent her life nagging him about money. She felt her life was supposed to get better—like Cinderella's—not worse, like it got."

"Yeah?"

"Well, she took the cheesy earrings and threw them right at his filthy suit, and he said, 'Is this the thanks I get?' and the battle began. She ended up with a broken collarbone—not broken exactly—fractured, but the dishes were broken and the chairs and furniture all kicked over and kids crying and Mummy screaming, Daddy yelling and screaming and Mummy crying and screaming and Uncle Dudley running over from Winnetka to chase Daddy with the fire iron."

"What did he do?"

"He got back on the train. He had ruined our Christmas," Margaret said, "so he could go home."

Loretta considered: "Why do men do things like that?"

"You should have seen some of the things she did to *him!* It was mostly *her* fault. She has no style. Her father earned all his money, but *his* father came from real money. With real money, it doesn't matter if you have it or not. That's what she never understood."

Loretta waited for Margaret to finish. "And he came back five years later?"

"No, five years ago. It was right after my college graduation—I wasn't exactly graduating. I had a few papers from freshman year, and from the other years, I hadn't done. I can hardly remember, but I was nowhere near finished. I told him I was graduating anyway, and he believed it. He came up on the train."

"Your father was pretty loyal, all things considered," Loretta said.

"Loyal! You call that loyal?"

"I don't know, there's something about it that's loyal."

"You're weird, you know that?"

Loretta smiled. "So what else happened?"

"Well, he called us up from the station. She was still in love with him, you know."

"Why?"

"What do you mean 'why?' He was so *loyal*," Margaret said as sarcastically as she could. "She's still in love with him now."

"She is?"

"Well, she's been living with the troll for over five years. She was with him then, so she couldn't exactly invite Dad in."

"By 'the troll,' you mean your stepfather?"

"Loretta! Can't you follow a story!"

"Go on."

"Well, by then, he was cheating on her too."

"Really?"

"She found out because she liked to go in on the train during the day and surprise him. Big mistake. One time she went in there and surprised herself. He was out on a date. Someone in the office must have told her. See?"

Loretta waited.

"You don't see, do you? She was human. Would *you* like to get kicked out of bed that way? She went insane." Margaret paused to collect herself. "Well, she didn't go insane immediately." Loretta understood this part of the story because Margaret was always talking about it: psychiatric hospitals, crash diets, fat farms, the sleeping pills, the anti-depressants, the tranquilizers and the booze. And this was *after* the troll was in the picture. "She wasn't like us, you know. She had no ambition, no plans. All she had was him."

"Oh."

"Anyway," Margaret sighed, "before too long, she started to like the troll because he was at least stable, and talk about loyal! He was gross but he makes lots of money. She loves money. So does Daddy, but he hates to work. I told you that already, didn't I?" She had, but Loretta couldn't decide about this mother and father, Mrs. Eikenberg and Daddy. Partly, it was because Margaret changed the story slightly each time she told it, depending on which parent she was mad at; and partly, it was because they didn't *act* like a mother and father, they acted more like boyfriend and girlfriend. Never in her life had Loretta seen a mother and father act so young. Her own mother and father were old from the start, and Aunt Rita, although more immature than they were, at least looked her age. Aunt Rita wasn't in love with Uncle Ted and didn't expect to be. Uncle Ted had never been in love with her. He did have regrets—there was no doubt about that—but wasn't it true that they all had more important things to think about than love?

This is a point that Daniel would not discuss, dismissing—as he did—her description of the parents' struggle with daily life. It was exaggerated, he thought, and more of a "screen memory" than any reliable account. Their "struggle" was part of the pathetic story of the child abandoned—a true story, he acknowledged—but overdetermined and too useful in her psychic economy to be simply "factual."

Listening to Margaret now bragging about Dad that night over dinner, Loretta watched to see how Daniel was taking it. He was taking it fine; there was not a single line of tension on his face. Mrs. Eikenberg, on the other hand, had heard enough. She did not want to hear one more word about Dad. Margaret was starting on Dad's new job at the Famous Writers' School and bragging about that, although she had told Loretta, along with the earring story, that this was his fifth job in five years, and it wasn't five years of steady working, either. But Mrs. Eikenberg had clearly had enough of Dad. "Do you think we can go now?" she said, and they all felt the chill. She had settled the check and the tip and they followed her out of the restaurant.

And to a wine bar for an after hour. Everyone breathed a sigh of relief. Daniel sipped a seltzer water while the ladies enjoyed their brandies and cordials. They were listening to a jazz song, sad and sweet. "Duke Ellington," Mrs. Eikenberg announced. "Charles Mingus," Daniel corrected. Loretta looked at their placid white faces against the murky background, thinking about the perfect fish and the delectable veal, the amber wine, the silvery wine, the finicky waiter and the desserts set on fire, confusing the tongue with tart, creamy, brandied and sweet without ever blending. Nothing too bad had happened; the conversation had had its stiff patches of laughter and hollows of monotony, a stripe or two of anger and sarcasm, less now that Margaret had forgotten Dad and Mrs. Eikenberg had dropped the subject of the homely man. No one said anything for a while. They listened to the music and tried to fight the stupefying effect of the alcohol. Mrs. Eikenberg, still sitting next to Daniel, roused herself first. "I didn't think they did philosophy anymore," she said, returning to an earlier part of the afternoon, and a remark made then.

Daniel didn't answer.

"Didn't you say that was what you did, Daniel?" the mother persisted.

"I might have said that," Daniel said drily.

"Well?"

"Daniel doesn't want to talk about his work to you, Mother. You're too stupid," Margaret said, quickly adding, "Don't feel bad, I'm too stupid, too."

"Daniel doesn't—" Loretta began.

"Don't talk for me," Daniel said.

"Don't be snappish, Daniel. It was my fault," the mother said. "It was a stupid thing to say, wasn't it? I had a feeling it was. I wasn't thinking."

Loretta looked at Margaret and Margaret looked at Loretta. Margaret's eyes were slowly starting to cross. Mrs. Eikenberg was still talking. "That's the problem, isn't it? I understand. Margaret doesn't think I understand anything, but I do. It's very hard to do something important that no one will recognize." Mrs. Eikenberg paused to catch her breath. "Either because no one's interested in it anymore, or because people have moved on."

"Not *on*," Daniel said. "Backwards."

"Well, maybe they have," she said. "That's something only you could tell us, Daniel. You're the specialist."

The amity of this, the peacefulness was impressive. Was that what age could do—take a Hopkins with diamond earrings and turn her into an Eikenberg able to offer a soothing word to Daniel? Was it soothing even if Daniel would never admit its efficacy? This was a philosophical point Daniel was forever trying to explain, but Loretta was forever, he said, fixated on intentionality. Didn't she realize how naive that was, even for a Catholic? She had 'laughed when he said that. Catholics are too sophisticated for good intentions? she asked him. "Don't mock me" had been his reply, and what can you learn from such a reply, especially if personality is illness?

"That was fun, wasn't it?" Loretta said, when they had been packed into a pre-paid cab and sent home. There was a pause, a click that Daniel made with his mouth, a sign of impatience.

"I think it's sometimes possible to talk to people like that, don't you?" Loretta pressed on. "They're not on your level, but it's good to be able to talk to them, don't you think?"

"You're not saying I'm a snob, are you?" Daniel said carefully.

"No, I'm saying—" It was not the time to talk. She had miscalculated. "Never mind," she said.

"Don't 'never mind' me," Daniel snapped back. "If you've got a criticism to make, make it!"

"I don't."

"Well, stop trying to read my mind."

This made Loretta laugh.

"What's so funny?"

"I don't know. It sounded funny." Loretta looked out the window. A set of dark office buildings went by, a bright block of bars, now Times Square. How could life be so hard after such an evening? This is what she would never understand, no matter how much philosophy she read.

"I don't mean to bark at you," he said. "It's just that that woman was driving me insane. Couldn't you see that?"

"Don't you think she's had a hard life, Daniel? She seems to think so."

"She never stopped patronizing us for a minute. Even you could see this, couldn't you? That's what's most important to a woman like that."

"She liked *you*," Loretta said.

"Don't tell me that!" he bellowed.

"Why? It's a compliment."

"I don't want to hear about some fat cow's perversions. Spare me. You get off on things like that, not me."

Loretta considered. "Didn't you find her sympathetic in a way? She's 'coming to consciousness,' as you would say."

"No, I didn't find her 'sympathetic,' and she has no consciousness to speak of," Daniel said. "She's a lazy bum whose job it is to sit on her ass and make the homely man work for her."

Loretta laughed. "That's a little like my job."

Daniel laughed, too. "It might be your job," he said, "if you could find a homely man to go out and work for you. Instead you found me. Too bad, huh?"

Daniel was changing the subject. It was funny, yes, but anyone with eyes could still see that Daniel knew that Mrs. Eikenberg liked him—and he liked it, no matter what he said. It made him feel good, so he was in bad faith. No wonder he was so grouchy.

"Are you listening to me?" he was saying, "or are you asleep?"

■ ■ ■

That was sometime in the winter; now it was spring. One April day, Margaret decided it was time to re-charge their batteries with a dose of pre-Renaissance art, something soaked in religion and superstition. Loretta wasn't feeling friendly toward Margaret; she wasn't feeling unfriendly either. She had been spending a lot of time by herself in the apartment, trying to get the yellow-painted bathroom, small and filthy, clean. It wouldn't come clean, no matter how much she scrubbed it or how many bottles of ammonia she threw down the toilet. But Margaret insisted: "Come with me, please. I can't stand being alone." So they took the subway up to the Cloisters. They were going to hear excerpts from the *St. Matthew Passion*, arranged for a small orchestra and chorus.

It was nice to be out and zooming uptown to the Cloisters. "And I very nearly a cloistered nun," Loretta bragged to Margaret, who said, "You might have had a religious vocation, but—" and the rest was lost in the screeches of the IRT express. Margaret was solemn-looking. She had a black cape hanging off her shoulders and a limp, black cotton blouse under it, ankle socks and Chinese maryjanes. "*I* should have been a cloistered nun," she said, when the train stopped at 59th Street, "not you."

Things were not going well for Margaret. She had finished, or was about to finish, an ambitious project: "Moon Ova," fourteen canvasses filled with interesting holes of various sizes, some that looked like they were gouged out of flesh, some out of milky liquids, some out of sand, beans, cloth and tire treads—a project that no one was paying attention to.

"You mean 'taking seriously,' don't you?" asked Loretta, "Because everyone's noticed it."

"Who's noticed it?" asked Margaret glumly. Margaret's boyfriend, finally, was Mr. Aschenbach, an important art teacher and exponent of the New York School, but it wasn't what she'd expected. He used to pay some attention to her work until Margaret started going downtown to his loft in the afternoons and sleeping in his bed. Now he either treated her like the old ladies who sat in the reception area, volunteers from the Upper East Side who donated money to the school and called everyone Miss or Mister, or he treated her like the models, who were working for money. He knew Margaret's family had once had money, so he didn't treat her exactly like the models. Loretta said it was still better to get some attention than none at all.

"He's noticed *your* work," Margaret said. It was true; Mr. Aschenbach had noticed it, making some snide comments like "strong draughtsmanship" and "hyper-representational." Loretta started out with landscapes, imaginary and from life, but now she confined her art to fine pencil-and-ink drawings of Daniel's face and torso, sometimes extremely small format (two- or three-inch squares), other times on big sheets. Loretta was attacking one of these sheets one day when Mr. Aschenbach noticed her work again. Loretta had already told Margaret why the teacher, an "actionist," didn't like her work. "He thinks I'm an illustrator," she said. "I should go work with your Dad at the Famous Artists' School," she went on. "I could draw that little picture for the matchbooks. Don't laugh. Who else here *could?*"

"No one," Margaret said, when she noticed that Mr. Aschenbach had entered the cold studio of death masks and statuary, eating a wet Greek sandwich wrapped in a cone of paper and dripping oil and a tomato wedge on his ragged tennis shoes, "would call this"—she pointed to several hand sketches in the corner of a large sheet—"an illustration." Mr. Aschenbach looked closer, then he pointed his greasy finger at Margaret's head. "She's not completely wrong," he said. "She's got a nose."

Loretta gazed at Mr. Aschenbach studying her sketches. Did he think her work was better than an illustration, or just tasteful (something Margaret's work never was, and neither was his)? It didn't matter what he thought. This work wasn't real work. Behind her eyes a beautiful idea was forming, but there wasn't much around to train and encourage it. The current styles and approaches were too personal, too aggressive, so she had to wait for the idea to work itself out on its own. By then, maybe what Mr. Aschenbach said would matter. He had finally finished looking at the sketches. ("You're a good student," he had said once. "Too bad for you." What he meant, Margaret explained, was she needed more sex.) "Your work does not speak to me," he said, facing her, his back to the sketches. "It doesn't tell me what I want to know." Mr. Aschenbach wiped his hand on a rag hanging from the pocket of his black chinos and guided Margaret—"Moggit," he called her—out of the room, placing his wiped hand around Margaret's clean and perfumed neck.

Loretta watched them. Daniel, whose opinion she valued, had liked her work, even in its early stages, until she started using him as a subject. "Fine, go ahead, do it," he said, when she showed him the first series of drawings: his figure and his face. "Just don't ask me what I think of it, and don't go showing it to anyone we know." He wasn't that interested in art, except for art theory, although they did make one trip together to the Metropolitan, after she had been a student for a while, and he had said, "Show me what you've learned."

They toured the museum: they looked at Impressionists and Postimpressionists, they looked at old masters, they looked at still lifes, they looked at landscapes and they looked at portraits. Daniel said he couldn't stand another minute—his eyes were burning, his feet were sore and his brain was half-dead from looking at too many paintings of too many subjects by too many artists in too little time. And he was disappointed. They trudged to the cafeteria for sandwiches and coffee. After Daniel had eaten a little and lit a cigarette, he looked coolly through his eyeglasses at Loretta's head, and then over it. He waited another minute, and said, "That was very boring."

"I know."

"I don't think you know," he said, sending a smoke cloud over head. "A blind man could have given me a better tour of this museum."

"A blind man?"

"What kind of selection did you make that he couldn't make? To him this museum is just rooms, one room as good as the next. Nice smooth floors and wide doorways. It's airy, a museum is airy, not too crowded, good acoustics."

"I don't see why you have to be so sarcastic," she said.

"Let's change the subject. Maybe it isn't your fault." Daniel flicked a crumb off his pantsleg and looked around the noisy, crowded cafeteria. "This is a ritzy kind of zoo," he said.

Loretta was trying to formulate something. "Being selective isn't that important to me right now."

"That I know. Tell me something I don't know."

She told him that styles and periods were not that important. What mattered were the masterpieces, and whether you could find them on your own. One way to do it was to stand in a room full of the same thing—paintings by the same artist, or similar kinds of paintings—and *look* at them. "It doesn't matter whether you like the style or not," she said. "If you just look, if you stop thinking for a minute and just look, the best pictures—one or two maybe—will come forward. The others will fall back and fade. It won't happen right away. It takes a little time. That's what I like to do."

Daniel considered. "What makes the others fall back? Or can you say?"

"A lot of things. People look at Manet and they say, 'Oh, these are good, I like these.' But they're not all good. Some of them are less vivid, less full of contrast." She stopped to think. "'Weakly realized,' our teachers would say. Do you know what that means? I'm not talking about Manet. The subject could be unclear, or *too* clear. Not as complex in its composition, yet not perfect in its unity either." She added, "This is a very old-fashioned view, Daniel, keep that in mind. No one thinks this anymore."

"I don't care about that," he said. "You're talking about aesthetic judgment. I'm interested. If we went back in there, could *I* see this? Or would you have to point it out to me? How soon would I learn it?"

Loretta pushed her chair back and got up, dusting her chair of crumbs. "You have to see it for yourself." People were pouring past them, eager to get their dishes and push past the steam trays and dessert trays and the glasses of ice water. "No one can point it out to you. If you don't work it out for yourself, you never really see. It's just a lifeless tenet."

They walked out of the museum. Daniel said: "What you're saying sounds a bit like Kant, but let me ask you this. Apply your theory to writing, to thought. Am I seeing for my-self, for instance, in my work, or is it just lifeless tenets? In your opinion."

"I don't think you can compare them," Loretta said.

"That's right," he nodded. "You're right!" A few minutes later, when they were sitting on the downtown bus, he said: "This is the kind of experience I always thought we could have, a real exchange, something that blows my mind. That's the way you used to be."

They both looked out the window for a while. There was a neat division: the park on one side, a solid wall of apartment buildings on the other. "Tell me this," Daniel said. "You might be right to draw the line between what I do and what you do. But, I bet, deep down, that you think I'm the lifeless tenant—isn't that right?—and you're the landlord. "But that's okay. Go ahead, I like that. I like that, Loretta." But he couldn't have liked it that much, because he clammed up and read non-stop all weekend, writing not a word of the 2nd-and-a-half. In the strange, tense air of the one-room apartment, she was afraid to draw—Peewee, too, seemed edgy and stayed in bed, even after Loretta had flung the Murphy bed into the wall. Cantilever Roof tried to visit, but Loretta nudged him back onto the fire escape and closed the window. The Burmese looked in the window. It looked at Loretta and it looked at Daniel; it licked its paw and looked some more, but Peewee was nowhere to be seen.

The subway rattled and then swerved and Margaret's portfolio—which she took everywhere—flapped against her legs, then slammed against Loretta's. It was too noisy to talk, so Loretta watched the shadows playing on the window and the racing strips of light. Margaret read an advertisement, in Spanish, for Planned Parenthood. "You can tell what this is from the picture, but everything written in Spanish is so hysterical. That's what I like about Spanish." The train speeded up and clattered its way between two stations. When it slowed again, Margaret took up the irritating subject of the still-married Mr. Aschenbach. She was never far from this subject; her mind sought it as a tongue seeks a pitted tooth. She opened by outlining her plans to devastate Alfred and his family, pitch them down the sewer of beggary and despair, shame, impotence, bankruptcy, scandal and suicide. He was a European man, and so "an act of spite from a woman," she said, pink with pleasure, "he wouldn't survive with his face still on. Or his cow of a wife."

It was a familiar routine. Loretta picked up the beat: "His wife, Lard?"

"His wife, Lard," Margaret replied, "and his daughter, Horse, his son, Watercolor, his son-in-law—"

"Gumball?"

"Yeah, Gumball, and his Arab grandfather, Salvage."

"Good," Loretta said, and she thought it was funny, but it meant that Margaret intended to prolong the affair, to do nothing about the two-timing Alfred except vent her spleen at odd moments. "Is he worth the trouble, Margaret?" she asked.

Margaret waited until the braking subway calmed. "I can't believe I'm hearing this," she shrilled. Loretta realized she'd cut off the riff too soon. "Do *I* think it's worth it? What about you? Do *you* think it's worth it, Loretta?" Margaret snatched the portfolio away from Loretta's legs and set it against her own. "What are you telling me? Since when is *your* life so worth it?"

"I didn't say it was."

"You implied it." Margaret's cape—which she had shoved through the overhead strap—started slipping out. Now it was on the filthy subway floor. "Get it," she said, "will you? Thanks. Would you put it back up there if you can? That's good. Is it dirty on your side? I was saying something. What was I saying?"

"You were saying my life isn't so great."

Margaret laughed. She was studying Loretta's face. "I don't get you," she said. "You act like you know everything, but it always turns out you know less than I do. Strange. Yet, people still go on thinking you know something."

It was too noisy again to talk, so they just stood, hanging onto the straps. Enough time had passed so that Margaret could reintroduce the subject of killing Alfred. At first, Loretta resisted the conversation—it was only going to prolong the agony for Margaret. Was it possible that something so painful could be funny? If it were funny once, like now, could it be serious again?

Margaret could make the shifts, she had done it before. Did that mean there were airtight divisions in her mind? Loretta considered the task of installing some in her own mind: Daniel would find them, and pull them right down.

They were laughing now at the helpless Alfred, butt of a thousand stupid jokes and snares—his studio a shambles, thousands of the famous splattered canvasses floating down the East River, the Aschenbach wife and daughter blasted, each sitting in a different welfare office, or in jail, and Alfred himself shambling once a day in paper slippers to O. T. at Bellevue to make an ashtray out of a shell. "No," Loretta said. "Yes!" Margaret insisted. Pasting macaroni on a styrofoam donut and painting it gold for Christmas. And now they were done: they had exhausted it.

And, exiting the museum an hour or two later—after hearing the music, and after looking at a portal and a triptych for twenty minutes each because they were told in class to look until you've worked through your pain and boredom and can see that the artwork is the only interesting thing in life—as the day was folding in, the Hudson a beautiful blue carpet with black stripes, it was clearly no fun anymore. Margaret's pretty, wisecracking face was pinched and pale with anxiousness about the whereabouts of Alfred Aschenbach and how, if ever, she could house him somewhere with herself, could become the sole object of his attention and his only gatekeeper. This project, they both knew, was a fantasy and Margaret, Loretta thought, would be left with her pain, and with the mental labor of making a chain and circling Alfred's leg with it over and over. Or she could distract herself with thoughts of Loretta's and Daniel's chains clanking on their warped wood floor. "I wouldn't be married like you," Margaret said, as she had said many times before, "and Daniel—I'm not saying that Daniel isn't interesting. He is. And mysterious. Isn't that why you like him? And a genius too. That must be why. Still, it's a living hell, I can see that.

"Of course,"—the subway was soon to enter the tunnel of Manhattan, so they both turned for one last look out the window—"I don't like not being married either. Who would?" Loretta said the solution might be to get married and then divorced. "That way," she said, "when you start to feel this lousy, you'll think back on the ordinariness of it all, and the irritation, and that—" The sun was setting, as it always did and always brought on longings, sliding its circle across a body of placid water, idealizing the day and the city's beauty. "Forget it," Margaret interrupted. They were sucked into the tunnel. "I live to long and nothing will stop it." Loretta repeated to herself the words: I live to long, and nothing will stop it.

■ ■ ■

That was the spring, then came the summer. The summer was when things fell apart. It started when Alfred went back to his wife for good—he had done this before, but this time it sounded final—and Margaret went and found Louis Malone. Louis was like Alfred, Margaret explained, but a little older. "He's *old*," she said, before Loretta had met him. "You'll never guess how old he is."

Louis was a filmmaker (ads and the occasional documentary when he could get a producer, but mostly ads) turned milk-bar owner, who owned a handful of beautiful white restaurants on upper Lexington which sold only dairy food, hand-milked from cows whose Long Island farm he had bought with money made on the market and through embezzling. "Which is why he quit making ads," Margaret said, although no convictions so far: too many so-called independents in New York were guilty of the same thing—all his friends and his whole age group, according to Margaret—and the jails were not big enough to hold them all.

Loretta and Daniel had gone up on the train to visit.

Daniel milked a Bessie and then drank the milk; he was the only one who could get the hot, clotted liquid to go down. Loretta tried, Margaret tried. They tried again when Louis offered them some milk that had cooled, but still they gagged. "They ain't so tough," Louis said to Daniel, who tried it hot and cold, no big deal, and he didn't even *like* milk. Loretta thought Louis might have been fifty, possibly a little older. He was tall and fat with thick glasses and yellowed white hair pulled into a pigtail. Daniel liked him. They talked for a long time about Flaubert and Maupassant—Louis was planning someday to adapt "A Ball of Fat" and other stories for TV, once he got back into TV. They talked about hobbies and travel and Marxism—Louis had been at Columbia, he said, when they were all reds and even he was a little pinkish. They talked all afternoon, tramping the length of the paddock and into the open meadow. Loretta and Margaret sat in the kitchen with a bottle of flat champagne and some snacks left over from a dinner party, then moved to the sun-room, waiting for the two men to appear against the sunset, as Margaret said, "like the Lonesome Ranger and Tonto."

Shortly after, Margaret moved in with him and they nearly got married. He asked her. She was getting ready to tell her mother, and had already sublet her apartment. What happened? Loretta had asked. They were having dinner, the three of them, and Margaret suddenly said the wedding was off. "He's selling the farm," she went on, "he's moving to L.A." To do what? Loretta wanted to ask and was getting ready to ask—not only that, but a lot of other questions (was he a gangster? suddenly gay? did a film project come up, or an indictment?), when Daniel, who was there, grabbed her knee under the table and dug his fingers into it.

It was the start of a terrible night, a night that seemed to last a year. In a way, it was still that night. She tried to ask another question and the hand came down again, like a claw, and stayed there. What was wrong with these questions?

It was Daniel's birthday. He had just turned thirty and they had planned to have dinner, just the two of them. "Is Margaret coming?" Daniel had asked. "No," Loretta answered.

"Good."

"Why do you ask?"

"Don't cross-examine me. I just asked you."

"Do you want her to come?"

"She comes to everything. I thought you were twins. When did you break up with her?"

"She's busy these days."

"Doing what?"

"She's going to get married."

"Did she tell you that?"

"How else would I know?"

"Oh."

"I'll call her if you want. It's *your* birthday."

"Don't bother."

"I will."

"Well, do it then. Don't keep bugging me about it."

So it wasn't a question of Daniel's resenting Margaret's presence. Was it the usual thing? That Margaret still wasn't worth the trouble of a question about her marriage, that her mental circuits, as Daniel once put it, were too elementary, that even her lies were banal? Was it that Daniel liked Louis, and maybe didn't want to see him getting fried and boiled by Margaret's ugly temper? Was that it? Maybe Daniel had talked Louis out of marrying Margaret, and was afraid to admit it. Or Margaret out of marrying Louis? They were sitting in the Blue Moon Cafe, Margaret, in her black flats, a polka-dot dress with little lace cape around her shoulders, seemed too relaxed, almost torpid. Either she had a fresh boyfriend already lined up, or she had worked out her disappointment—she was thinner now and hollow-eyed—on someone else. Who?

Daniel stopped talking a minute. He presented Margaret

with a copy of *The Critique of Judgment* ("If you're an 'ottist,' why
don't you read this?") and a gloss to go with it, and Margaret
had laid a ten-dollar bill on top of the beautiful purple paperback. Daniel was putting away the ten and suddenly tossed a
new dime in Margaret's glass of white burgundy, untouched.
"Now what am I supposed to do?" Margaret squealed. "Drink,"
Daniel ordered. Margaret drank the wine and balanced the dime
on her lower lip. The dime fell on the table. "This is too much,"
Margaret said to Daniel. "Everything you do is *heavy*. Can't you
just relax?" But he could see—who couldn't see—that
Margaret enjoyed the special attention. Here was the waiter
with the dessert tray. "Nothing for me," Margaret said, but
Daniel ordered her a white cake with almond frosting. "It's my
birthday," he said to the waiter, "so let them eat cake."
    "Did you hear what I said?" Margaret said, smirking.
Daniel picked up the wet dime and tossed it in Margaret's water
glass. "I think you're asking for it," she said, and she took a
penny out of her change purse and flipped it onto Daniel's
chocolate cake. It sank into the cream frosting. "Pick it up with
your tongue!" Margaret brayed.
    They dropped Margaret off at her building and waited un-
til she locked her door, then they filed down the steps and out
onto East 4th. It had been a long night, an interesting night in
some ways. Daniel had talked a lot. He was feeling better since
his advisor had convinced him not to die a pure neo-Kantian,
and Daniel had halted work on the 2nd-and-a-half. He still had
the pages; she wouldn't let him throw them away. "If you don't
want these anymore," she said, "I do." There had been a
struggle, but Daniel said: "Take it, I can see you want a sample
of my impotence to keep forever." She kept it in her school
locker, in case he had the idea of sending it down the garbage
chute with the garbage. A few weeks later, he went back to it,
and worked his way word by word through chapter two. The
advisor accepted and praised chapter one, although he still

thought Daniel could not make a career in the 18th century—
the Age of Light had dead-ended, the 20th-century mind had
become no more interesting than a simple machine, Daniel reported to Loretta. "The age is unworthy of Kant."

"Two things I want to ask you," Loretta said, on the way
home. "Why didn't you let me ask her about Louis? And—"
"Shh," he said. "And why were you throwing things in her
glass?" They were walking fast, the street was silent and two of
the streetlights were out. Someone on the third floor of a wreck
of a brownstone was screaming out the window and throwing
things: a sheet floated out, a pail and broom handle, but there
was no one on the sidewalk for them to strike and kill.

"Don't look!" Daniel hissed, taking Loretta's arm and
hurrying her away. They fled down the middle of the street, a
bottle smashed behind them. One more block and it was perfectly quiet. They crossed Cooper Union Square, empty and
bleak, and were home on the West Side, people pouring out of
movie houses and out of the doors of bars and cafes.

Now that they were safe, Loretta started over: "Don't you
remember when I was trying to ask her?" The subject already
seemed a little unnecessary, annoying even, but she pressed on.
"Why did you stop me?"

Daniel slowed his pace, dropped her hand and lit a
cigarette. They were walking into Washington Square, the
street was empty again. "Why did you throw a dime into her
wine glass?" It was cooler now, walking under the trees along
the park, the leaves dusty and black, but ripe-smelling. Most of
the houses were in darkness. Once or twice they passed along a
sidewalk into a rectangle of light and Loretta, without turning
her head, could see that his hair was drenched in sweat; the ends
had curled around his ear and stuck in places to his forehead. It
was hot, but not that hot. "I'm not criticizing" she said. "I'm

trying to figure it out." He was silent. "Well, maybe I am criticizing," she went on, and right over the line, "but you still
ought to tell me."

"Why didn't you just bull your way through and ask her?"
he said, in a voice that was louder than necessary. Or maybe it
was because she hadn't heard that voice in a long time. "Since
when do you listen to me?" he shouted.

"Why are you so mad at me all of a sudden?"

"I'm not," he hissed back, then started walking a little
ahead, and a little more ahead. Loretta tried to keep up. He was
up at the corner and turned. "Why don't you just get the hell
away from me," he said in a croak. "Just stay away!" and he was
gone.

Daniel didn't come home that night. When, out walking
with Loretta, Margaret finally told the story of the Louis break-
up, the whys and the hows—it was about a week later; Margaret
had gone away for a few days and then was too busy to talk—she
also told Loretta that Daniel had spent the night of the birthday
dinner at her apartment. She rushed onto another subject, but
Loretta slowed the story down so she could get the details. She
still didn't get it, even with Margaret going word by word.
Margaret had stopped short on the sidewalk to look into
Loretta's face for a reaction, but there was none. She told Loretta
to wait, then ran into Nathan's, came back a few minutes later
with a large Orange Julius and two straws, peeled one of the
straws and handed it to Loretta. Then she tried the story once
again. The account was interesting but incomplete. There was
no more emphasis on one detail than on another. Loretta listened, more curious than nervous, while the facts of the story—
or what Margaret thought of as the facts—rolled out. Since that
day, Loretta's curiosity had sharpened, and she often scanned
Margaret's tense face for signs of a lie. Margaret rarely—in spite

of what Daniel said—lied and got away with it. Mostly she didn't think it was necessary to lie: if the truth hurt, let it. Yet this one time, it might have seemed necessary. He had ended up at four or maybe five at Margaret's place. Where had he been between one and four, then? Having, Loretta answered her own question, the first half of his nervous breakdown. (He put the second half off, as far as Loretta could tell—and he was still having it.) Daniel and Margaret had talked in Margaret's tiny kitchen, drinking coffee, then beer and smoking all the cigarettes, even the clove cigarettes. Margaret had offered to go out for more, but Daniel said no. They needed more, the conversation had broken down, Daniel couldn't find the words for what he wanted to say—"He wanted to sleep with me, Loretta, he made that pretty clear, but he was holding himself back for some reason he couldn't explain"—and Margaret couldn't help him. She put an old album on, brought out what little grass she had in the house—"But no, no dope, no rock 'n roll, no blues, no album of mine, no anything of mine," so Margaret had to turn off the stereo. "I was just looking out the window out of sheer boredom, and he said to me, 'Sorry, I don't want to go home either, if that's what you're thinking.' But I wasn't, so I offered him my couch for the night. He said he didn't want to sleep. I asked him what he wanted to do. I said I could make coffee or tea, if he wanted tea—it was almost morning. I turned around and he wasn't even listening to me, he was reading a book.

"I don't know what book it was. Who cares what it was? Oh yes I do, I remember. It was *Mysteries*, you know, by that guy you like—the Norwegian, Knute. By then—it was about 8 or so—I had to get ready for my class. And I went to my class. And when I came back, I found a little string tied to my doorknob—why do you look so bored? Are you bored? Am I boring you? A string and a bouquet of flowers, ordinary flowers, daisies and things, tied to the end of it. Their heads were dangling onto the floor. Now what kind of a gesture is that? He was gone. The house was all tidied up."

Loretta was starting to understand the story. "Why didn't you tell me this before?" she asked.

"I haven't *seen* you to tell you," Margaret replied. "Oh, I almost forgot. He said one more thing. You're going to like this, I think. I'd like it if someone said it about me. He said it early, about six a.m., I don't know exactly, but it was morning. Are you listening? He said, 'I have to go see what delicate little hollow of pain Loretta has dug out of her part of the night.' I hope I'm remembering this right. I wrote it down, but I lost the paper. It was so weird. 'If she's still there,' I think he said, 'if she's managed to make a hollow big enough to hold her.' That was it. At first I thought: what is this bullshit? Who does he think he is? But he meant it—I turned around to see, and I could see he meant it."

Loretta and Margaret separated at the art school. "Now you're pissed, aren't you?" Margaret said to Loretta's back. "Even *you* get pissed sometimes, right? Are you just going to walk away, or are you listening to me?" Margaret's voice was getting louder, and Loretta stopped, but didn't turn around. Margaret was beside her, with an arm around her shoulder: "You're the one who's my friend. Daniel isn't dirt under my feet." She paused, trying to catch Loretta's eye. "Do you believe me?"

Loretta felt no need to answer. Somehow, none of it made sense: it all seemed too elaborate and artful: what was any of them going to get out of it? And, as with anything that involved Daniel, it was also too deep: either they had betrayed her, or they hadn't. If they had, it was one thing, and it was easy to understand; if they hadn't, there was something subtler and more creepy going on, and they were both in on it. Margaret's nervousness had erupted into tears, now streaming down her hot, flushed face. Loretta looked at her: now she wanted pity.

After treating Margaret to all she had—a few harsh

pockets of silence—Loretta went home, calmer. Daniel was out. She flopped on the bed face down and Peewee, after watching her, leapt up and settled in the gap between her knees. All was quiet. Loretta could hear the sewing machine next door whirring; the heavy zipper foot going up, now down.

She lay with her face smashed into the pillow—it smelled a little like Daniel, but so what? And she drifted. It was when she was fourteen, wasn't it, that she had her first birthday party? This was nice to think about. They had a photograph of the party at home: Loretta and the Whites in paper crowns, so giddy they looked drunk, and Gloria making a face at the bottom of the frame. She recalled Aunt Rita's living room—yellow and brown, smelling of pot roast and boiled cabbage. A birthday party for herself and for ten friends, that's what they had said. At first, it had just been for five friends, but Aunt Rita had begged her to include her cousin, and one of her cousin's friends, and said that if she did it willingly, without letting Gloria know her mother had interfered, Loretta could go ahead and add a few more guests of her own—the White twins, and Frances Farley. "Let me see if you can do it," the aunt had said, and Loretta was so sure, she went ahead and called the Whites and Franny, who said yes, and was it a party with presents?

Loretta told them it was, but had to explain who else was coming. She remembered the scene—they were walking to school, and Deedee White stuck her tongue out at the mention of Gloria. Frances added that Gloria would spoil any party. "Well, you don't have to come," Loretta said to them all.

Then Christine said, "Shut up, Deed," giving her sister a little push, so she bumped into Franny, who gave a push back, then Christine gave Deedee another push until the three of them were laughing so hard they stepped into the street in front of a milk truck, or were going to, until Loretta screamed, "Look out!" and when they were back on the sidewalk, white and popeyed, but still laughing like goons, she had to say, "You fat fools!"

Then they all got involved in an argument about Gloria, and why Gloria had to be included in everything when she was such a queer.

"Why is she queer?" Loretta asked.

"Why is she queer!" Christine squealed. "She's always with that Charlene, they do *every*thing together. I bet they go to the *bath*room together. Do they?"

"Chris*tine,*" Loretta said, "don't *we* do everything together, stooge?"

Christine laughed to think of it. Franny was pressing, then punching the walk button. "Yeah, what of it?" Christine said. "Besides," she added, while they crossed the street in step, "we're different."

"Why?" Loretta asked her.

"They're ugly."

That got Franny laughing, and then Deedee was laughing. They were all laughing and made stupid jokes and laughed all the way to school.

The party was on March 19th, a Friday, 7 to 10. Aunt Rita made a pineapple upside-down cake and a pan of brownies with harlequin ice cream to go with them. Loretta remembered wanting an all-white cake, white with white frosting. She also remembered the rigmarole about that cake. The first time it came up, Aunt Rita corrected her: "You mean a yellow cake with white frosting." Loretta said no, white with white. "Angel cake, then," said the aunt, who must have been working a crossword puzzle because she wasn't paying attention. No, Loretta said: she knew what angel cake was, and it wasn't angel cake. She told her aunt to think of a coconut cupcake and take the coconut out: that was white cake and white frosting. Aunt Rita must have thought that was fresh because she said that never had they had white cake in this family. "Your uncle doesn't like a white cake, it's too sickening sweet."

Loretta said she liked it, and her aunt asked when she had ever had a white cake in her life. Loretta said she'd didn't know, but she knew she'd had one. The aunt was too distracted to continue working on her puzzle: she did what she always did—closed the big, flapping book and pinned her mechanical pencil to the cover. She sighed and went out to look at supper.

Once the cake had become an issue, the way trivial things always became an issue with her aunt, Loretta wondered if she *had* ever had a pure white cake, or even seen one. Even a wedding cake was sometimes yellow, and she had never had a wedding cake. Aunt Rita was back and resettling herself in the upholstered rocker, putting her feet up on the footstool with its petitpoint cover. Loretta had prepared a look, and was going to deliver it as soon as the stocking feet plumped on the footstool. She raised her head, the fierce and hateful look already in position, but when her eyes found the pale head and soft face, and the aunt's eyes, blue and magnified behind the rimless glasses, Loretta's hard glance fell away, down, the way it always did. "If you had asked," Aunt Rita said, pulling the lampcord and turning the bluish air of the room to a hazy yellow, "you could have had one." She picked up the crossword book, and put it down again, relaunched herself out of the rocker and into the kitchen, turning on the fluorescent overhead light, which gave the parlor doorway, where Aunt Rita was standing, the look of a fresh miracle with dust still settling. The aunt turned and walked into her kitchen; Loretta could hear her removing lids from the pots, shiny from thousands of buffings and scourings. Now she was back in the doorway. "But it's a little late to be asking—don't you think, or do you, Loretta?"

Where was Gloria? Gloria must have been at Girl Scouts. There was still time before Gloria came home for Aunt Rita to begin a discussion of how she had gone to the trouble of fixing a special dessert like pineapple upside-down cake, and it still wasn't enough to please Miss Loretta, a girl so flighty and demanding that nothing and no one could please her. Instead of this, Gloria did come home and was treating her mother to a full account of what Mrs. McIntyre had said at Girl Scouts about how many badges she needed for whatever award she was after. One year, it was the Marian Award, and she needed too many to get it that year, Mrs. McIntyre had said, just like she said the year before. It wasn't fair, Gloria said. And that year, like the year before, Gloria was excluded from the procession that marched up to the bishop and received the medals on blue ribbon. Gloria was saying that she wanted it so bad, she could taste it. ("What does it taste like?" Loretta yelled from the living room.) It was never clear why—if she wanted it so badly— Gloria was so unwilling to work on badges. She hated working on badges. She tried to get Mrs. McIntyre to give her badge credit for things she already did, but she had collected the badges for schoolwork, and the one for housework, and what else did she do?

Aunt Rita was always a good listener and Loretta heard them settle at the kitchen table while Gloria drank her chocolate milk and ate two peanut-butter cookies on a napkin.

"Hello, everybody," Uncle Ted always said when he came in from work, but by then they were all engrossed in some TV program—Aunt Rita, too—and nobody would answer him.

When they were seated at the supper table, Uncle Ted had to be told about the birthday party on Friday ("Tomorrow," Gloria had said, putting her round face close to Loretta's. "It's tomorrow, Retta"), and who was coming, although someone had already mentioned it to him, hadn't they?

"I told you, Daddy," Gloria said, "don't you remember?"

Uncle Ted looked at Loretta; nobody told him anything. Loretta looked at her aunt, who was pouring chicken gravy into a hole in the middle of her mashed potatoes where there was already a pat of butter. Gloria reached for the gravy boat, but her mother tapped her hand: "Let your father have some first, and don't reach."

Uncle Ted was still waiting for Loretta to tell him; the gravy boat was handed to him, but he didn't take it.

"I thought I *did* tell you," Loretta said.

Uncle Ted took the gravy boat and poured a thin stream on his chicken leg, then passed the gravy boat to his daughter, who had flattened things out on her plate and now made a jiggly line over potatoes and meat. "Don't play with it," her father said. Gloria was starting to fill in the silence with a story about Girl Scouts, a different story from the one she told her mother: the troop was planning a field trip to New York with another troop in the spring, right after Easter.

"That's not too far off," her father was saying. "How much does it cost?"

"See, Loretta," he said, "what you're missing not being a scout?" He was mad, Loretta figured, because he was bringing up the subject of Girl Scouts and how she had quit Girl Scouts right after flying up from Brownies. Everyone was disappointed, especially Gloria, who wanted to do everything Loretta did. She tried to quit Girl Scouts too, but her mother said nothing doing. Uncle Ted said Loretta was a born teenager. Gloria said she was a teenager, too. No you're not, said the aunt, and so on.

After this discussion, the only sound was Uncle Ted breaking the joint of his chicken leg and Gloria gulping her milk, then Gloria started in on the party again. "I'm invited, Daddy, and so is Charlene and we're both going. It's a nighttime party."

Loretta saw that Uncle Ted's small glass was empty and she got up to fill it. She put the full bottle and the nearly empty one on the counter and went back to the table for the glass, but Uncle Ted took it out of her hand. "No thanks, I've had enough." Loretta started back to the counter to take the nearly empty and the full bottle and put them away—"Don't bother with the empty one," Aunt Rita said—but Loretta left both bottles on the counter, pushed open the swing door and vanished. This was happening every night—Loretta getting up from the table and leaving it, and making everybody else either nervous or aggravated. At first, they tried to understand, but it was almost a year and a half now, and time to shape up, she had heard her aunt saying. Loretta heard a lot of things they said because she was often "skulking" around when people didn't know it: she heard that "the girl" was using the situation to get her own way and she *was* getting it; that this was bad for her character, it was hard on the family, and set a bad example for little Gloria, so gullible, especially when it came to the cousin, whom she adored. Uncle Ted always said the same thing: give her some time, don't be so hard. "I'm not hard, I'm not hard on her, do you think I'm hard? I think it's you that's too easy," Aunt Rita said, working herself up. "You're easier on her than you are on your own daughter, and you know it. Don't think," she said one time, "Gloria can't tell. She's no fool."

Loretta turned on the light in the room she shared with Gloria and Gloria's cat, Mikey. The cat was stuffed into the opening between the window and the sill. It had spread itself out to fit smoothly in the three inches of space, but it was wedged in so tight, it couldn't turn its head to see who had come in to scare it. Loretta laughed to see the wriggling mass of fur, headless and wild. She opened the window an extra inch and the cat scurried out and under the bed in two leaps.

Not five minutes later, there was a tap on the door. "L'retta? Can I come in?" It was Gloria with a tray: milk, brownies, two napkins and the candy egg she had bought on her way home from school and hidden in her schoolbag. "Open the door, Retta," she sang out, kicking the door. Loretta opened it and saw the silly grin with orange lipstick and a hat of Aunt Rita's. "I'm your maid," Gloria said. "How come you're here in the dark?"

And the party, even with the sickening cake that was dessert, was a success. It was the best time Loretta had ever had: they danced, they laughed, they ate, they screamed, they told stories, played games and took turns singing like Elvis. Even the aunt had enjoyed the party, she told Uncle Ted Saturday morning when they all went off for the weekly outing, a breakfast at the pancake house. Aunt Rita was wearing the blue ruffled blouse that Loretta had ironed for her right before the party, when the girl, as Aunt Rita was saying, had heaped the laundry basket full of clean clothes without being asked, and sprinkled them all, rolled them up, then ironed the work shirts and handkerchiefs, the blouses and dresses—one for Gloria and one for herself to wear to the party—and sheets and pillowcases, things the aunt herself didn't always bother to iron, bureau scarves and a tablecloth.

"It was five to seven," Aunt Rita said, "and I had to go in there and unplug the damn thing, or she would have kept it up until the guests came pouring in and tripped over the ironing board!"

Uncle Ted laughed. He opened his red paper napkin and dropped it on his knees. They all looked down at their placemats, maps of the world, to see how many countries they could remember from last time, before the waffles and pancakes were plunked down.

"Are you interested in what I'm saying?" Aunt Rita said, like she always did, as she picked through the basket of syrups until she found the one she liked: claret—they didn't always have claret—and then drenched her buttermilk pancakes in a purple stream, "or should I change the subject?"

"What are you talking about?" he said, taking a bottle of maple syrup from the basket. He always picked the plainest thing.

"The party! And I have to say I've never in my life seen a man look so bored."

He said he was tired. He had gone straight from work to the Elks for a couple of beers, then supper. Aunt Rita told him again he could have come home, that Loretta wouldn't have minded if he had come to the party. Why not give the kids some privacy? he had said. What kind of privacy do they need at that age? she shot back, but it was the kind of question that you couldn't really answer.

"Well," the aunt said, "where did you say you went?" He went first to the Elks, he said again, and then. . . . Loretta stopped listening. She was looking at Aunt Rita eating the purple-soaked pancakes and drinking milky coffee. The aunt was listening intently. He was tired, Loretta knew, not because of the Elks, or whatever he did after the Elks; he was tired because he was up half the night talking. She knew, because she was up too. Loretta woke up every night with dreams—sometimes they were nightmares, mostly just strange dreams—and went downstairs for a glass of milk or a piece of candy. Sometimes she turned on the television, but usually it was too late or too early for television, so she just sat in the living room on Aunt Rita's rocker and read a magazine until she felt sleepy again.

The night of the party, after they had cleaned up—washed dishes, swept and pulled crepe paper and pieces of popped balloons off the walls—it was late and they all trundled up to bed, but Loretta couldn't sleep. She tried talking to Gloria, but Gloria couldn't stay awake to talk, so she lay there and looked out the window at the spidery branches of the oak tree lit by the streetlight. She heard the car door slam and waited for Uncle Ted to creep up the stairs, but he didn't come up the stairs. She crawled out of bed, careful not to wake Gloria, and crept to the top of the stairway, without turning on lights or creaking any floorboards. It was dark down there, he must be sitting in the dark. She waited, but no lights came on, no TV set, nothing, so she sat down on the top step and slowly let herself down each

step, silently, carefully, until she was all the way down. Then
she got up and let her feet be heard padding into the kitchen,
opening the refrigerator door, pulling the cord for the overhead
light. "What are you doing up?" Uncle Ted said from the living
room. "Did you have a good party?"

Loretta fixed a plate of peanut butter crackers and two
glasses of milk and carried in the snack, napkins, a jar of jelly
and a knife, on a painted tray. Uncle Ted said thanks, none for
him, he was going to bed, but he ate a couple of crackers and
drank all his milk. They talked. Loretta said the party was fun,
that everybody had a good time, they had danced to the 45s that
the twins had brought over, and they stuffed themselves with
brownies and ice cream. No one ate the upside-down cake, so
Aunt Rita said she'd just save it for Sunday dessert. A miracle,
Loretta remarked, and Uncle Ted laughed.

He thanked her for the midnight snack and for the nice
visit. He wasn't tired, he was going to sit up for a while, but it
was late, shouldn't she be in bed? It's not late, it's early, she said.

And that's how they had had their first real talk—not like
family, but like people. He said he liked having her and Gloria
as his kids, that he didn't like babies much, but he liked older
kids, teenagers, because you could talk to them. They talked
about a lot of things that night. Mostly, he talked. It started to
rain and rained hard for an hour, the water pouring down the
side of the house where the gutter was broken, and splashing in
a puddle right outside the living room windows. It was a cold
sound and Loretta shivered, so Uncle Ted got up and covered her
with one of the afghans from the couch. They talked so long,
they saw the night slowly change to morning and the morning
grow lighter every minute. The rain would wash out the grass
seed Uncle Ted had planted last year, he said, and they got up to
see. There was a puddle near the drain pipe, one corner of the
lawn was flooded, and dirt streaking across the sidewalk. A lot
of the time he spent telling the story of how he came to marry

Aunt Rita. It was kind of a sad story, but maybe that was just because of the rain and the lawn all washed away in the gloomy light of morning. He hadn't had many girlfriends, he said, but he had had one in the days before he met Aunt Rita—that's where the story started. He still thought about that one, Anne Walters her name was. When he met her, she was already married, married with twins. He met her at a restaurant where she did part-time waitressing, a blonde with a full round face and glasses, attractive in the black uniform with a starched apron. He went back to the restaurant a week or two later and sat at the bar. They had a drink after her shift and another the next week. She showed him pictures of the twin boys and one of her husband, Bobby. It was some name like that, Bobby or Jimmy, looked like a kid with thin hair and buck teeth. He was in and out of the hospital, a heart condition with complications. "She talked about the guy like he was her son, and I mentioned that. I shouldn't have, but we'd been drinking, and you know how it goes. We were feeling no pain."

She didn't want to leave a disabled man and he wasn't going to ask her to. Bobby Walters died—he saw the obituary about five years after, just before Gloria was born—of a long illness. He learned from someone else that Anne Walters, who still waitressed at the same place, had remarried, someone who owned a nightclub, and they bought a split-level home in a new development in Seekonk.

It was right after he broke off with Anne that his own problems had started. First his mother died, then his father—not six months after—was killed by a car while he was crossing the street to buy his paper. Uncle Ted spent night and day at St. Joseph's and it was there he had met Aunt Rita—a girl he'd known since grade school—who ran up and down the stairs with bedside reports. His father was all broken bones and internal injuries and in horrible pain, dopey and half insane from the drugs and operations. Everyone wished he'd just die, which he did, one day when his son was in the room to see him, just as he had been there when his mother died. Aunt Rita was also there and that was one reason—if people ever need a reason—he had said. She had chased him a little, too; she was forever turning up in his father's ward. I swear, Uncle Ted said, she let the other patients die just so she could spoonfeed my father his cereal and keep his window decked with flowers she stole from other rooms. She almost lost her job for that.

He ended up marrying little Rita Sullivan and a year later they had Gloria. Loretta knew the rest of the story, didn't she? They lost a child a couple of years after; Aunt Rita had a hard time—she was nearly forty—and when the doctors delivered the baby, stillborn, they put her in for a hysterectomy. He was lucky she was alive, so torn up she'd been by the second pregnancy and the birth. What he didn't say, but she knew because she had eyes in her head, was now they slept in separate beds.

"So now," he said, "you know something about your old uncle. You're a good kid," he said. "I'm glad you had fun at your party. You should have more parties. You're only young once."

It was still raining hard. Loretta was tired now, as she traipsed up the steps in the ashy morning light and jumped into bed, burying her head under the pillow. It was a happy day, but now it was a different day and she was excited because in less than a week, she was going out on her first date. She hadn't told anyone yet, not even Gloria, but Carmino, a boy from the pizza parlor, a boy with a beautiful new car who went to the public high, had asked her out.

But next morning, Loretta told Gloria about it, and as soon as Aunt Rita was finished finding out what Uncle Ted had done to be so tired, she was asking Loretta about the date. This boy was not the kind of friend she would have picked out for Loretta, but since when did Loretta listen to anything *she* said? Aunt Rita talked about the date and about what you could expect from bad boys. Uncle Ted said, let's wait and see, give the kid a chance. They were still talking about it on the way home from the pancake house when Uncle Ted stopped the conversation by doing what he sometimes did when only his pals, Gloria and Loretta, were in the car with him. He made a sharp turn into the driveway, jumping on the brake—the wheels screeched on the blacktop—and Aunt Rita was thrown against the door. They were always surprised when he did this, and a little scared. Uncle Ted braked hard right in front of the garage door, and they all pitched forward. Loretta and Gloria were giggling in the back seat. Uncle Ted shifted and turned off the ignition. They were all alert, waiting for the reaction and the hotball of harsh words that would follow, and the nagging that would follow that. But in the rear-view mirror, Loretta saw not the sourpuss she expected to see, but Aunt Rita's face smooth and pink, round eyes and a giddy smile. Loretta looked at Gloria, and Gloria looked at Loretta. She had enjoyed it?

"Wake up!" Daniel was saying, pleading. "Loretta, wake up. Why don't you wake up?"

Roto-Futurists

■ ■ ■

"CARMINO P. LUCA," Margaret intoned. She lugged a can of blue paint over to the "set" and slapped her paint brush on the mound of gray paper that was meant to suggest the dark cave of a subway station. Loretta was making the subway and Margaret was putting the graffiti on it: "The Godforsaken," one rockface said, "Fukku," another one. The set was being made for *Fuckernauts on Plastic Fruitcake*, a play "written" by a gang in Bronxville for performance on Off-Off-Off by a company called the Roto-Futurists. The little theater group had called the art school and Margaret had volunteered herself and Loretta as designers. Margaret ended up filching the materials from school because the Rotos had no budget, hadn't even paid their authors. Loretta wondered how they could build a set knowing nothing about set designing, but Margaret dismissed her doubts: Alfred would help them, and even if he didn't, who would know the difference?

Margaret didn't have much respect for the Rotos, a company of five, newly formed from the remains of defunct companies from the Lower East Side: the Juke, the Phylogenetic

Feminist Lucrative Theater (PHFLT) and Rainer & Eddy, a "two-man autobiographic vortex." Margaret had talked to Miss X and Miss Y of the PHLT. They didn't use names, so Margaret distinguished between them simply for the sake of telling Loretta about the conversation. "They're a couple," she said. "They're all couples, except for the Juke."

The only person Loretta had met was the director, an ex-ballerina with a talent for doctoring scripts: she could turn any kind of drivel—obscene, vulgar, malevolent, insane, scrawled by moron, felon or psychotic—into clear, if hectic, dramas. Everything she touched with her emaciated hands was reviewed in the *Times* and would run for weeks, earning the actors more money than they had seen outside of the dives and massage parlors where they were often employed. *Fuckernauts*, about Hispanic and black homosexuals in the Vietnam war, would be staged in a rickety storefront space for an audience of twenty, some sitting on folding chairs, some sitting on the floor with their backs pressed against the cold, moist walls. Part of the set had already been transported to the storefront, where the actors were rehearsing. Loretta hadn't met any actors. They were always working somewhere else; one of them was wanted by the FBI and slept in a different place every night. "Maybe I *have* seen them," Loretta told Margaret while they worked in the ballerina's place, "and I don't even know it."

"You'd know it," Margaret replied.

In addition to the subway, the designers were making a Kansas cornfield and a used-car lot in Saigon—all settings the director had dreamed up out of nothing. The script was a mere stream of threats and insults, filthy, apocalyptic, but mainly—the ballerina told them—boring. Everything had to be changed. First the ballerina made up the sets, then thought of a story to arrange in front of them, then she typed up choral lines to be droned or spoken by the actors to provide "a filtrate of sound." The play would work like a silent movie with the Rotos serving as mimes and as mighty Wurlitzer.

Loretta liked the director. She treated them as equals, describing the nature of each set, then letting them work on their own. When she saw what they were doing, she seemed pleased. It was only later they saw that what she did to their jumbled and confusing set ("Hopkins and St. Cyr, designers; Aschenbach, consulting artist") was not unlike what she had done to the script: wiped it out, pressed it against the damp wall, upstaging it with the many beautiful props she bought or made herself—a toy car, a ticket booth and turnstile and a beautiful silk-screened wheatfield with a real red tractor, built for a child. Margaret, who went to opening night with her mother, said she didn't recognize a thing. And then, when she did, there it was all shoved in one corner and crumpled together. Nonetheless, Hopkins and St. Cyr were cited next morning in the *Times*, and Margaret—less put out when she called Loretta at 8 a.m., woke Daniel—said they would probably receive a lot of calls now for their work, because they were fresh, no one had heard of them, yet they were in the *Times*, they were known, they had a track record.

But that was later. Now they were still working on a corner of the first set, creating blue-painted paper rocks to suggest an underwater grotto, which in turn was a metaphor for a subway station in the stone jungle of upper Manhattan. To make the tedious work more interesting, Margaret had been trying to get Loretta to tell what life was like in Providence back in the days of madras shorts and ditty bags. The story was interesting if she could get Loretta to finish it, but Loretta only wanted to tell so much, so Margaret had to keep going over with her sodden paintbrush to slap more blue paint on the rocks, and to egg her on.

"They're starting to look like kitchen walls," Loretta said.

"Kitchen walls, for your information, don't have words on them. At least not in my neighborhood."

Loretta stood up to rest her back. Margaret had flopped down on the drop cloth. "What did the *P* stand for?"

"Are we still talking about that?"

"Just answer the question."

Loretta told Margaret that it stood for Padraic, but even Margaret knew that Paddy was an Irish name and that Carmino was a guinea. They had already gone over all that in a previous conversation. "Where I come from, if an Italian had a *P* in his name, it could only stand for one thing."

"What?"

"Pass Squally. Or Pass Squall."

Margaret lay back on the drop cloth. "Pass Squally," she chanted, "or Pass Squall."

And in walked the ballerina, not to check on them, but to use the bathroom. She was in there a long time, so Margaret and Loretta worked silently and made one rock face dripping with blue paint, no words, although Margaret tried printing PAS and Loretta grabbed the brush out of her hand. The ballerina came out, pale and sick-looking, with a glass of water in her hand.

"She's squalid too," said Margaret, when they heard the front door shut. The ballerina would be off—they knew her schedule—to her dance studio, practice for three or four hours, eat a pathetic lunch, then walk over to the West Side to see her biofeedback lady, followed by tea (black, no sugar, and no toast either) with her gay friends, Jerry and Larry (Loretta couldn't believe they knew each other: Patrice had even boarded C. Roof, as she called him), then back here and work all night on plays and other things: she reviewed restaurants and movies for some arty magazines and newsletters. The movies were one thing, "but what could she possibly do in restaurants," Loretta asked Margaret, "when she's always on a 10-calorie diet?"

Margaret thought the ballerina's eating disorders were beneath contempt, and said so, but she still wanted to investigate. The set designers had examined the kitchen and turned up a library of cookbooks and supplies for cooking, although the kitchen was clearly never used. They found only coffee beans, mustard and bottled water in her refrigerator. Her shelves were filled with vitamins and prescription drugs. She was taking everything they had ever heard of: ups, downs, anti-depressants, estrogen supplements, tetracycline, pain-killers, purgatives, antacids and lots of different sleeping pills. Margaret checked all the dates and they were all new prescriptions, or fresh refills. "Wow," said Margaret, when they had been through both bathroom cabinets, "some of this stuff, *I* don't even recognize!" She did recognize some strong tranquilizers. "These would put a horse to sleep. My mother used to take these," she said, taking a handful of the shiny orange pills—"You never know when you might need these"—and stuffing them in her pocket.

At first, they admired the ballerina: she was so tense and so perfect, so busy and so important. Her phone was always ringing and her mail was full of personal letters and thick brown envelopes from art magazines. Everything she did, she did fast. She never relaxed. She was dying of starvation, Loretta pointed out, but Margaret said that that was the price you paid for that kind of control. Unfortunately, their time spent working for the ballerina coincided, for Margaret, with a fat phase. She was converting the strain of Alfred Aschenbach into nightly forays to the New Deli for treats, and the New was open all night long. Margaret's latest food fad involved anything white and soft: macaroni salads and rice puddings, quart cartons of vanilla yoghurt, five-packs of pale macaroons, baby marshmallows, pecan sandies, tins of white frosting and those little rolls, Margaret reported to Loretta, packed into a cardboard cylinder that you pop open, then arrange the sliced rounds of dough on a buttered cookie sheet; these often came with a tin of frosting which you could eat separately, as needed, or spread onto the steaming toasted surface of the little buns. "Or," she said in the solemn tone of a food-maniac, "you could eat the dough raw, and cook the frosting on plain bread, if you had any left over—"

"Enough," Loretta said. Margaret never got too fat, and Loretta hated to think of the things she inflicted on herself to keep her weight stable while gorging on the sweet white things.

These binges gave Margaret a sharper eye on the ribbon-thinness of Patrice Fallows, but Patrice was as oblivious to this scrutiny as she was to everything else pertaining to the set designers and the Rotos, business she relegated to the early hours of her long nights.

Margaret was standing near the window so that she could watch as Patrice issued from the metal basement door with its ring of garbage cans, ran up the steps and trotted down the street in her small white tennis shoes, a rope of hair swinging down her straight back. "I despise her, did you know that?" Margaret said, turning away from the window.

"Yeah, I know that," Loretta said.

"I have contempt for anyone who's all show, but underneath a mass of squirming pathologies."

Loretta nodded, but she also thought that could apply to anyone they knew. Margaret slumped down to the floor near where Loretta had slumped. "I don't want to think about her," she said. "Tell me about your date with Pass Squally."

Loretta was sitting on the floor surrounded by mounds of expensive paper, folded, crumpled and painted. They had overdone it; they had enough for ten subways. Margaret sighed. "Would you go and see what she's left us to drink?" (Margaret liked to drink the ballerina's wine and didn't consider it stealing because they weren't being paid for their work. Loretta had pointed out that Patrice herself wasn't getting paid, so why should they steal her wine? "You always take her side," Margaret snapped.) Loretta didn't get up, so Margaret marched into the kitchen and returned a few minutes later with a half bottle of something and two crystal glasses.

"You could at least use the everyday glasses, Margaret."

"You can't drink good wine out of glass."

They sipped the wine, a nice dark-red one (Margaret had announced the grape, its year and vineyard, and the price-tag, $35, still on the bottle), and already opened and aired. "I'd still rather drink a cheap bottle," said Loretta, "since we're stealing it." Margaret said there were plenty of open bottles in the kitchen, and all of them pricey. The ballerina had had a party. "By tonight, she'll have to throw it all away," Margaret said. "It'll turn fast. Besides," pouring more wine into both glasses, "she doesn't drink by herself, so this would have all gone to waste."

"Do you want to hear about Pass Squally, or don't you?" Loretta said, after a long pause. She hated it when Margaret got onto a jag.

"I said I did, didn't I? You're the one who's always changing the subject."

"Well," Loretta said, pressing her sore back against the cold wall, "picture the arrival of a 1969 Corvette Stingray, white with white upholstery, customized, no muffler, at 54 Canton Street. It had been to the carwash that very day and had had a whole can of Turtle Wax applied to its coat with a chammy rag. Then braking with a screech that would have killed Aunt Rita dead on the spot, if she'd been there to hear it."

"Where was she?"

"That doesn't matter." Loretta looked at Margaret to make sure she was paying attention. "You could see skid marks on the street."

"Don't exaggerate."

"All right. My uncle was out there by the time I got down. They were talking. Pass Squall didn't even get out of the car."

"Did he like Pass Squall, your uncle?"

"Yeah, I guess he did. I don't know."

"How was he acting?"

"He was acting okay. There'd been a big blow-up."

"About what?"

"About my going out with him."

"How come?"

Loretta paused to think. She knew why, but she didn't want to get into it. "You know, the usual thing."

"Oh."

"I wore my white linen pleated skirt—"

"I remember those. Those were nice."

"—black pumps—"

"You should have worn white with white. But you didn't know any better, right?"

"Margaret."

"Sorry. Go on, I'm listening."

"And a turquoise shell on top."

Margaret wanted to know what a "shell" was. "It wasn't like the shells Bloody Mary wore in *South Pacific*, was it?"

"Haven't you ever heard of those sleeveless sweaters called shells?"

Margaret said she hadn't.

"Well, that's what I wore, a tight sleeveless sweater and a pleated skirt."

"What did you weigh then?"

"Same."

"Oh," Margaret said, gazing at Loretta's long, rangy body. "It must have looked pretty good then."

Loretta wondered if it did. Her aunt had said she looked lovely, Gloria had whistled, and her uncle had said she'd become quite the young lady. It was embarrassing.

"What's that?" Margaret said, when the door suddenly slammed shut. They looked at each other, then Margaret covered the wine bottle and glasses with a paper rock and snatched up her paint brush. Loretta just sat there. Not that the ballerina noticed: she swished in, her string bag filled with supplies—Loretta saw oranges and chives, a loaf of French bread and a few wrapped packages—and then the kitchen door swung shut. They could hear her opening and closing cupboard doors. What telltale signs Margaret had left out in the kitchen, Loretta didn't know.

Patrice swept through the workroom a few minutes later, carrying the leather tote bag filled with her dance clothes, and holding a can of Coke. "If you're hungry," she said to Margaret, "I bought some things for lunch." She turned toward the door and pulled back the heavy bolt. "I won't be back till late, so good-bye. If anyone calls," she said, pulling a ring of keys from her handbag, "I'll call them tomorrow." She shook loose the key she wanted. "I looked at your work last night, and you're doing just fine. I'm getting lots of ideas from what I'm seeing." She closed the door and locked it.

"She's on something," Margaret said, not even waiting for the ballerina to emerge from the basement door. Loretta sat still. "Don't you think?"

There was no answer. "Well?" Margaret insisted.

"I don't know." Loretta got up and headed toward the subway set and started pulling off chunks of charcoal paper from the mounts.

"What are you doing!"

Loretta pulled off another sheet and threw it on the floor.

"Tell me what you're doing!" Margaret shrieked, pushing herself between Loretta and the set. "Have you gone berserk?"

Loretta looked at Margaret: "Can't you see that Patrice is criticizing us? Either she's criticizing us," Loretta sidestepped Margaret to pull off another sheet, "or she thinks we're too stupid to be *worth* criticizing."

"I don't get it. Tell me what you mean."

But Loretta refused to explain: by then, Margaret knew. She was very quick in these matters.

"How exactly do you know this?" Margaret demanded, studying Loretta's rigid face. "Did she say something to you in private?" Margaret's eyes were two hard points. "I'm looking at you," she said, "just the way you looked at her, but I still can't read your mind." Loretta laughed, and that eased the tension a little. "You always know more than you say," Margaret complained. "Sometimes I don't trust you."

"Oh really?" Loretta returned, in a tone ever so slightly arch.

"Okay. All right," Margaret said, turning her back so that Loretta couldn't see the look on her face, or the shade of it. "Well, tell me about your boyfriend. Tell me about Carmino. It was Carmino, I think, who taught you how to see right through people."

No, Loretta felt like saying. You know who it was. She didn't say, but she found Margaret's eyes and looked into them, until Margaret, still flushed, looked away. Loretta then felt free to re-launch her story, having made the needed point efficiently, and almost painlessly. "I looked out the bathroom window and there was this blinding white car with a teenager in it."

Margaret was thinking, her face paling to its normal color. "You hadn't already seen his car, Loretta?" she asked.

Loretta watched the face: the car was *not* the issue, and she wanted to make sure that Margaret saw this. "I was young. The year before I was in the Girl Scouts. I had never been asked *out* on a date."

"Really? I thought you were so popular."

"I went to an all-girls school, remember?"

"That's right, I forgot."

"So—"

"So, did you *do* it?"

Loretta looked at Margaret and waited until Margaret's smile faded a little.

Margaret said: "Go ahead, hurt me."

"I'm not going to 'hurt' you, Margaret. I can see, though, why you don't understand Patrice Fallows."

"You did it. You hurt me."

"Can I tell my story, or should we change the subject?" Loretta said sharply.

Margaret sighed. "Go on, tell me."

"You got to understand," Loretta said, standing up and stapling the ripped sheets back onto the mount, "we're talking

about the sixties: '68, '69." (The story was a good story, and
Loretta was feeling good. This was how the ballerina must feel
every minute of her life.)

"The sixties," Margaret said, "I remember. Go on."

"In Providence, there was already a head shop on the East
Side, and a shop for India imports, a theater that showed only
foreign movies and a few kids from Boston starting to grow their
hair long and criticize the president."

"I was criticizing him, too. We were criticizing him where
I was, too."

"Right. Well, you have to understand that Pass Squall had
never seen any of this."

Margaret laughed—Loretta had taken such a serious tone.
"You sound like a social worker. Was he one of New York's
neediest?"

"No, but he was never going to enter the sixties the way
we did."

"*You* didn't."

"I didn't, true. But I did more than he did. He was never
going to see it. It never hit his neighborhood."

"What neighborhood was this?"

"My neighborhood."

"It missed your neighborhood?"

"Carmino was my first date of the sixties."

Margaret picked up the wine bottle. "It was different for
me," she said. "It was the sixties when I was in high school." She
poured a full glass for herself and a splash into Loretta's untouched glass. "The only time it wasn't the sixties was when my
parents were still married and I was a kid—no, that's wrong.
For my father, it was always the sixties. He was criticizing the
president from the time I was born. Or even before."

"He's still in the sixties now, isn't he?"

"You can say that again," Margaret said emphatically.

"It's not a criticism."

"Tell your story. I'm growing a root here."

"This *is* the story. Tell me: what was I wearing?"

"Shell."

"You remembered! What else?"

"I don't know: skirt."

"Yeah, my uncle said how pretty I looked. Gloria came out to the car too. She wanted to get her eyeful."

"She was wearing—?"

"Oh, I don't know. She'd dressed up for the date, I suppose," Loretta said.

"Oh, right!" Margaret said sarcastically.

"Yes. She had a skirt and blouse on, like me. She looked normal, except for her head."

"Was her head in the sixties?"

"She had on a plastic headband."

"You don't mean headband, you mean sweatband, or freak flag."

"No, I mean headband—'hairband,' you might have called it. One of those brown plastic strips with teeth. Her hair was pulled straight back and she had mascara under her eyes."

"What do you mean, '*under* her eyes?'"

"She put it on and rubbed in it. She looked like a raccoon with a little patch of Clearasil right there on the chin." Loretta reached over and pointed her finger at Margaret's rounded chin.

"Did she have pimples? You didn't touch my skin with your hand," Margaret said, feeling her face with her fingertips, "did you?"

"She had a few."

"Gross."

"My uncle sent her right inside."

"Why? She doesn't sound so bad."

"She was being punished."

"You have a good memory. For what?"

"I don't remember. Anyway, to get back to the story—" Loretta took a sip of her wine; it had already started to turn. "Where were we?"

"Go on your date."

"Oh yeah. We went to the pizzeria."

"T'eat?"

"No. We just parked in front so Carmino could see his friends."

"How'd you like the car?"

"Nice. I remember how it smelled. It smelled of leather, plus Carmino had poured some men's cologne all over himself, and I had on perfume, too."

"What?"

"Emeraude." Loretta looked to see if Margaret recognized this. It could make a difference.

"What's that?"

"Some crap of my aunt's. It stunk."

"Why'd you wear it?"

"I don't know. It was pretty-*looking,* green cream in a bottle with a little ribbon on it, very Loretta Young.

"We drove around. We stopped for gas. We cruised up and down River Avenue, then up and down Atwells Avenue, then swung up to Cranston where his aunt lives and we parked in front of their house for a while. The uncle came out in his tee-shirt—an Italian one, with the skinny straps—to talk to Carmino about the car, and then one of the cousins came out. They didn't pay any attention to me, and Carmino didn't introduce me. Finally, the mother came out to ask Carmino 'why dint he invite the girl in.' Carmino said he dint, that's all. So then we went to the show. I think we saw a war picture—*The Green Berets*. And then we went back to Providence to park."

"This is the part, this is the part! Tell me."

"No."

"Why?"

"This is the part you already understand."

"What do you mean?"

"You can picture it. You did it every night of your life in high school."

Margaret laughed. "There, you're wrong. But you did let him, didn't you?"

"I dint."

"Then, what are you saying?"

"I'm saying that he was all over me and I let him until—"

"Until what?"

"Until he got sick and tired of it."

"When was that? You're lying now, aren't you? He wasn't sick and tired of it. Nobody at that age gets sick and tired of it. Just the opposite."

"It doesn't matter. After a while—I'm not saying when—he got off me."

"Where was this? On the back seat? I can't picture it."

"He got up and put his face right into my face and said: 'I don't turn you on. Why dint you say so inna first place?'"

"Carmino said that! How old was he?"

"He said: 'You don't have be a bitch about it. I'm not stoopit!' I told him I was sorry, it was my first date. I was probably too young for him."

"You didn't say that."

"I did say that, and he started to bawl."

"You're making this up!" Margaret was feeling around for the cigarette package. "They're under your leg," Loretta said. Margaret said, "It doesn't sound even remotely possible. What did I do with the matches?"

"Yeah, but he did. He was lying there with his head on my lap and telling me things about his life and his old girlfriend. She didn't like him either. Either that, he said, or she was 'a fuckin' ice cube,' like me."

"That's funny."

"In a way. He stopped blubbering after a while and started giving me a kiss. It must have been a little better because he asked *me* to be his girlfriend."

"He did? What did you say?"

"I said yes."

Margaret reflected. "That's a weird story." She stood up. "no one but you would tell a story like that. What was wrong with that guy?" She picked up a *Dance* magazine and went into the bathroom.

Loretta took the dirty glasses into the kitchen. She had bragged about Carmino. It wasn't really that funny. What was so funny about it? She hadn't been nice to him. When he was upset about his old girlfriend, she didn't say anything to help. It was a shock just to see a boy crying. Still, there was no reason to ignore him or look down on him. He had a reason for crying: now that she was older and married, she understood the reason better, although she wasn't sure she could explain it.

"You were too mature for him." Margaret was back. She was leaning against the kitchen doorpost. "Don't you think that was it?"

"I never understood what was going through his head." Loretta was looking into the sink, into the mouths of the wine glasses streaked with soap—an iridescent soap skin formed across the lip of one glass.

"He was from another planet, Loretta." Margaret came to the sink and looked at the soap bubble. "He didn't understand *you.*"

"What was there to understand?" Loretta said, rinsing the glasses in cold water, after pushing Margaret's arm out of the way. "It was just a date."

"That's what *he* thought," Margaret said. "He thought it was just a date."

"Well, what was it then?" Loretta asked, ripping sheets of paper toweling and upending the glasses on a double layer.

"It was—" Margaret stopped. "Well, you know, you did it. He got in his car for the date, his white 'vette, he was okay when he got in, but when he got home after it was over, he felt like the ignorant greaseball that he was. He knew his name was funny. You're telling me he didn't? *You* did it to him."

This was the payback, Loretta figured, for noticing that

the ballerina didn't like their sets and would use them only to spur on her own more vivid, practical imagination.

The phone rang; it was an actor friend of the ballerina's. They knew him because he had come over one day and kept them company while they worked. They pumped him about Patrice; they knew this much already: that the ballerina had quit dancing professionally one year ago because of an injury; they wanted to know what and how. At first, the actor was reluctant to say, but when it became clear that Margaret was going to make up a story if he didn't tell, he said tendonitis and bone spurs.

Margaret said the ballerina must be living off unemployment or disability: that was why she could afford to be so idle. The actor said no, Patrice was rich. She had planned to quit dancing anyway, and then she had viral pneumonia twice in one month, enough was enough. But the ballerina herself, one afternoon when she felt sociable, told them a different story: she had been fired by Mr. B himself.

"Why?" Margaret asked.

"He said I couldn't work well with people, but it was exactly the opposite. I'm better with people than he. The dancers were coming to *me* for help in reworking their steps."

"Really?"

"I was doing choreography, too, and was thinking about starting my own dance company. It was a question of finding the backing. The dancers were there and the material was all in my head."

The story grew more elaborate over time: the actor added details about the illnesses, and the ballerina episodes in the battle between her and Mr. B, and the stories never came together. Margaret checked in the library and, sure enough, Patrice Fallows—never a principal dancer—had worked for Balanchine, yes, but mostly in the corps. Nothing was said about why she had quit. Margaret was very much affected by the story. For a week, she hardly criticized the ballerina. The subject of Balanchine came up a few times, as Margaret worked it over in her mind.

When Margaret hung up the phone that day, they discussed the actor and whether the ballerina was now having an affair with him. They discussed her dancing career—as they always did—and what it really meant. "She thought she was something she wasn't," Margaret said.

"I was thinking just the same thing," Loretta said. "You mean the ballerina and Balanchine, right?"

"She was never as good as she thought," Margaret said in a monotone. "She still thinks she's a good dancer, and I bet she *never* was."

Margaret went on: "And notice how quick she is to judge what other people do. How would she know? And why do you believe her?"

"What we're doing *isn't* good," Loretta said. "It stinks."

"Well, thanks for telling me." Margaret wheeled around and walked out of the room.

"Let's get our stuff," Loretta said, when she came back. "Are you going out tonight?"

Margaret had a date with Alfred—not a date exactly, but they were going to meet somewhere after he finished doing something else. If it wasn't too late, he was going to call when he was done. "Are you and Daniel staying home or what?" Margaret asked, annoyed at the reminder that she didn't have a real date, just a worthless promise.

"I guess so. I haven't heard from Daniel since this morning. In fact," Loretta said, pulling on her coat, "I'm dead late. I should have been home an hour ago."

"Really. Why?" asked Margaret coyly, but Loretta was already out the door and halfway down the steps.

Turning back to watch Margaret flying home to see if Alfred had called, Loretta wondered exactly how much trouble

she was in. It could be a big deal, or it could be nothing. She
started home. It was a cold night, a metallic taste to the air, and
a scud of red clouds in a dark sky, the street sunk in soft gloom.
Loretta raced along a crosstown street, fast and then faster. Too
bad, because this kind of walk in the changing light was the best
part of any day; the worst part of any day was going home. Was
that true? After she was home awhile, things became easier, but
re-entering, not knowing what kind of mood Daniel was in, was
hard. It wasn't all his fault. He was probably just as surprised to
find her there every day, at home in the small apartment, and
forced, night after night—. She took in a deep draught of the
gray air, cold and smoky, and went in.

The apartment was empty. "All this time," she read when
she found the note—neat script on a yellow legal page—"I've
been waiting for you. Since 4. Isn't that when you said you'd be
back? I can't wait anymore. I'm tired of waiting." Loretta put
the note down on the table, fed Peewee, went to splash some
water on her eyes, tidied the room, patted Peewee, made the bed
and filled the kettle for tea. She watered the plants, talked to
Peewee, and opened the two windows a crack. She picked up the
letter ("You always make me wait") and sat down on their one
comfortable chair. She stared at the page until she saw only
yellow with veins of blue script. Daniel was angry. This time he
was angry because she was late, but behind that was the real reason: that she was always out, that she preferred anyone else's
company to his, that she wouldn't lift a finger to call him and
say she'd be late (she'd rather he agonize alone, wondering
whether she'd been mugged, raped or killed); she just didn't
care, that was all. He had said all this before. In his eyes, she was
his only friend, his lover; to her, he was "just another pain in the
ass. Admit it. Everything you do shows how little regard you
have for me."

Loretta threw the letter on the floor. Peewee jumped up on
her lap. ("And that bastard! You'd rather have a cat than a

husband. ") She stroked Peewee's long yellow back until the cat, perfectly relaxed, produced the low rumble of his contentment. Loretta closed her eyes. To come home, to get a letter like this, to have every little thoughtless thing she did magnified into an agony for him: this was too much.

Once she had asked Margaret what she thought of this marriage. "Why are you asking me?" Margaret had said defensively. Then: "At least you talk to each other. You and Daniel can talk about anything. No man I've ever been with wanted to talk to me."

Another time she had said: "Don't you even *like* Daniel? He's so attractive! Don't you find him attractive?"

There was no answer to this question. Or the answer was: Sometimes, not that often. Loretta wouldn't like to admit this to someone like Margaret, or even to herself. Wasn't it better just to resign yourself to nothing? Nobody she knew experienced attraction after marriage in a way that wasn't dangerous; sometimes they didn't even experience it in their affairs. People always seemed to get involved for reasons other than sex, whether they knew it or not. Loretta pushed the comfort-loving Peewee off her lap and picked up the letter. Daniel liked to say how he had eliminated everything in his life except her, and that he had given her his whole life: I'm yours, he liked to say, and I don't want anyone but you.

In a sense, this was true. Once they were married, Daniel got rid of his friends, and then he tried to get rid of hers. And, when she had gotten herself a part-time job laying out classified ads for a local paper, he said: "What do you want to do that for? I thought you wanted to be an artist. Do you want to be an artist or a wage-slave?" But after she quit the job, she had nothing to do and no one to talk to. Daniel spent his time reading and studying. He wrote long research papers for his classes, and gradually dismissed each of his professors, once he recognized their various intellectual limitations. His mother sent enough

to pay their rent, and his fellowship covered expenses. They
didn't have to worry about money, but Daniel liked to worry: he
organized periods of austerity and periods of spending, however
the mood struck him. He fixed up the apartment the way he
liked it: comfortable but with no trace of indulgence, nothing
bought for the sake of being like other people, or just to be tasteful. He built bookshelves and tables out of odd pieces of lumber,
and covered the windows with Indian textiles. He taught
himself how to cook cheap, one-pot dinners with canned soup,
rice and beans.

He loved being married, or at least he did in the beginning. He was always in motion, full of enthusiasm. He changed
his program once a term, sampling every branch of Western
thought until he found a period rich and rigorous enough to sat-
isfy his longings: the eighteenth century, apogee of man's belief
in rationality, as he put it, before religion, romanticism and
mass culture dealt the mind a fatal blow. This—and everything
he did in the beginning—seemed wonderful; she followed
along in his wake, reading what she could understand, and listening while he built, refined, tore down and re-built his
theories, his readings. Daniel was a puzzle to most people he
met: where did he get the drive, the burning intelligence, the
eloquence, where was he going to invest these talents, and what
was he going to get out of it? And Daniel couldn't say because he
didn't like this kind of question. He couldn't accept a description of any of his qualities; it sickened him to be pinpointed in
any way. He didn't want to know—to know was limitation, to
know was death. She wondered if Daniel could recognize *his* face
in a mirror—he hated mirrors almost as much as she did, but
where she saw only pieces and no pattern, he saw nothing at all,
or so he claimed.

Peewee jumped back on her lap and sat on the letter.
Daniel was happy the first year they were married, and he
wanted her to be happy. First he arranged her easels, paints and

chair in a sunny corner of the one-room apartment. "Now you can paint all you want." He himself left early in the morning for school, after making the coffee and discussing his plans for the day. His days were all filled up: he had barely enough time to attend his classes, read in the library, practice his guitar with the little band he had formed and try and find them gigs. (The little band—Chokecherry, it was called—played a few gigs in a small bar, then broke up. The members couldn't agree about anything—material, arrangements, solos, practice time, fees, drugs, girl singers. But for a while, before the fights got rough, it was fun and Daniel was content just to stand behind the singer with an amplified guitar around his neck.) In addition to music and school, there was shopping, scrounging for junked furniture and bits of wood, and riding his bike all over the city to gather material for the novel he was writing.

Loretta stayed home and penciled, painted, crayoned, chalked and inked the lone trees out the window—sometimes pictured through the bars of the fire escape, sometimes without the bars. She sketched the radio, the pots and pans hooked to the wall, the telephone with its kinked and knotted coil, many views of Peewee. Tab cans and bottles, books on the table, coffee cups, the drafting lamp, and whatever else she could find. But no matter how enthusiastically she began, after a few hours of steady work, she was bored with drawing.

There were only a few things to do then: stare out the window, which she did when she felt peaceful; solitary walks, or a visit to the library—she never went shopping because Daniel kept what little money they had. In the dead of the afternoon, hours before Daniel returned home full of the day's excitement and variety, ready to cook a one-pot dinner and drink a jug of wine, argue the themes of his papers, or something someone had said in class—before all this, Loretta would dig out the sole cookbook they owned, wedding present from a destitute relative, in and out of mental hospitals all his life, who didn't come to the wedding but sent the present from a nursing home: *The Young Bride's Cookbook*, "Cooking for Two on Pennies a Day." It contained many color photos of dishes: bright yellow and brown casseroles, desserts sprayed with Dream Whip clouds, grayish icebox cookies and hamburgers done with 101 different tomato sauce garnishes—some of these were photographed, some were merely sketched in pen and ink. Everything in this book was sickening. So why did she read every word of every recipe, and all the little stories that introduced the recipes? Each story was about a happy but poor woman who had, say, $2.50 to spend on dinner, and what she did with her money to make the dinner on the page. Other women had $3.25 to spend and so could be a bit more lavish, or $4, even more extravagant, or there was one who had $1.25 and had to dig deep into her pathetic staples, and, worst of all, the poor idiot who had 45 cents, and yet even here *The Young Bride's Cookbook* had a cheery solution. All these women were given names and addresses, in addition to their budgets. There was a Mrs. Dorothy Thomas from Norwalk, Conn., Mrs. Celia Allen of Brockton, Mass., a Mrs. Eunice Green from Topeka, Kansas. They could, of course, shop for regional specialties, cheaper in season, and part of the charm of living in America. One of the regional recipes ("Dixieland Delight") was "Butterbean Porkchops with Potatoes St. James, Homemade Apple-Rhubarb Sauce and Canned Pears for dessert, with Sugar Cookies, Instant Coffee or Sanka."

Loretta never made a single recipe from this book, although she memorized a few from repeated readings, and she had sketched some table settings, trying to achieve the dullish sheen of plastic plates and bowls, the ruffle of paper napkins in their napkin holder, the cheery flowered tablecloths with spongeable surface and the odd vase of "Spring Flowers," which may have been a code word for "artificial."

She hid the book from Daniel. He wanted to throw it out, it depressed him, but at the last minute she always rescued it

from the trashcan. She liked to soak for a good hour in the atmosphere of the *Young Bride's Cookbook*, and by then, the worst of
the afternoon would be over; there'd be a sense that everything
would come to an end, the monotony and the empty, gloomy
hours.

Then, one day, when even the cookbook didn't ease the
boredom of three in the afternoon, she broke down and did what
Daniel warned her not to do, for her own good: she called
Margaret Hopkins, after months of ignoring Margaret's calls,
notes and invitations. Margaret was home. She, too, was bored.
She was in between boyfriends and had left her job as a
receptionist at NBC. Margaret said she'd been thinking about
getting it together to go back to school, to become a real artist.
Loretta liked that idea. There was no money to do it, but at Margaret's suggestion, she brought a portfolio of sketches to the
school, and the admissions office got her a tuition scholarship on
the merits of the *Young Bride*'s dinners, pots and pans and the can
of Tab. They were modest yet witty, one of the art teachers said;
he could picture them on the pages of the *New Yorker*.

That changed everything. The days now had more of a
shape, and Loretta read less of the cookbook. Eventually she lost
it. Around that time, Daniel went into one of his slumps, feeling sick of school, discontented, hopeless, angry and frustrated
with the limited prospects of an academic philosopher. Now *he*
spent time at home, watching hours of TV or practicing his
guitar. He still worked on his papers, but only at night, when
the fires of philosophy were fed by a long dinner and discussions
with a person naive enough to swallow whole a lot of cut-rate art
theories that were "threadbare, self-contradictory, and already
bankrupt 500 years ago."

That was the phone. Loretta pushed Peewee and the letter
off her lap. It was Margaret. Did Daniel and Loretta want to go

out with her and Alfred—Margaret sounded so excited—a film, dinner? Loretta said no, Daniel wasn't feeling up to it. "Can I talk to him?" Margaret said. "Put him on." Loretta said Daniel was still asleep; he had a migraine and a stomachache and had just fallen asleep.

"Too bad," said Margaret.

"I'm sorry," Loretta said. "Talk to you later."

"Why do you sound so funny?"

"Me?"

"You know you do."

Loretta got Margaret off the phone with difficulty, and there was Daniel in the doorway. He took in the letter on the floor, but made no comment. "Did you just get home?" he asked.

"I don't know what time it is," she said. "What time is it?"

"Seven-thirty."

"I got home at six."

Loretta thought he might sit at the table and ignore her, but instead he stood in the middle of the floor with a peculiar look on his face. It was something like a smile, but it didn't go with the way he was standing. Daniel had put on weight and was always riding his bike, so he had a layer of shapely muscle on his legs and arms. Even his neck had filled out and wasn't so delicate-looking.

"What do you want to do tonight?" he asked.

"I don't know," she said. "Shall we eat something?"

"Not yet."

It was then, looking at him posed in the middle of the floor, that she realized that he might still have a fight planned, or at least an argument, in spite of all the time that had passed.

"Why were you so late?" he asked. "Were you having *that* good a time?"

"Are you mad at me?"

"I asked you a question."

"I was having an alright time. We're still making the first set, you know the one—"

"I'm not interested. That's not why I'm asking you the question. Does it look like I'm in the mood for a chat?"

She didn't answer.

He finally moved from his spot. He walked to the refrigerator and got a beer. "Want one?"

"I don't know. Yes." He carried the beer and a glass to the bed—the bed was made but not flung into the wall. He sat on the bed: "Why don't you sit here next to me?"

Loretta didn't get up.

"Why are you afraid of me?" he said in a quieter voice. "What do you have to be scared of?"

She started to get up, then sat down again. He got up instead, and handed her the beer and glass. "You don't have to sit next to me or do anything, if you feel that way about it."

She sat still in her chair, and waited. Then: "What way?"

She knew what the argument was going to be about. It was going to be about the thing that was at the bottom of all their problems. They were going to have a talk about sex and why they never had any. He already knew the answer: she was completely uninterested, and even if she were interested, it wouldn't be in him, he made her sick. Why did she marry him? Had she wanted to leave home that badly, or did she just like grinding someone down? "Well," he was saying, "you've succeeded at both, haven't you?

"You're a cruel person," he went on. "I know you don't believe that—and nobody who *thinks* they know you would believe it—but it's true." He was putting his coat on. "I'm going out for cigarettes, and when I come back, I want to talk to you like a human being. You'd better decide whether you want to stay married or not. I'm not going to live like this anymore. It's not worth it."

When he came back, she met him at the door, removed the

bag of groceries from his arms. She walked him to the bed and pushed him onto it. Then she put the whole bag of groceries into the refrigerator, walked to the bed and lay down next to him. He lay perfectly still, his eyes were alert and wary. But eventually he closed his eyes and she ran her hand around his neck and under his shirt and sweater. He was very warm. "The trouble with—" he was saying. She kissed him to stop him from saying it.

A bit later, when it was over, he was still mad. There was a residue of anger because nothing dramatic or satisfying had happened. His back was curled, turned away, encased in an air of gloom. Loretta turned away from him. The kitchen light was on, but the rest of the room was sunk in darkness. She had hurt things before, this wasn't the first time. She had begun hurting things when she was little. Spite and indifference. She was like that: harsh, mean, indifferent to the pain of others. Maybe she even enjoyed their pain. She closed her eyes.

She remembered, when she was very young, hurting that nice black dog that lived on the second floor of their tenement on First Street. She liked that dog, Bells its name was. It sat on the concrete stoop with her every day. They sat side by side in the hot sun with nothing to do. Some days they'd listen to her mother screaming at her father, or her father yelling at her mother, or both of them talking at the top of their lungs, while drinking pot after pot of coffee, iced coffee in summer, and bottle after bottle of beer. Her father liked beer; her mother preferred a highball, when she could get it, and Loretta liked Coca-Cola in a bottle.

She would either listen to them, or try not to listen. One time her mother came flying out the door, clattered down the steps, just a housedress and her pocketbook, and tore into the garage, backed the car out. Her father followed close behind, opening the car door and dragging the mother out, punched her right in the mouth, the pocketbook fell on the dirt (the driveway wasn't paved yet) and opened. Loretta sat there. Her mother tried to smack her father back, but he grabbed her arm and— "Let me get my pockabook, you big slob!" she yelled, but her father grabbed the pocketbook and marched her back up the steps and into the house. Loretta and Bells had moved to the sidewalk. "What are you looking at?" her father bellowed. "Why don't you mind your own business!" The door slammed and Loretta stood on the sidewalk, then sat down on the curbstone. The dog huddled next to her, shivering.

Everyone heard the ruckus. The door across the street opened and slammed shut, and another neighbor was looking out her front window. Mrs. Matusiewicz, the Polish lady, was standing on her porch looking, and then sat down on the rocker. Loretta's friend, Helena, was out there with her. They were both gaping. Eventually, Bells stopped shivering and went back up the steps to sit on the stoop. Loretta heard the porch door slam and Helena appeared, finished with housework and ready to play, but not to sit in the gutter, if that's what Loretta was planning to do all day. "My mother says," Helena whispered in Loretta's ear, when her mother went back into the house and couldn't see her sitting in her clean pink shorts on the filthy curbstone, "to tell you that you can come over to our house when they're raising a stink. You can either come over to our house or if we're not home, you can sit in our yard. You don't have to sit here on the sidewalk. Okay?"

Loretta turned to the house. "Bells!" she screamed, and the dog leapt up and started barking. "Get down here," and down it came.

Helena jumped up from the sidewalk. "Don't let that dog get so close to you!"

"Why not?"

"It's filthy. Can't you see that its fur is all covered with dirt?"

"That's not dirt," Loretta said.

"Then what is it, wiseguy?"

"It's mange."

Helena squealed, although she had heard this story many times. "That dog"—she had jumped into the street—"has *mange* and you're hugging it like a baby!" Then, Mrs. Mats must have seen, because she called Helena home. Helena must have forgotten to clean *under* the plastic slipcovers that clung to every stick of furniture in the Mats' parlor and den, just like they did in Loretta's house, though they were never cleaned, inside *or* out. "What's the point," Loretta's mother had said, "of getting goddamn slipcovers if you have to go and clean them?" Loretta remembered how she used to tell her mother about the work Helena had to do every single Saturday and how carefully she had to do it: how the girl had to use a wet sponge with ammonia, then a damp sponge with water, a dry rag and a soft polishing rag, and then her mother would come and criticize her for the slipshod job she was doing. "Get out!" Loretta's mother always said. "You're making this up!" "Cross my heart," Loretta said, spitting on her fingers and drawing a cross on her chest, "and hope to die." "Don't do that," her mother said. "That's disgusting."

What were they fighting about? Daniel asked her once, when she had told him one of these stories. Loretta said it was about money, although she didn't always know what they were fighting about—it was different every time. "They were always on each other's back, snapping, criticizing, making cracks and giving digs."

"Did they give you digs?"

"No, they each tried to get me on their side."

"Whose side were you on?"

Loretta laughed when he asked that question: it was a stupid question, and Daniel was never stupid. "I was always—"

"I know," he interrupted, "you were always on *her* side. I can see that. You think your father was a criminal. Well, I don't think your mother was such a saint. It sounds like she drove him to do the things you're so quick to criticize."

But Daniel was wrong—her father *was* a criminal, worse than a criminal. But her mother was no saint. "Loretta," she'd sing out in that silly voice, when the coast was clear, "come in now, it's all blown over. Your father's taking a nap." Once it was over, her mother saw the whole thing as a joke. "Come on, Loretta, don't be a fraidy-cat." As soon as she heard that sickening voice, Loretta would go and hide, often behind the garage, sitting with Bells in the weeds. She would force poor Bells to sit still, and then—in a surge of anger she never understood because the fight had blown over by then, and it never concerned her anyway—she would hold him down by digging her nails into his sides. (It wasn't mange he had, he was just dirty.) It was a mean thing to do to a dog who was that friendly, but she did it anyway, digging her fingers in until Bells whimpered and cried. The dog struggled to escape, but she held him down and scratched and poked until she could feel his ribs and yes, he did have fleas, she could feel the fleas crawling over the ribs (but not mange). Bells would squeal and whine and eventually wriggle away, speed around the garage in a frenzy and out into the open.

Later on, he'd come back, he always came back, he never held a grudge. He'd go and sniff around for a cat until he felt better, and her mother would lug out a couple of kitchen chairs to the backyard and a pitcher of lemonade, cards for Old Maid or War. Everyone would be trying to make up for it, let bygones be bygones. All except Mrs. Mats, who'd talk about it for a week, or at least every time Loretta went over there to watch Helena clean house, or peel a million potatoes for dinner, just so her mother could check each one, nag and criticize.

Life was easier then, it had a predictable rhythm of bad times and good times. Nobody was smart enough to understand what they were doing, or how many times they repeated the same things; they were surprised every single time, and once something was over, it was over forever.

She looked over at Daniel: he was asleep, or just had his eyes closed shut. Not asleep because he suddenly threw an arm and leg over her and pulled her closer. "Even when I hate you," he said in a dull whisper, "I love you." She understood, but what good did it do to spell things out like that? Every time you spelled it out, you pushed things farther along and hurt everybody's feelings.

An hour later, Margaret called again: their plans had changed—had Daniel and Loretta changed their minds yet about going out? (It was Daniel who answered the phone. He was sorry to hear who it was, or that's the way he was acting.) "Better than what?" Daniel said. "I'm not sick." He put the receiver down and reached for his cigarettes on the counter. Lit one with a kitchen match and turned to the bed: Loretta pretended to be asleep. "I'm not *better*," Daniel was saying. "I'm fine. I never was sick."

"She wants to know," Loretta said in a tired voice, "if we want to go out with her and Mr. Aschenbach tonight."

Margaret must have been saying the same thing in a different way, because "No," Daniel said, "we don't."

"That's what I thought you'd say," Loretta said, and turned over. She could tell from his phone voice that he wanted to have the rest of the fight before doing anything else. But she was wrong, his mood suddenly changed. When he hung up, he stooped over his bookbag, naked, and pulled one book out, then another, piling them up on the floor. He chose a book: he was reading Wordsworth and Hölderlin these days because philosophers, his advisor had told him, were starting to turn their attention from logic and pure thought to literature, as yet virgin territory for systematic thought and in need of philosophy's grave and self-certain method. ("Here," the advisor had said, "is the break for someone like you, with your gift for putting odd things together.") Daniel laid a book on his table and wrapped himself in a robe. He read for a while, forty-five minutes, an hour, making stars in the margins, or asterisks, sometimes underlining important passages, using an empty envelope to draw each line straight and not obscure a line of text. After about fifteen minutes of labor, he was comfortable; she could see him relax and yield to it.

Then he was finished, he had read enough. Loretta got up to make dinner, chopped vegetables and boiled water. She turned on the lamps and put a bowl of pretzels on the table next to his book. She poured a beer into two small glasses and put one of them next to the pretzels. He picked up the little dish of pretzels and examined it. "When you're mad at me," he said, "I wish you'd just say so, instead of finding subtle ways to act out."

"I'm not mad," Loretta said. She was running water in the sink.

"Sure."

"It doesn't matter," she said, her back to him.

"I didn't even give you a chance to put in your thing."

She thought a minute. "Why are you calling it a 'thing'? You never called it a thing before. You always call it by its name."

Daniel ignored the jest. "I guess it doesn't bother you to be treated that way. Anyone else could see I was completely out of control. Not you, you're too hard-boiled to see it."

Loretta turned the faucet on and off, on and off. "I think you shouldn't use me to get yourself into a rage," she said.

"I'm not using you. But you're right, I am mad. Why am I mad?"

She smiled, but he couldn't see this. "You're mad because—" She thought of the reasons, she knew them by heart, and recited a couple.

Daniel laughed to hear his own words coming back—coming back right, but somehow they still seemed different. "Yes, in a way, you're correct. It *is* a trivial thing, but it is important. Why else am I mad?"

"I don't know."

"You do know, tell me. You know everything."

"I don't know."

"Yes you do." He was behind her. Then he turned away, and walked to the end of the apartment and walked back, paced back and forth for a minute or two.

"You sound just like my father when you say that," she said.

"When I say what?"

"When you say that you're mad and it's my fault, or I should know why."

"You're a coward," he said.

"*I'm* a coward," she shrilled, "because I won't tell you why *you're* mad!"

Daniel could see—anyone could see—that he had finally gotten a rise out of her. He laughed, and sat down on the bed. "I'm tired of having these scenes. We always patch things up, but I don't think anything ever gets settled. It's just put off till the next time." He paused. "You're too scared to tell me what you really think. That's always been your problem."

It was hard to read his tone, but something in it had softened. She didn't know what he was saying, but he was no longer angry. He was putting his clothes on. When they were on, and the shoes out from under the bed, his wallet taken from the bookcase, he unlocked the door. "I'm going out," he said. "I never go out anymore. I'm going out with Maggot and Alfred Ashcan. Do you want to come? No? Fine."

Loretta looked at the door closing. She waited for it to open again but it didn't. She took the boiling water off the stove. The phone was ringing, but it was a wrong number. She put the rest of the dishes away, then made fresh tea and a peanut-butter sandwich and got into bed. Too bad she had thrown out the cookbook; she could use a good read. If she had had a psychiatrist like she used to, she'd call him up—just like Margaret always called them—at home, while they were eating dinner or screwing, or whatever they did. But what would she say? Something is rotten here and I can't tell whether it's him or me. The doctor would say: Do you feel guilty about something? They always said that, and so things always got off on the wrong foot. Why was that?

If her mother could see her now—which she couldn't, she was long gone—she'd say: "Sister, you'd better change your tune, before somebody changes it for you." But no one was changing it: this was the tune. She felt herself grinning and went to the mirror to check the grin: it was a grin—some would call it a rictus, never mind. Around this tight grin was a young-looking face, no lines or other tracks visible, except for the ones the grin was making. Life—if you could call this life—was making no mark on her, no inroads. She had the same face she had had as the little girl who woke up in the middle of the night and both parents were gone, strangers banging on the door: Wake up.

What look did she have on her face then? No look: the worst thing on earth was happening and there was no look, no mark, no tears, no lines, no screams, no nothing. There was no grin then; she was too young. A grin is a more sophisticated response, and that thought made the grin get even tighter.

She left the mirror and lay on the bed facing the window. Even in the first few days, right after they died so suddenly, she did nothing more than sleep: she was always asleep, and fell into a deep sleep just sitting in a chair. Everyone had noticed it, but they mostly let her sleep. All except Gloria, who *watched* her sleep and waited for her to wake up. Until she couldn't stand to wait any longer, and she woke Loretta up, to tell her she was sleeping. Fool.

She Remembered a Night

■ ■ ■

"**W**AKE up, Retta!" Gloria always said, "you're talking in your sleep."

"I'm not talking, I'm not even asleep, dummy," Loretta said to Gloria. Sometimes Gloria woke her by laying a hot hand on her face. She would open her eyes and all she would see was a fleshy chin and gap-toothed mouth, Gloria was that close, and breathing.

"Get up, Retta! Ma wants you to get up and go sleep in your own room."

Loretta would try to get away from that voice by wedging her face deep into the couch crack, but she could still hear Aunt Rita's voice booming in the background: "Well leave her there, if she's such a stubborn mule." Loretta grabbed the hot hand and twisted it. "Why can't you leave me alone? Quit hanging around me all the time." Gloria pulled her hand away. "Don't you have any friends your own age? Who *are* your friends?"

Gloria would shrug, another stupid grin spreading on her face, and Aunt Rita would fly into the room to shoo Gloria out the door. If there was one thing she hated, it was the daughter mooning on the cousin, and she discouraged Gloria in every way she could, but Gloria stuck, she was curious about the orphan, both parents dead in a car crush. *"Crash,"* Loretta had to correct her.

It had just happened, and Loretta was new in their house. Uncle Ted brought the last of her clothes and furniture to the bedroom she was now going to share with Gloria. There had been a discussion about what to do with the rest of her parents' possessions. Uncle Ted thought Loretta should help make that decision, but Aunt Rita said she was too young. "Is there anything," she had asked Loretta at the funeral home, "special of your mother's you'd like to keep for yourself?" Loretta, who was trying to keep certain thoughts out of her mind and stop more of them from coming, wondered what Aunt Rita meant by "special." Did her mother have things she didn't know about? "Well," Aunt Rita had said, spotting a group of people signing the guestbook in the doorway, and then waiting for her to return to her place beside the caskets, "you think about it. You don't have to decide this minute."

Thinking about what was "special" of her mother's always flooded Loretta's mind with the kinds of thoughts she was trying to avoid. Even ordinary things, like the grimy pink robe hanging on a hook in the bathroom, pockets stuffed with kleenex, hem all ripped and shredded, did that. Where do people go when they're dead that they can't take their old crummy things with them? Not enough room in the casket—was that the answer? It was a babyish thought, but at least it wasn't a thought about crushed things, or about her mother's "chest"—as someone late at night had described it, and Loretta wide awake, standing right there on the stairs, had heard—with a hunk of metal from the car buried in it. What part of the car went in there? Loretta wondered, and how did it get there?

She saw the pictures in the paper, although the aunt and uncle had tried to destroy all the papers, once they had looked

themselves. Loretta saw the papers at the 5 & 10. She went looking for them and there they were, stacked next to the check-out
counter. On the front page was just the article: "Two Dead in
Dawn Crash." The picture was in the second section, Metropolitan News. "Can I help you?" a lady said. Someone else said,
"She's the little girl—don't you recognize her?—the one who
used to come in here with her mother." "Honey," the first one
said, taking the paper out of Loretta's hands, "don't be looking
at those." Loretta snatched them back and laid them flat on the
floor, putting her feet on them. This was her mother's favorite
store, where she bought her lipstick and nail polish and bought
Loretta her ten-cent rubber balls and paper dolls. Loretta could
look at these papers if she wanted to, it was a free country. By the
time the manager had come, after they had rung the bell and
helped her up and led her back to his teeny office and made her
sit on the stool for a minute while he ran and got her—no, the
check-out girl had it already—an orangeade, she had seen what
was there. It wasn't how people had described it. There were no
bodies and no people either, not even cops or rescue workers.
There was only one car on the dark street. Loretta didn't think it
looked like their car.

    She took the orangeade, a Nehi, from the girl and then the
manager said something, but she didn't pay attention: he wasn't
saying anything. One side of the car was gone—it was all
squeezed together, and folded over the back tire. There was no
front seat left, only a back seat. The back seat was empty, just a
dark space, not even any pieces of broken glass in there. There
was a lot of glass around the car, small pieces like you sometimes
see on the street, and near them was a big rag dropped in a pile.
She knew what this was. She didn't want to look. There was
something under the car too, and sticking out. It looked like an
old tire, but it was clothes—was it clothes? That was when the
manager took the paper away—no, it wasn't the manager, it

was the girl, but the manager led her back to where he had his
office, behind the toys.

"What did you see?" he said, and this wasn't the usual
thing people said, so she heard it better.

"What?"

"I said: what did you see? Your name is Costello, right?
What's your first name?"

She didn't answer.

"How old are you?"

She didn't answer that either.

"This isn't your mommy and daddy," the manager said,
"so don't think it is."

"Who is it?" Loretta asked.

"It isn't them," he said smoothly, "they were already gone.
When they died—I know the sisters taught you this in school,
Miss Costello—the soul leaves the body and instantly flies up to
heaven."

Not always, Loretta was thinking.

"I know what you're thinking," the man said, "but your
mom and dad were decent folks, and they went up. They're not
in that picture, so don't even bother looking."

Loretta sighed at the stupidity of it, and the man talked
some more. Then he told her that he couldn't visit with her any
more, he was busy, but that she could pick out one toy in the
store, anything under five dollars, and keep it for free. Loretta
said she didn't want toys.

"Pick out one anyway," he said. "You might change your
mind later on."

"Okay," she said, but she didn't go near the toys. She went
over to the knitting and sewing and looked at the skeins of yarn,
stopping to squeeze a few, then over to make-up—they were
watching her—where she found Perfect Pink lipstick and nail
polish: "nail *enamel*," it said, same thing. Her mother always

picked a red—Fire Engine Red, Cherries in the Snow, Oh! So Red—but pink was more for girls, so Loretta picked a pink and the salesgirl waved her through the check-out counter. She didn't even get a brown paper bag or a sales slip.

When Loretta was on the sidewalk, two doors down from the 5 & 10, she ripped the polish and lipstick from their cardboard backings and dropped the cardboards down the sewer, one didn't make it, fell on the sidewalk, litterbug. Then she started home.

No one lived there anymore. *Wrong,* the lady on the third floor was still there, stupid, and Bells, and so was the lady on the second floor. The first floor—no one lived *there.* She would be living now and forever more ("How long will I stay?" she had asked her uncle, and he said, "Now and forever more," like a prayer and then he said, "Till you're sick of us, Loretta, and want to go and live in a house of your own") with the Gillis family at 54 Canton Street. The old house, 132 First Street, was for rent, although there was no "For Rent" sign yet, her aunt had reported last night. Loretta decided to go look.

It was at the top of a hill and she dragged her tired legs up the bumpy sidewalk. She watched her feet until she reached the top of the hill, and there it was—blue and green shingles and three porches, one on top of the other. The big driveway was all dirt with tire tracks going into the three garages. The first garage had its door open and no car in it. The other two garage doors were closed. Loretta liked to play there, although it wasn't exactly a yard. Some of the kids she played with were coming to the funeral to say goodbye, Aunt Rita had said. They knew she'd be moving. Someone had either told them, or they had guessed it—no nine-year-old girl, even one as smart as Loretta, was going to live by herself in a two-bedroom tenement and park her car in the garage. She laughed to think of it.

Everything looked the same. No, it was different, because old Bells wasn't sitting on the back steps. Where was he?

Loretta looked in the back yard and behind the garage. They were keeping him inside, maybe; they were afraid he'd get hit by a car.

The windows were all shut, even the bathroom window, a skinny window with bumpy glass you couldn't see through, so what good was it? The shades weren't pulled; you could see in, and Loretta—first by climbing up the chain-link fence and trying to peek, then leaping for a second and grabbing onto the window ledge, then by climbing the drainpipe, and finally by leaning off the back steps and hanging onto the railing—could see that everything that used to be there was still there. Even the clutter on top of the refrigerator—glasses case, spool of thread, bottle of cough syrup and an old envelope—was untouched. Part of the broom was sticking out of the broom closet, like it always did, and a shell her mother used as an ashtray was on the windowsill, with a butt still in it. Loretta jumped down and circled the house. When she got to the front porch, she went under it, opening the loose panel of latticework and squeezing through. No one could see her, so she sat down on the dirt.

This had always been a place—dark and small with spy holes—she wanted to live in. She could be near them, yet have her own apartment down here. It was a stupid idea: no person lives under a porch on a dirt floor. She didn't even own this porch anymore. Still, it was hard to believe, sitting there, trespassing, that she couldn't squeeze out from under the porch, inch around the side of the house, shinny up the bannister, push open the outside door, knock on the inside door, test the knob, kick the door open and land with both feet on the kitchen linoleum and see her mother folding the dishcloth, with a cigarette in her mouth, or one burning in the shell.

If she wasn't in the kitchen, she might be taking a nap in the little bedroom, with an arm shading her eyes and one stocking foot over the other. Or in the bathroom, reading the *Reader's Digest* that cooked on the radiator all winter long because no one ever thought to throw it away. Or in the parlor sunk in a big green chair reading a knitting pattern with her feet up on the hassock and the lamp cord swinging over her head.

This was something—Loretta sat down again on the damp, bumpy ground—she would never have thought of. She had thought of other things. When they were fighting and her mother throwing a shoe, a plate, even a full bottle of vinegar one time, at her father, who would duck into the little bedroom, and these things would smash against the wall, and one time against the window and broke it, she thought (Helena agreed) that her mother might murder her father, or that her father might tear across the kitchen floor, sick and tired of being hit with things and not fighting back except with words, and strike her dead with his bare hands.

"How?" Helena wanted to know, because her parents never fought, she claimed, although Loretta could hear them all the way across the street, screaming in Polish, sometimes in English. At first, Loretta thought of telling her to mind her own beeswax, but instead—feeling smarter than a dumb ox—she said, "By squeezing her neck," putting her hands around Helena's scrawny neck, "like this!"

"Don't scream!" Helena said. "I'm not deaf, you know." She gave Loretta a look that meant, "I'm not like *you*." When she did this, Loretta knew that one of these days she was going to be left flat—which she was, the day after her parents drove into a pole and were instantly killed and Helena came over with her mother to pay her condolences (her mother holding her hand, that's how scared she was). Her eyes said, "I'm leaving you flat, I'm going to play with the girls from the Polish school and the Polish girl scouts. I'm staying on my porch or behind the fence with the fruit trees and I'm never playing again with the likes of you, living in bedlam, family fighting like cats and dogs, mother and father punching, screaming and cussing . . . "

Loretta had heard Aunt Rita say the same things. "They

don't," Loretta wanted to inform her, "fight every day of their lives, and they're *not* animals!" But she knew from experience that this kind of talk wasn't meant for children's ears, and that children weren't expected to answer it.

"Then how come she says it right in front of me?" Loretta had once asked her mother.

Her mother laughed. She had no respect for her sister.

"Just because I'm a kid and she's an add-ult?" Loretta went on.

Her mother laughed at the tone. "I guess you'll have to find some other way to get back at her, won't you?" she said to Loretta. "And don't tell me you don't have a hundred ways of belittling people without even opening your mouth. Don't look for sympathy from me.

"You can take care of yourself, my girl," her mother went on, as she always did, if she was in a talking mood. "You don't need help from your rotten mother or your rotten father, even if they could give it to you, which they can't." Her mother paused and looked to see if Loretta was hearing what she was saying. "Instead of feeling sorry for yourself, my lady, you should feel sorry for me. I'm the one that's married to him." Her mother was still talking. Had she been drinking? "I never come whining to you, though, do I, when my feelings get hurt? Don't tell me I do."

So now it was only Gloria who wanted to be friends. All the other kids were scared. "Will I be your friend now?" she asked. "I don't want any more friends," Loretta told her, "and besides, I'm too old for you." When Gloria still didn't get the message, Loretta yelled in her ear: "Dry up and float away!" Gloria looked at her cousin. "Why do you hate to talk to me?" she asked. Loretta got up from the couch and was making her way up the stairs, Gloria close behind. "I'm talking to you!"

Gloria shouted. Loretta sat on the radiator in the bedroom, and put her feet in the windowsill. "Are you feeling sad?" Gloria asked, but not in that pitiful voice everyone was using and makes you sick to hear it.

"Aren't *you* sad?" asked Loretta.

"Sometimes I am."

"Close the door," Loretta said. Gloria kicked it shut, then sat on the floor with her back against the dresser. "How do you think *you'd* feel?" Loretta said, but not in that sharp voice she was using on everyone. Gloria didn't answer. She slunk down, her body sprawled across the floor. She slanted her eyes up to look at Loretta, who was crying. "You got nose trouble?" Loretta sobbed. "No, but I've never seen *you* cry. I thought you never cried." "Well, that was a stupid thing to think, wasn't it?" Loretta bawled through a curtain of tears. There were even tears in her mouth.

"I'd feel worse if my father died," Gloria piped up, after a few minutes, "than if my mother died."

The sudden flood was starting to let up and Loretta answered, "You can say *that* again!"

"I'd feel worse if my father—" Gloria said, and they were both laughing at the stupidity of it when the door flung open and there was Gloria's father, home from work with two small paper bags. In one was a Bolo ball and in the other a set of heavy jacks with a maroon ball. They talked to Gloria's father. He didn't have much to say and they didn't have *any*thing to say. He emptied his pockets. In his jacket were some comic books: Betty and Veronica, Reggie Rich and Wonder Woman. Gloria bounced down on one of the twin beds and Loretta on the other. They put Reggie Rich between them, and that was Aunt Rita screaming up the stairs to tell them to wash their hands and not lollygag, dinner was getting cold, and call your father too.

At the table, Aunt Rita offered a prayer for Loretta's mother and dad, and while Loretta mouthed the prayer and listened to her aunt intoning and Gloria lagging a little behind, she noticed that Uncle Ted wasn't saying anything. His hands were resting on the table and he was looking at Loretta. When she caught him looking, he moved his eyes to Gloria, and when Gloria looked up, he turned to something on the wall, but there wasn't anything there, so he moved his eyes again and by that time Aunt Rita noticed. He wasn't Catholic, Loretta knew that, but she didn't know he didn't pray. When the first prayer was over, Aunt Rita started saying Grace. Uncle Ted didn't know that one either.

In Loretta's house no one said Grace, but if they *were* to say it, they would all say it together—no one would get out of it— but they hardly ever said it. "What do we have to be thankful for, Loretta?" her father said one time, when she asked him why they never said it. "The garbage she cooks, she should thank us for eating it." That was the time his plate of beef chuck, lima beans and overboiled potatoes ended up in his lap, and Loretta's mother locked herself in the bathroom crying but mostly screaming: she called him a goddamn cheap bastard and a complaining son of a bitch, lucky to have someone to put food on the table. He called her names and shouted: "Don't you call me cheap, you're the one that's cheap!" and no one ate that dinner. Loretta fixed herself a peanut butter and marshmallow fluff sandwich and took it to her room.

She thought her mother cooked things okay when she didn't burn them, but she burned a lot of things—not deliberately, like he said, but from paying no attention, from reading or talking on the phone, polishing her nails or going out to the store and forgetting she had something on the stove. "I've got other things on my mind besides the goddamn cooking," she liked to say, but Loretta's father blamed it on the drinking.

"Look who's talking," her mother would jeer, "the world's biggest sponge."

They were both drinkers, Loretta's father explained to

Loretta, when she was old enough to understand—he had had a
few and was feeling good—"and I think you *are* old enough," he
said, "aren't you? What are you, seven? Eight? We drink, I admit it. But we're not drunks, like the rest of them." They drew
the line at suppertime—they didn't drink during supper, although sometimes the father would finish his glass of milk fast
and ask for a can of beer. They did drink before supper, a highball or two, and they drank after, right up until the time they
went to bed. "Beer," her father repeated, "it's just beer,
Loretta." They didn't hit the sauce that often.

At Aunt Rita's they never hit the sauce. Aunt Rita had
taken the pledge and Uncle Ted had a thimbleful of Canadian
Club one night of the weekend, big deal. And there were never
any fights at dinner, and nothing was ever burned. That was the
difference.

One night at dinner, they had a homemade chicken pie.
Loretta could tell it was homemade because there were no little
foil plates thrown in the garbage and there was a big slab of the
pie in a glass dish. They had it with peas and carrots on the side.
Loretta hated peas and carrots mixed together, but she thought
it might be more noticeable if she picked the carrots out with
her fork. She didn't eat the chicken pie either: it was too hot and
when it was cool enough to crack the thick crust without steam
rising out, the inside—chunks of chicken (some still had the
skin on) and celeries and carrots—were soaking in a thick white
gravy whose greasy surface gleamed under the kitchen light.
Loretta tried a little of the gravy with her spoon; her aunt told
her to please use her fork, the spoon was for dessert and didn't
she like dessert, or was she "a little girl who didn't like
desserts?"

Gloria answered this question for her and Loretta put the
teaspoon down and picked up her fork.

"You'll have some salad too, both of you," said Aunt Rita,
and Loretta noticed that each person had a saucer with a few let-

tuce leaves and a quarter of a tomato with orange dressing poured on top. Her mother never made her eat a salad. ("When you grow up," she always said, "you can eat salad, so what's the rush?") Loretta put down her fork and took a sip of milk from the gold plastic glass—the milk was okay, it was cold and you couldn't taste it. She picked up the fork and drew it through the soupy gravy, lifted it, and watched the gravy slip through the tines. What was left on the fork she put in her mouth. No one would have noticed this if Gloria hadn't copied her with that stretchy grin on her face.

Uncle Ted, by then, was finished with his dinner and his glass of milk, and Aunt Rita with most of hers—Gloria half-finished, although she had toppled the heap of peas and carrots with her fork and a few cubes had dropped and some balls had rolled under the dish, and when her aunt finished scolding Gloria for being such a little slob, she suggested that if Loretta were not hungry, she go to Gloria's room and lie down.

Loretta *was* hungry, but she went anyway and Gloria tried to follow, but was stopped, told to finish eating, then to clear the table, if she wanted to watch any TV that night, or do any playing outside. Loretta turned around to listen. "Go ahead, Loretta," the aunt said, "do what you're told. I'm putting your dinner in the oven and you can eat it by and by." But Loretta walked only as far as the stairs and stopped again. Through the doorway she could see Uncle Ted wrapping up his newspaper with a string and carrying it and the garbage outside. She could hear Aunt Rita telling Gloria to do this and to do that, how to do it and how fast and what to do with her heavy feet, her slumped shoulders and her clumsy hands. Gloria whined and Aunt Rita told her not to talk back to her mother.

Loretta moved to the parlor window, a window covered with two curtains, a heavy drape and a see-through lacy curtain. Uncle Ted had put on his garden hat and was dragging the hose across the lawn to the little patch of tomatoes and lettuce he had

planted next to a bed of flowers: marigolds, he had told her, are
the ones with the short, mustard-colored petals, petunias wear
floppy petticoats, pansies are flat as a butterfly's wing and
dahlias, taller than marigolds, have round heads; peonies, he
said, looked like snowballs on a bush and hollihocks grew up the
side of the garage a little like cornstalks. Uncle Ted dropped the
hose and was kneeling in the grass near his flowerbed, pulling
up weeds, some with big dirtballs stuck to the roots. He threw
the weeds in a pile on the grass. Gloria came up and kicked the
pile until he told her to stop. She spun away, twirled away across
the lawn and fell over near the tree.

Loretta laughed. Aunt Rita came through the swing door a
minute later with her library book and glasses and a piece of pie,
and settled in the armchair. "I remember telling you," she said,
"to go upstairs. Isn't that what I told you?" Loretta started
toward the stairs. Her mother used to tell her that Aunt Rita
was an unhappy woman because she let every little trivial thing
drive her nuts. She was a trivial person, this was her gift, "and
no one appreciated it," said her mother, "boo-hoo-hoo!"

"Wait just a minute," Aunt Rita was saying. "I didn't tell
you to go, I asked you to tell me what I told you to do. Do you
act like this at home?"

Loretta didn't answer.

"And do you refuse to eat the good food your mother puts
in front of you?"

Aunt Rita sat back and started on the pie; Loretta thought
the crust must be awfully tough because the fork kept smacking
against the plate. "I know you're upset, honey," Aunt Rita said,
"but in this house you have to mind. That's what's expected
of you. All right," she concluded, putting her feet up on the
hassock, "that's all I have to say. Run along now, play outside
with your cousin, and tell her to stop aggravating her father."

Aunt Rita pulled the lamp cord and opened her library
book to the spot held by the handmade potholder, the kind with

the spongy loops that Loretta used to make at camp. Aunt Rita looked up: "Hurry up now," she said, "before it's dark and I have to call you back in."

Loretta closed the parlor door and stood in the front hallway. Gloria was sitting under the tree playing with the Bolo ball. That's something her mother would never do in a million years, Loretta was thinking—Gloria spotted her looking out the screen door and called her—use a potholder for a bookmark: that was too stupid for words. Her mother didn't read library books either, or anything heavy: she read paperback novels from the 5 & 10 and sometimes a *Photoplay* magazine or the *National Enquirer*, which was like a newspaper, but filled with stories— Loretta liked reading it too—about mysteries and coincidences sometimes happening to famous people, movie stars or freaks. Loretta's mother had to hide these because the father threw a fit if he saw trash like this coming into the house. ("It's the only thing he cares about," her mother said, "and why? Why is it important? He's afraid one of the neighbors will see this," she said, pointing to a movie magazine, "and think I'm cheap. We *are* cheap! That's what I keep telling him. He doesn't like to hear it, though.") So these papers and magazines were hidden in Loretta's closet on top of her old pink phonograph, the phonograph that played red plastic records, so thin you could bend them. Or smash them, like she had dreamed last night: the phonograph was smashed and all the records smashed. A tire was still stuck right in the phonograph and the wall of the bedroom was knocked down, the picture frame broken, the bed flattened right to the ground and squeezed like an accordion. Next, her mother walked into the crashed room. "Who did this?" she said. "You tell me who did this, little girl, and don't lie," but she didn't say it in a mad voice. She said it sweetly, like she sometimes did.

In the dream everything happened like in real life, except she felt the crash, but didn't hear it, when in real life all she heard was the man from upstairs banging on the kitchen door. "Open up!" he said. She went to the door and it was locked. The key was kept in a cookie jar and she found it. She had only one slipper on; she couldn't find the other one. ("Don't open the door," they had said, "for anyone." They said this every time they went out and left her to babysit for herself. "Nobody you know will be knocking, so keep the door locked. If you hear any knocking, don't pay attention.")

No one had ever knocked before. It did sound like Uncle Ted and Mr. Monahan from upstairs, but it could be a trick. They were saying: "Loretta, Loretta, do you hear me? Unlock the door." Loretta was all set to unlock it—who else but Uncle Ted would say it was Uncle Ted?—when the phone rang. She ran for the phone. It was the police and they wanted to talk to somebody in charge, but there was nobody home. She was scared. People were banging on the door and the phone was ringing. She put the phone down and went back to the door. Who is it? she asked and they answered together: "Uncle Ted and Mr. Monahan from upstairs!" So she let them in, and it wasn't only them: Mrs. Monahan were there too, in her bathrobe and slippers, and the man next door, a fireman. They looked at her a second and then they all crowded in the door. Mrs. Monahan took Loretta by the hand and walked her to the bedroom. "Let's find your robe and slippers, honey." Loretta knew something bad had happened.

It was Uncle Ted who told her, Loretta remembered, but she already knew by then. There was a crowd of people in the kitchen, some of them strangers, and Loretta had been put to bed a dozen times and told to stay there, but she kept getting up. After a while, no one made her go back. Uncle Ted took her by the hand into the den. He told her to sit in her Daddy's chair and he sat on the hassock. She had no slippers on at all and he wrapped up her feet in an afghan. Then he put her feet on his lap and held them there. He had closed the door and it was nice and quiet, peaceful, with just one lamp on and no TV. She knew what had happened, but no one had told her to her face, so when Uncle Ted told her, she wasn't that surprised, but she still didn't believe it.

"Loretta," he said, "while you were asleep tonight, a very bad thing happened." She already knew it, but that made it seem scarier. His face was worked up and he tried to begin again. Loretta pictured all the faces in the kitchen and in the dining room, drinking coffee and drinking whiskies, red faces and teary faces, strained faces and every light in the house, as her father would say, blazing.

Then a cop wandered in. He looked at them, and walked out again, shutting the door tight. They waited for the click, then Uncle Ted went on. He said that he and Aunt Rita were going to take care of her now, so she wouldn't be alone. She could live with them and Gloria and, in a little while, things would be all right. Loretta didn't realize it meant having to move. Her arms were stiff beside her when Uncle Ted leaned over to give her a hug. "I'm taking you to your aunt's house right now," he said, "so you can get some sleep."

Loretta said she didn't want to go. Couldn't she stay? Absolutely not, he said. There's no one here to take care of you. That was the first time she realized that they weren't ever coming home. She told Uncle Ted that she could take care of herself, that they always left her to take care of herself when they went out. It's very late, he said, and people here are talking. It was then that she started to cry, but it wasn't because of what happened, it was because they were making her leave.

Mrs. Monahan found a slicker in Loretta's closet and put it on her. She made Loretta wear her school shoes and carry her slippers. She didn't give her any socks to put on.

When they got to Aunt Rita's, there she was out on the porch, her hair in pink curlers with a white hairnet and strings hanging down her back. She stood by the bannister as they

walked up the path. Loretta could see Gloria behind her, standing in the doorway. She stayed there, even after her mother
yelled, "Go back to bed, you!" There was a dish of cherry vanilla
ice cream waiting for Loretta in the pantry, Aunt Rita said.
That's all she could think of to say. They were all standing in the
hallway, Aunt Rita sobbing and Gloria asking questions. Uncle
Ted said he had to go back but to give some of that ice cream to
Gloria and the two girls could keep each other company.

The ate their ice cream and sat in front of the empty bowls
until Aunt Rita came into the pantry and said it was time. They
walked upstairs together, got into the twin beds and Gloria said
not a word.

Next day, Loretta woke up late and Gloria was gone, the
house was silent, and Loretta saw all her clothes packed in a box
at the foot of the bed. Next to them was a box of books and
comic books, and next to that some dolls and games. On a chair
in the suitcase were her brush and comb, her St. Joseph's aspirin
and liquid vitamins, her bathroom cup, a Peter Rabbit plate she
hadn't used in a long time, her old red sneakers, new white
sneakers, some school books, her lunchbox and a shoebox full of
things like report cards, chart of vaccinations and polio shots,
her birth certificate and other things her mother kept in the scarf
drawer.

Hidden in a pile of sweaters and winter pajamas was a
white cardboard box from Cherry & Webb with an elastic band
holding the lid on. Loretta slid off the band and opened the box
to find her Daddy's high school ring—a flat-top ruby cut with a
thousand sides and set in a thick band carved with lions. When
Daddy was at work, Loretta liked to sneak into his room and
into his dresser and open the blue box with a cover like a snapping turtle to find this ring. It was always there because he never
wore it anymore. ("Why don't you wear this ring?" she asked

him. "What ring?" he said. "What ring? I asked you," he said again, "what ring?")

In this drawer with the ring were other things: a chain with two small metal plates—Daddy's name was on both of them. Loretta hung the chain around her neck and paraded into the kitchen. "When did you enlist?" her mother said, and they both laughed. She told Loretta the plates were dog tags, but this didn't mean Daddy used them for a dog, although he did have a dog, Bruno. Loretta couldn't get this idea out of her head and every time she saw the chain she pictured Bruno or Lucky, the dog he had before Bruno, a beagle, with this thin chain hanging around its neck and the plates dangling on the ground. They were a little like license plates and Loretta asked her mother if she could nail them onto her bike. Her mother said it was illegal, then told her to ask her father. Loretta put the chain back.

There was other interesting stuff in this drawer: the cufflinks with the blue stones and the ones with the red stones. She brought these down to show her mother, who was bleaching something in the sink. "See these?" she said.

"I remember those," her mother said, after she put her glasses on. "He used to wear those before we got married, your father." Her mother lifted the shirt and let the blue bleach stream and then drip down the sink. "He used to own a couple of fancy dress shirts with French cuffs, very handsome. He was quite the dressy man, you know. Nothing like the rag bag he is now.

"Don't tell him I told you that," she added. Her mother poured herself some coffee that had been on the stove since morning. It was burned from re-heating but she drank it anyway.

"Beautiful shirts and shoes," she said, sitting down at the table across from Loretta. "He was very particular about his clothes and had them done up at the Chinaman's." She lit a cigarette and sat back with her elbow resting in her hand. "Always looked like a million dollars."

Her mother was going to tell the story—Loretta recognized it—of how they first met, right after the war when "we girls hadn't seen a guy older than fifteen and younger than sixty," but her mother had known her father from before the war, too. He had a job delivering groceries for Ike's. "We had ours delivered only once in a blue moon, but I still remembered him. What a sport he was, even then, and by '45, he had his own car—imagine that! He was good-looking, your father, even my girlfriend Margie said so and she was so particular about men, she jilted them all, and ended up an old maid." Her mother still found that story funny, although she hadn't seen poor Margie in twenty-five years.

"Your father started coming around in—oh, I must have been nineteen or twenty, so when was that?" She paused and tried to count up the years. "Who knows, after the war. I had just graduated high. No one thought I'd make it through, the nuns had it in for me, and I admit I was no ball of fire as a student.

"I was smart, though, I was no dumbbell. I took the business course and they had a lay teacher then, a woman who'd been in business—smart and a sharp dresser—and she taught me everything I know. She even told me I should go on to business school, imagine that, your dunce of a mother. I must have been a lot smarter then. I don't know where it's all gone. Too bad."

Her mother would pause in the story, sink into herself, then begin again after a few puffs of her cigarette. "But there I was, fresh out of high and making my own money. And a boyfriend. My sister wasn't married. No one thought she'd ever get married, she never went out to work, either, you know."

When her mother finished her stale coffee, she sometimes asked Loretta to start a pot of tea. "Anyway, your father started coming around. He had traveled, he was in England for the armistice," she said, sipping the black tea. "He even knew a few words in French and he could say them. And what a dancer!

"Well, you've seen the pictures." Her mother got up,

drank the rest of her tea, doused her burning cigarette under the faucet and flipped the butt into the wastebasket. Now she was ironing, and arranged a dress of Loretta's on the board. "Here I am," she said, "gassing when I've got all this ironing to do. Don't be distracting me with your questions, let me get my chores done, then we'll run down the avenue and get something nice for dessert." She was working on the plain cotton skirt, gathered at the waist. The iron made a smooth path up a fold and pointed its nose into the waistband. Then she lifted the iron—"This is what tires you out," she said, "the lifting, not the pushing"—and began driving up another fold until the skirt was perfectly smooth and limp. She pulled the dress off the board and pressed one of the little puffed sleeves, making a crease in the middle of it, ironing the top side, the bottom side, and when she was done, the sleeve opened like a jack-o-lantern. The collar was easy, a simple flat circle with a lace border, then her mother fed the dress onto the board again and ironed the bodice with its few rows of smocking. "I don't know why I'm taking the trouble," she said. "You don't even like this dress."

Her mother was a good ironer and she liked to iron. She hated housework, dusting, scrubbing, mopping: a dog's work, she'd say to anyone who was listening. But she liked everything to do with ironing and didn't feel like she had to gape at the TV while doing it. She was happy to concentrate on the work itself. "I see you working on your arithmetic problems," she said to Loretta, "and you're just like me—you concentrate, you do one thing at a time. You got this quality from me, don't you think? *He* can't concentrate on anything. At least you got something good from me. What did you get from him? Do you think you got anything?"

Loretta was thinking.

"Oh, you must have gotten something. I know—you got that beautiful handwriting you have from him. You know that beautiful handwriting?"

Loretta laughed. She had terrible handwriting: you

couldn't read it and it was ugly to look at. It slanted to the left *and* to the right and it was very faint and jiggly.

"But you can draw pictures," her mother was saying. "Your pictures are nice. You're way ahead of your age there. Why do you think that is? Your father and I don't have an ounce of talent for anything. We're not arty, none of us in this family is the least musical or theatrical.

"Nope," she corrected herself, "I take that back." She was laughing now. "We're very theatrical in this house. We have the gift here for theatricality."

Her mother had finished the dress and was unrolling another damp ball. First, she would take the basket of clean clothes, dry and stiff from hanging on the line, and shake out each one, stretch it on the tabletop and dampen it with the sprinkler she'd made herself from a ketchup container and the spout from a watering can. The first one didn't work. The spout, when her mother tipped the jar, came flying out and the water poured all over the table and the floor. Then she tried taping the spout with electrical tape and for a while it worked, but it flew out again. Loretta laughed. Her mother said it wasn't funny, but she laughed too. They went down to Benny's and her mother discussed the problem with one of the salesmen, who found a better spout, one made of cork, so it fit into all openings, and it worked fine.

Loretta cut out paperdoll clothes while her mother ironed—they were both boring jobs—or she worked on a jigsaw puzzle, but mostly she just sat and watched. Sometimes she pulled out the box of photographs her mother kept in the kitchen cabinet with the wrapping paper and ribbon. "If you want to look at them, look at them," her mother always said, "but don't get me involved. It's ancient history. I'm not interested." But after a while she would come over and look at pictures. They had stopped taking pictures when Loretta was born: why? "I don't know, the camera broke, I think." So the pictures were all old. The mother and father looked different then. The picture Loretta liked best was an old brown-and-white snapshot. They were married and standing together in a big field in front of a house Loretta didn't recognize. "Yes you do," her mother said, "that's your father's Aunt Mary's house in Haverhill. You've been there." Near the couple was an old cardboard suitcase—"It looks like cardboard, but it isn't. Who'd take a cardboard suitcase on vacation?"—tossed on the grass.

"Is that all you brought?" Loretta asked.

Her mother looked at the picture, looked at the suitcase and looked at the couple. "No, I don't know." She sniffed: "Look at us," pointing to the couple leaning on each other, "we must have been in love. Your father looks pretty good, doesn't he? And look," her mother nudged Loretta with her elbow, "at your old mother. See how slim I was. I was just a girl. My mother bought me that suit in Boston, $25. That was a lot in those days. That's why it looks so good.

"Well," she sighed, "doesn't it show you how life can change?" Her mother handed her the picture—May 8, 1946, it said on the back in pale brown ink—and walked around the lip of the ironing board, filled the sprinkler with fresh water and set it on the board. "And look at us now," she said. The clothes had dried up in the meantime.

Her mother liked to tell about all the boyfriends she had had and the good times "before I got married to that bum, your father. But he wasn't always a bum. He used to be pretty peppy. He liked a good time, just like the rest of them." Her mother was unrolling a dry bundle, looked at it, rolled it up again, dropped it in the basket and selected another. "He was peppy, Loretta, not like he is now, drinking beer all the time.

"I wonder what it is happens to people to slow them down?" She had stopped ironing to think. "What do *you* think? You're young." She didn't wait for an answer. "You know what I think? I think people do it to themselves. And when they finish doing it to themselves, they start in on the people around them." She paused. "Everyone ends up the same: pooped and sour. And defeated, too. Why are we so defeated at our age? That's what I can't understand."

Sometimes her mother would talk like this, and Loretta didn't know what to say. Once her mother had said: "I like to talk and I have no one to talk to but you. And *you* don't say a word. I don't blame you. Who wants to hear bellyaching day in and day out?"

Ironing a basket piled as high as this—three loads of laundry, enough to break the pulley line if it weren't propped by the pole—could take a full afternoon. Loretta would sit and listen. Then she'd fix her mother a snack: raisin-bread toast and milk or more tea. If Helena came to the door, her mother would shoo Loretta away: "Go out and play with someone your own age. Take a walk, go to the library. Don't waste the day inside with me."

But her mother wasn't finished talking until she had gotten to the part about all the good times they had had in the old days, and Loretta liked that part best. When they had run with a crowd who knew a good time when they saw it, and had a few bucks to spend. What did they do?

"Oh, the VFW had times and your father belonged to some of the clubs. The Elks, he belonged to the Elks. Plus we went out night-clubbing. That was a big thing then. And roller-skating. We ice-skated in the winter and—I almost forgot, the best thing—dancing under the stars, that's what I used to love. Nothing on earth—would you get me a glass of water, Loretta, I'm dry as a bone—nothing was more romantic than dancing in the dark to a big band playing outdoors."

"Beautiful? It was out of this world. Thanks," she said, gulping down the water. She ironed in silence, then put the iron up again. "And what do couples have to do today that's fun?

Nothing. There's nothing for us to do either, but it doesn't matter—we're old, we don't mind staying at home.

"But what do they have to do? There isn't a good movie for them to see, not like we used to see—good stories, romances." Her mother reached into the basket, but it was empty. "I'm done, my girl. See?" She unplugged the iron and wrapped the cord around its handle. Thick layers of shirts and dresses hung from the cellar door and the dining room door, piles of blouses, hankies, pants, shirts and pillow cases were stacked on the table top and counters. Her mother sat down and sighed. "Pour me a short one, will you?" Loretta jumped up and poured a little beer from the Narragansett bottle into a juice glass.

"Oh, get me a good-sized glass, will you? Did you see the big pile of ironing I just did? And get yourself something. We'll sit here and have ourselves a tea party, just the two of us, before Mister gets home grouchy as a bear."

Her mother watched as Loretta gulped her red Kool-Aid. "You don't mind spending time with me, do you? He can't spend a minute in my company without blowing up. But you like to talk to me, don't you? I can see you do, you don't have to say it." Her mother reached over and patted Loretta's hand, giving her that crinkly smile that seemed phony but was the only one she had. In the old pictures she had another smile, more relaxed, more teeth, but now she just had this rubbery smile where she pulled her closed lips across her teeth and closed the eyes. Loretta had tried it in front of the mirror, but it didn't look much like a smile.

Loretta closed the box of cufflinks, after slipping the ruby ring on her finger. Who had brought all this stuff? Where was she supposed to put it? "Put it all away," her mother would say, pushing her out of the kitchen, loaded down with piles of wash. "You put it away and put it away right! Don't wrinkle what I

just broke my back ironing." Loretta would drift in and out of
the rooms, dropping a pile on one bed, a pile on another. She
didn't like going into her father's room. His room was small,
just enough space for the bed and a dresser. It was right off the
kitchen, and if he was in there, sleeping or lying on the bed
smoking a cigarette, Loretta and her mother stayed away. He
never closed his door because he was listening for fires, he said.
Loretta's and her mother's rooms were side by side, but that
didn't mean Loretta could barge into her mother's room and pry
into her personal things. Her mother kept her bedroom door
shut, but the door didn't close all the way.

In the old days, when Loretta had a babysitter, she used to
sneak in there. First she waited for the sitter—Frances was her
name—to fall asleep. Then, on pajama feet, she snuck down the
hallway to her mother's bedroom. "Hey!" she sometimes yelled,
just to check, but Frances was a sound sleeper and nothing woke
her up. "Look at the goddamn mess you made! Pick up that underwear! And hang up those dresses you just threw on the floor
before I take a stick to your legs!" After talking in a loud whisper, or yelling into the empty room, Loretta would collapse on
the bed laughing. If her mother had been hiding in the closet,
she would have jumped out on the spot. "I'll horsewhip you,"
she had said when Loretta had wet her pants in grade one for the
16,000th time, just like a baby, the tinkle running down her
legs and collecting in the seat of her wooden chair, there for anyone to see. She pretended to cry. "I'll beat you black and blue, if
you pull that stunt again!"

Or the babysitter might sneak up behind her. Loretta
looked in the mirror to see if Frances was coming. No: the coast
was clear. She ran back on slippery feet, soundless feet, to the
parlor and there was Frances, fast asleep on the couch. One eyelid opened. "I was going to the bathroom," Loretta said. Frances
looked like she was going to say something, but the eyelid
dropped. Why was she so tired all the time?

Frances came to the wake, too. She shook Loretta's hand. Loretta was all dressed up in navy blue with navy blue knee socks and maryjanes, a flat straw hat with no flowers (Aunt Rita had removed the band of paper flowers), just a ribbon. Frances wore a limp cotton skirt, brown, and a faded print blouse. Loretta's mother liked to criticize Frances's "rig," but Frances had informed Loretta that she was going into the convent and just biding her time until graduation, a year and a half away, so big deal. "I'm not getting involved with boys," she informed Loretta—and Loretta reported it to her mother, who laughed: "Fat chance!" she hooted.

Loretta liked Frances. Frances wasn't interested in anything. She liked to relax and she liked to sleep. She spent her free time helping the nuns at the convent. When she wasn't at the convent dusting the pianos or folding serviettes—"Folding *what?*" her mother asked, but Loretta kept forgetting to ask what a serviette was, and why it was folded—she was napping or sitting on the porch with Mother and Dad, both retired and content just to sit and watch the world go by. "How much of the world," Loretta's mother wanted to know, "can they see from Box Street? Four houses and four garages and an Italian grocery store with cheeses hanging in the window."

Loretta thought it sounded nice: peaceful. Her mother said that Frances was throwing her life away, or whatever life a girl as plain as Frances could have. "Not like you, Lori."

Like me?

"You wait and see. When you grow up, they'll be lined up and howling at our door."

This is not what Frances said. Frances thought that if Loretta tried hard enough, she'd see that she had a vocation, too. But no, she was too selfish and piggy to make the sacrifice. "Get out," Loretta said to Frances. "Wait and see," Frances said, lying on the couch and waiting for Loretta to bring her a sandwich and a glass of iced tea.

Or waiting for Loretta to scratch her back with the Chinese backscratcher, which Loretta's mother hung on a rack and which, the minute she saw it, Frances coveted. You could scratch your own back—that was the idea—but Frances said she'd rather Loretta do it, it was more relaxing.

"Do you think," the girl said one time, when she was lying on the couch wrapped up in the afghan and holding the backscratcher, "your mother'd notice if I took this?" Loretta said she didn't know, probably not, but the answer was yes: her mother would miss it right away. She liked the backscratcher too, and she despised thieves.

"Are you lying?" Frances said.

Nobody knew—Loretta thought about this a lot when she was still young enough to have a babysitter—what a rat Frances could be. Loretta's mother had guessed some of it: slovenly, moody, idle, backstabbing, mental, greedy, lying, mean, selfish and grubby. She suspected something was off in a girl like this, so sulky and quiet, but nobody knew for sure. Loretta knew, but she was never telling, cross her heart and hope to die, she told Frances. Frances made her promise, then said what she'd do if Loretta broke the promise. Frances was smart. She said, "If this here thing was ever missing, you'd tell them *you* took it, right? Or you'd tell them you broke it." Loretta watched her: she was working herself up into a rage. "Because if you didn't, you know what I'd do to you, don't you?"

"What?" Loretta said.

Frances lay back on the couch and looked at the ceiling. "Well, the first thing I'd do is tell your mother how you sneak into her room and rifle through her stuff." Loretta wasn't scared. What did "rifle" mean anyway? Her mother wouldn't know what that word meant, and Frances didn't either. Frances pulled the afghan up to her chin. She had the backscratcher under the cover with its little hand on the pillow next to her head. Loretta was afraid to look because she knew she would laugh.

When the parents came home that night (a movie and a nightcap, her father said), Frances and Loretta were both asleep, Loretta slumped in the chair and Frances on the couch. Loretta's mother didn't like the look of this, but they let it go. Frances was odd, yes, but she was reliable, and would babysit for fifty cents an hour, sometimes for nothing. Loretta's father left it up to her to ask for her money on the ride home, and sometimes she didn't.

And Frances never did go into the convent. She ended up working for the phone company as a switchboard operator, a job she'd gotten—Loretta's father was certain—through pull, because she had never even finished high.

"Yes, she did," Loretta said. "You know she did, you saw her name in the paper."

"Maybe so," the father said, "but you know as well as I do she got through by the skin of her teeth, because they don't give jobs like that to dumbbells."

That was at dinner no more than a week before the accident. Loretta's father was upset and it was understandable, her mother said later when they were doing dishes together, because he was having a tough time finding himself a job, a skilled worker, and that Frances Griffin, a nothing. Loretta couldn't picture Fatty Frances the Talking Horse working for the phone company. Did she talk to people in that sarcastic tone? Wouldn't she lose her job, Loretta asked her mother, when they found out how fresh she was? (Loretta didn't mind talking about Frances, once Frances was never coming back to sit.)

"What?" her mother said, dipping a plastic plate in the soapy water. She had already washed this plate, and now she was washing it again—why? Her mother hadn't been paying attention to anything lately, and if she did pay attention, it was only long enough to get Loretta off her back. Her mind was always wandering, and she was mad if someone forced her, with a loud voice or a tap on the arm, to pay attention. She didn't like to be touched: she was too hot or too cold, it was too sticky out or too miserable and she preferred to be left in peace. This happened even if Loretta's father, who didn't like to be touched either, tried to give her a kiss or a peck, a harder kiss. "Leave me alone," she was always saying, "and let me get my work done. Don't be hanging on me. Go about your own business." When Loretta took the hint and walked away—once she slammed the door behind her and her mother said, "Look who's got a temper. I know where you got *that* from"—her mother always called her back: "I didn't say to go *away*, I just said to be quiet. Why can't you stay here a minute and keep me company? Do I have B.O.?"

But it was a waste of time to talk about Frances. Her mother didn't care about Frances, Frances was ancient history. Phone company or no phone company, the girl would never amount to much. She was just an operator anyway, so what's the big deal? Loretta noticed that her mother still had the same plate; she was rubbing around its rim. Her face was all red and tense. "What's the matter?" "Nothing," said her mother. Then she said, "Don't ask. You don't want to know."

"Yes I do," Loretta said.

"No you don't. You'll just feel bad, and then we'll all feel bad, and who'll cheer us up?"

"Tell me."

"Okay. You talked me into it. Go, run and get me my cigarettes and matches and pour us something to drink like a good girl." The mother left the rest of the dishes in the dishpan and sat at the kitchen table. She watched Loretta scurry around: the cigarettes weren't in the parlor ashtray and they weren't on the dining room table, they weren't in the bedroom and they weren't in her father's bedroom. "Wait," the mother said, watching Loretta with the same unfocussed stare, "I've got them right here in my pocket. Stop looking. You're making me dizzy.

I had them all along and I didn't know it." This made her laugh and Loretta laughed too, although she didn't know why it was so funny.

Her mother started out by telling a joke she had heard. "There was a priest, a rabbi and a minister, and they were all going to eat at the Automat. It was a Friday. The priest said to the rabbi—you don't want to hear this joke, do you?" Her mother looked at Loretta and made a funny face. "You're not in the mood. And neither am I."

The mother studied Loretta's face. "You look so serious, it's almost funny," she said. "We've got a few money troubles, my girl," the mother went on in a different tone. "I don't want you to worry about it, I just want you to know. You might offer up a prayer for your daddy and me. Are you still making your First Fridays?" She got up and opened the pocketbook hanging on the kitchen doorknob. "I've been keeping a novena. See?" She showed Loretta the little blue booklet. Loretta had seen it before. Every year the Franciscans came to their church and held a novena. The nuns told them it was obligatory, so Loretta and her mother went every night. Her mother enjoyed the singing and the Franciscans always sent a good preacher, someone good with words, not like their own pastor, stilted, tedious and always begging for money. These were holy men and their sermons were inspiring; you were interested and you wanted to go back for more, you didn't dread going. "And you really believe what they're saying, you really want to mend your ways," her mother always said.

But now she was making her own novena because it wasn't time yet for the Franciscans to come. She was up to the second day and was still keeping it. Did Loretta want to keep it with her? She did. And together, they had kept the novena until the eighth day—the ninth day was today, Loretta thought, as she closed the suitcase with the box of blue cufflinks in it, and clothes sticking out of the sides, because someone was at the door—that pest of a Gloria. Loretta was already practicing saying: Keep your hands off of my things. Don't touch anything of mine.

The novena was broken. The blue booklet was in her mother's pocketbook where she always kept it; it was in the wreck too. They had gotten up to the eighth day. They remembered it that day and said all the prayers sitting at the kitchen table after supper. Her mother played the priest and Loretta the congregation so they were able to recite all the lines: the blessings, the responses, the prayers, the litanies and the benediction. The first night it seemed strange for her mother to be the priest and they laughed each time the priest's lines came up, but they got used to it. Her mother, Loretta was thinking as the doorknob was starting to turn—it was locked, no it wasn't—could make anything, no matter how boring or ordinary, into something fun. "Don't come in," Loretta sobbed, but it was too late. There was Gloria's head in the doorway and, behind her, Aunt Rita's. It was the whole family, all three of them, and what were they looking at? They looked like they'd just seen a ghost.

1978

The End of the Rotos

■ ■ ■

*I*T wasn't always worthwhile talking to Margaret about problems with Daniel, but who else was there to talk to? "I'm guilty," Loretta said, about a week later, when she and Margaret were walking to a gallery where Mr. Aschenbach had a new installation of foam paintings and sculptures made of candy wrappers and popsicle sticks.

"Of what?" asked Margaret.

"Of driving Daniel crazy."

"Daniel was already crazy," Margaret said.

"No," Loretta said, "I think it's a real illness."

Margaret looked at her. "That's giving him the benefit of the doubt. I think he does it to himself."

"Does what?"

"Whatever it is you're talking about. What *are* you talking about?"

They were almost there: other people were gathered on the street, different kinds of couples, going to the exhibit. Margaret started talking in a louder voice: "What's wrong with him anyway? Is he suicidal?"

"Shh," Loretta said, pushing Margaret toward the door and through the doorway. "Don't talk so loud."

"There's nothing wrong with Daniel," Margaret was saying. "He's a typical man." Who was she talking to? Her eyes were all over the room. She saw someone they knew from school, then someone else, and then there was Alfred himself, dressed in a tuxedo jacket and dungarees with saddle shoes. He was standing next to Mrs. Iona Johns Morrison, Margaret said, the lady who owned this gallery and a few others, and who knew, personally, every artist in New York. She was a white-haired lady dressed in a white silk hood and long white scarf. "Stay with me," Margaret whispered, pulling Loretta over to a table covered with glasses of pink wine, a plate of Hostess Snowballs and a punchbowl full of something like Kool-Aid with marshmallows floating in it.

"Do you think this is really wine?" Loretta asked, as Margaret picked up a glass and sipped. There was no one else near the table.

Margaret groaned, and quickly put the half-filled glass back on the table.

"What?"

"Did anybody see me? No one saw me, did they?" Margaret pulled Loretta over to the far side of the room and cowered behind a knot of guests.

"*What?*" Loretta asked.

"Did you see what I did?"

"No."

"I ATE part of that exhibit!"

Loretta laughed, and waited for Margaret to laugh at how absurd it was, but Margaret didn't laugh. "This is exactly your problem," Loretta said.

"What is?"

"You take stupid things too seriously."

"Look who's talking!" Margaret shot back. "You're the one

that's so worried about men. Daniel is one of the biggest ass-
holes I've ever met and you treat him like a god. Talk about
absurdities." Margaret looked around. They happened to be
standing in front of an artwork that Margaret had had a hand in
making. It was an unprimed canvas laying flat like a shelf from
brass hinges. On it was a little fort made of popsicle sticks with a
flag on a flagpole. "I put the rugs in," Margaret said.

"What rugs?"

"The rugs. Look in the window there—see?" But the fort
had no windows. "I know, but look between the cracks. Don't
you see? Well, it doesn't matter. I made a braided rug for the
floor. I used a shoe lace and a little shred of grosgrain ribbon."
Loretta didn't seem to be listening, so Margaret stopped talking. "Are you thinking about what I said? I'm sorry, I just ran off
at the mouth."

Loretta was looking straight at Margaret. "Do you really
think Daniel's that much of an asshole?"

"I said it, didn't I?"

"Do you mean it, or are you just being defensive?"

"Don't psychoanalyze me, Loretta. I said it—just leave it
at that." Margaret dashed back to the snack table again, to catch
a woman with a glass of pink Kool-Aid in one hand and a Snowball in the other. First, Margaret took the glass, then the
Snowball, but the lady snatched the glass back. Loretta couldn't
hear what they were saying, but she could hear their loud voices.

"What's she doing over there?" Loretta turned and there
was Alfred.

"She's policing the fake wine."

Alfred strode across the room and took the glass from the
woman's hand, then he kissed the hand. The woman's face was
red; she was talking and Alfred was listening. Now Margaret
was talking. When Margaret started talking, the woman
wheeled around—Loretta caught her eye—and marched across
the floor and out of the room.

"She tried to eat that!" Margaret said. She had led Alfred back to Loretta, but Alfred was looking at the sparse crowd, then disengaged himself to talk with a man in jeans and a sleeveless red tee-shirt. Margaret and Loretta tried to engross themselves in a foam painting. The room was suddenly crowded and noisy. Loretta said she had to go. "Please don't go," said Margaret. "I'm sorry I said what I said, I really didn't mean it."

"What *do* you mean?" Loretta asked her, but Margaret didn't seem to hear. She said that Alfred wouldn't talk to her during a big event like this, so they might as well leave. When they were outside again, Margaret mumbled a long, chaotic statement whose gist was that she didn't understand Daniel or what was going on between the two of them. "I look to *you* for opinions," she said, as they made their goodbyes on the corner, "so how can you ask me what *I* think? What I think is what *you* think. Sometimes, Loretta, I don't even think up to that level, so what can you possibly get from asking me?"

"Did you say good-bye to Alfred?" Loretta said.

"No. You think he'd notice?"

Loretta watched while Margaret crossed the street and trudged home.

■ ■ ■

Not long after the Roto play had run its few weekends, Margaret was waiting for their next job based on the *Times* review and the mentions in the *Voice* and *East Village Other*, but they never got it. Patrice, who would have hired them in a minute, she had said on closing night at a cast party at Tonto's, wearing her plastic transparent dress—and a flesh-colored bodysuit, Margaret insisted, to cover the hair shirt—wasn't going to do any more theater for a while. She was going, she told Loretta, to a special European spa where you could have your blood restored, or replaced if necessary.

"Where does the other blood come from?" asked Loretta. She was dressed in forest green tights and a small black jersey dress. ("You've lost weight," Margaret had said, pulling the dress to get a clearer outline of the body.)

"It's fresh, whole blood," the ballerina explained, "and I don't know where it comes from. I can't go on with what I have now. I'm virtually depleted."

Loretta was studying this face: thin but pretty, and perfect as a cameo, hair scraped back with combs and drawn into a fat braid which the ballerina had wrapped around her neck. "Then what will you do?" Loretta asked her, although it was clear that Patrice didn't want to talk: she had gathered together a little pile of her belongings—purse, a library book on taxes, some make-up, costume jewelry she had lent the Rotos and medicines in a clear plastic bag—and was ready to go, having spent fifteen minutes at the party. Loretta didn't have to ask how many other projects and events the ballerina had planned for that night, a slack night with only one performance.

"Why do you ask?" the ballerina said.

Now that Patrice was looking at her, Loretta wondered if she knew who it was she was addressing. "Will you stay in Europe, or will you come back?"

"Excuse me a minute," Patrice said, "will you?"

Loretta watched her weave through the crowd, the plastic dress like a bubble. Patrice came back with a glass of water and a glass of wine, handed the wine to Loretta: "You drink wine, don't you? Now," she said—she had evidently dropped all the things she had been carrying—"what did you ask me?" Loretta took a sip of the wine. "You want to know where I'm going after my spa?"

"Yes," Loretta said, "but you don't have to tell me if you don't feel like it."

The ballerina took a step closer to Loretta. "Don't confuse me. Do you want to know what I'm going to do or don't you?

Was it a real question you were asking? If you want to know, I'll tell you," she said, her voice a little louder.

Loretta, looking back into this face so smooth and tense, wondered what Patrice thought her question meant. Was it that deep? "Wasn't I," Loretta said, her voice louder too, "just asking you what you're going to do next? That's what I thought I meant anyway."

The ballerina was still peering; suddenly she looked away, put her glass of water on the floor and showed Loretta her hands, covered with fine lace mitts. The hands were shaking. "See these?" she said. "Do you now see why I have to go? Or," she picked up the glass and bit the edge of it, "do I have to prove it to you?" The ballerina stared at her.

"I'm not criticizing you," said Loretta, "if that's what you're thinking. I can see that you're tired. I'm glad you're taking a break." This seemed to be the right thing to say, but the ballerina seemed not to comprehend a word of it.

"You *don't* see, do you?" she said, stepping back and laying one of the mitted hands on Loretta's black-jersey arm. "I was just asking"—her voice was different now, light and casual—"if you really wanted to know, or if it was just another bullshit question."

Loretta took a step back too.

"Well," the ballerina said, moving forward again, "I'll tell you anyway. My session at the spa lasts two weeks. I'll come out"—she smoothed her cheeks back with her fingers—"healthy and calm, completely relaxed. There'll be someone waiting for me, someone you don't know, an Italian, and we'll drive away from the spa and off into the cool, clear, forested part of Switzerland."

Loretta, seeing how different this story was from what she'd expected, took a sip of wine and then another one.

"Are you listening to me?" the ballerina demanded.

Loretta said she was and the ballerina told a long and pretty story of the tranquil, stark adventures she would have with the Italian against a beautiful pattern of Swiss and Italian lakes, culminating in a boat trip up the Rhine that would last a month with intervals of living in the countryside, music-making, samplings of the popular and haute cuisines, the purchase of selected art works at auction and in galleries, and various other occupations and diversions arising from the complex, civilized, yet passionate love of one woman for another. She suddenly stopped. Several people were trying to attach themselves to this conversation, and the ballerina was chilling them out. It gave Loretta time to wonder why she was telling this story. Did she think Loretta was being nosy? It was Margaret who wanted to know everything, not her. Again the ballerina stared at her. "So," Loretta said, "first you go for the blood, then a vacation with a friend. That's nice." "Not a friend," the ballerina said. "Lover." "Yeah, I know," Loretta said. The ballerina seemed to be waiting for something. "It's been nice talking to you," Loretta said, putting her empty glass on a table.

"Are you paying attention to what I'm saying!" Patrice shouted, "or are you just protecting yourself? That's what people always do, don't they? They never listen, except to their own thoughts. They can't spare the time to hear a fresh story, if it's the *least* bit threatening." The ballerina's eyes were like two pinpoints.

Loretta, even though she could see that Patrice was cracked, or at least high on something—maybe just starvation—thought she was partly right: this did happen all the time. People couldn't keep themselves separate from the stories they heard. Whatever you told them, they thought it was a message, or had a direct application to themselves. Otherwise, why would you say it?

"You're thinking about this," the ballerina said. "You're having your own thought, and that's good." She was smiling.

She took Loretta's glass from the table, and her own from the floor and carried them to the kitchen, then returned. "Goodbye," she said, "I enjoyed talking to you, and I almost never talk to people." She turned to go, then stopped. "I never asked you," she said, "what you plan to do next, did I? And I'd like to know. I can't stay to listen now, but I'll call you soon. I'll call you before I leave. Tell Margaret"—the ballerina had all her things gathered up again: the book, jewelry and the bag of medicines—"I'll call her tomorrow."

"Did she give you"—Loretta turned and there was Alfred Aschenbach right by her ear—"food for thought, Miss St. Cyr?" Loretta said yes, mainly the food of: were Margaret and the ballerina friends? How could that have happened? "I liked your show," Loretta remembered to say. "How did it do?"

Mr. Aschenbach said it had done well and asked if she had seen the reviews.

"No, but I'll look them up," she said.

"Don't bother. I'll give you a copy. What was she telling you all this time? She was talking to you for a long time."

The party was crowded. Loretta was looking, without moving her head, for Margaret. Was Alfred Aschenbach one of the ballerina's boyfriends—that's the way he was acting—from the old days, or more recent? Mr. Aschenbach was now asking about Daniel and whether he'd be coming to the party.

"No," she said, "he's not coming."

"Too bad. I kind of like Daniel."

He hovered a minute or two longer, but when he saw that Loretta wouldn't or couldn't give an account of her conversation with Patrice—she was too busy thinking about something else—he told her: "Look, I'm going to get another drink. Take care of yourself. You look thin, Loretta." He gave her arm a little pinch. "Put some fat on you. See," he said, confidentially, "if there's an exhibit somewhere you can eat."

Loretta had never heard Mr. Aschenbach make a joke. She

thought he might be losing a little more of his foreignness, and that was too bad. (Later that night, when Loretta found Margaret, she seemed already to know that the ballerina wasn't only interested in men. Did she also know that Alfred was a little interested in the ballerina? Margaret said she did know, but she probably didn't, judging by how quickly she began to abuse Alfred and his phony accent. He wasn't foreign at all, Margaret insisted: he'd grown up in the Bronx and gone to City College. He'd spent a few lousy summers in Germany, that's all.)

Three weeks after the party, Loretta knew something no one else knew, and she told Margaret. I might be pregnant with a baby, she said, and Margaret laughed. "Is that how you say it where you come from?" Then the message sank in and Margaret cried: "How could you be so stupid?"

Loretta said it wasn't stupid, it was an accident. Margaret listened as Loretta outlined the good points of the pregnancy: it would settle them down, her and Daniel; it would draw them together, around something besides analysis; it would give their lives some purpose ("You mean *his* life, don't you?" Margaret interrupted); plus it could be fun.

"Could it?" Margaret said. "I've never heard you say that before."

"It could," Loretta said. The reasons were starting to seem a bit thin, so Loretta said: "You know what the real reason is?"

"What?"

Loretta was thinking fast.

"Say it!"

"Well, it's fine for us now, isn't it? We're young and comfortable."

Margaret looked puzzled.

"What I mean is, we're fulfilling our possibilities."

"Not me."

"I don't mean as artists, I don't mean in a career, I mean physically. We're grown up, wouldn't you say? Our bodies are finished becoming what it was planned for them to be."

"What are you getting at?" Margaret said. "This doesn't sound like you."

"Let me finish: if we don't have a baby and put a dent in these finished bodies—"

"A 'dent'! I'd call it more than that!"

"—then when we're fifty or sixty, we're not going to be the nice, flabby, contented ladies we were meant to be." She paused. "With the horror of existence behind us."

Margaret was silent.

Loretta then said that if they didn't give themselves over to something destructive, there would be no way to begin again. "We'll just have these same old lives. And we won't even have those. Nothing lasts, so we might as well tear up our lives and start a new life, or we'll just go on living in the same junkyard." Loretta's eyes were filling with tears.

"You're talking about your marriage, aren't you?" Margaret said. "I'm sorry for you, Loretta, but now you've made it worse, haven't you? I mean, haven't you?"

"You're not helping, Margaret."

"I know. I'm just shocked. I can't believe you'd go and do something like this without telling me."

When Loretta told Daniel the news, he wrote a jubilant, extensive letter to his mother, who sent a beautiful white layette and a long note to Loretta. "You are happy about it, aren't you?" asked Daniel, when he'd read his mother's letter.

"Are you?" Loretta asked him.

He said he was. He didn't expect it, it was something he hadn't even thought of, but he was happy. It was interesting, bewildering, he didn't know how even to begin to think about it.

Loretta decided to wait to tell her family. It was early, anything could happen. "That doesn't mean you're thinking about an abortion, does it?" Daniel asked.

"If I was, don't you think I'd say something?" she said.

"I don't know. You might not."

"I'm not thinking about an abortion."

"Your life's going to change," he warned. He talked more these days, and less coherently. The baby was already changing things.

"So's yours," she said.

The ballerina called before she left for the spa, or wherever she was going. They talked for a long time, and Loretta wondered if Patrice was hinting that the solution might be to run away. She kept offering money, and at one point—in the middle of an unrelated conversation—said: "There are other men, you know." When Loretta didn't answer, Patrice said, "I'd like to meet this Daniel. I'd be impressed if he were even half as smart as you say he is."

At another point, the ballerina said she thought Loretta needed a change of scene. She suggested another country, another language, a different water. "You're living like a rat on a treadmill. I know it doesn't seem that way to you—"

"It does."

"Well?"

Loretta sensed that the ballerina would soon end the conversation. Patrice was going to urge something radical and cutthroat, then hang up. Encouragement from someone like the ballerina was a little like the beans in "Jack and the Beanstalk." They were useless in any practical sense, but powerful and unpredictable if any of them happened to hit the ground. Patrice was living in another world with her beans. She was safely barricaded behind something Loretta didn't quite understand, plus she had wrapped herself in thick vines of disguises, stories and exaggerations. That helped, too. She had a strong imagination and an even stronger will. This allowed her to alter the world she lived in to her specifications. She had only one foot in reality, and nobody ever challenged her.

And so, over the phone, the ballerina built a model world for Loretta. She said that Loretta was living a fairy-tale life, but had only gotten halfway through the adventures, the part where everything goes wrong. It would get better: there was a second half, when the fancy things, the miracles and coincidences would happen. And they happen, the ballerina added, when you *make* them happen. If you don't make them happen, it's your fault.

Loretta hung up the phone, after wishing the ballerina a good trip, good riddance, too. She went over to the kitchen sink and hung over it until the nausea passed. Peewee was rubbing the yellow fur against her bare ankles. The cat was purring. Loretta turned the faucet on and put her face under it, felt the coldness of the water. Loretta bubbled some words of incantation into the spray of silvery water and some of it went in her eyes, some up her nose.

St. Vincent's and the Afghan

■ ■ ■

*I*T was a foggy afternoon. You could barely see the street from the window, and the window was also streaked with dust. The room was hot, the sheets were stiff and had been treated with a chemical that irritated her skin. The hospital was quiet now after a nightful of noises—bumps and clanks and people groaning, the nurses talking in loud voices and the P.A. system turning on and off. Now was the time to sleep, but she was too tired to sleep.

She had been in the hospital for two days and two nights. She had finally graduated from the IV liquids to a diet of bland food—pale, quivering things and mashed things, and smooth white things that came covered with silver lids. Most of the time she had to stay in bed, but was allowed to hobble to the bathroom, and to sit for an hour in the sunroom with a couple of skeletal old men. One was meek and silent, the other stared. At first this seemed awkward, but after one visit the two seemed glad to see her. They exchanged greetings and then lists of symptoms.

Daniel came in three or four times a day, never for very long; Margaret popped in and out and the ballerina sent flowers from Chamonix. When Gloria heard that Loretta had been rushed to the hospital, she sped down from Providence on the train and begged Margaret to put her up on the couch so that she could be close by until Loretta was well. Gloria came over to the hospital that morning, lugging two bags of groceries. Loretta was surprised that a person could walk right into a hospital with grocery bags, but Gloria said that people gave her the right of way as a matter of course: she had that look of authority. She also happened to be wearing a nurse's uniform—she even had a little starched cap with a velvet stripe. "The nurses were glad to see me. They didn't care what I brought," she said, unpacking candy, cigarettes, a fifth of Jack Daniels, a bottle of Coke.

"Is that all for me?"

"It's all for you."

"Thanks."

Gloria unpinned her cap and set it on a chair. "I can tell you're depressed," she said.

"Really?"

"Yeah." Gloria sat quietly for a minute, then said: "Remember what the guy in the 5 & 10 told you? He said, 'Separate the soul from the body.'"

"What guy?"

"Don't you remember? The guy who gave you a bonus the day your parents died. In the 5 & 10? I forgot what he gave you, but he said that when you die, your soul rises and the greasy part falls down to hell."

"How do *you* remember that?"

"I remember every important thing that's ever happened to you," Gloria said calmly.

"I don't understand what that has to do with depression."

"Separate the soul from the body—don't you see?" Gloria said, as meaningfully as she could, but Loretta still didn't see.

The cousins sat in silence. Gloria scanned the tiny room: two plastic chairs, a TV set chained to the ceiling, and the spotless linoleum floor—no more than ten inches of it bordering the white bed with its metal appendages. There were three vases of flowers on the windowsill. Gloria looked at these, and said: "I see he's making up for his sins."

"Who?"

"Who do you think?"

"I wish you wouldn't talk about him that way, Gloria."

"Sorry," Gloria replied, and let her tired eyes fall with their full weight on Loretta's face. Loretta looked away.

"Aren't you glad to see me?"

"I am," said Loretta.

"You don't act glad."

"I'm sick!" Loretta shouted.

Gloria threw an arm over her eyes. "I think I'm having a déjà vu, Loretta. Am I?"

Loretta wondered if Gloria was trying to reestablish the old tone. There was no basis for it—things had changed too much. Since the wedding, the cousins hardly saw each other: they lived too far apart, they didn't write letters, and Loretta had married someone who didn't believe in wasting free time visiting relatives. "How's Margaret?" asked Loretta.

"I don't know," Gloria said. "We're not exactly girlfriends, you know. I've barely laid eyes on the whore." She tapped out a cigarette and lit it with her silver lighter, dug out of the small picnic basket that she used as a pocketbook. "Do you mind if I smoke in your face?" she asked, kicking the door shut so no one could see. "You don't have emphysema, do you?"

"You're just saying that to get even," said Loretta, "but I never asked you to stay with Margaret. I would never ask you to do that."

"Shut up," said Gloria, enveloping herself in a cloud of smoke. After two quick puffs, she stubbed out the cigarette. "So, how are things going? You don't look well," she said.

"*You* look pretty good."

"Don't change the subject." Gloria peered over Loretta's head and squinted at the dirty window.

"I'm sorry this isn't interesting," Loretta said, watching her.

"Who cares! Nobody has to be interesting when they're sick!"

"Why are you so worked up?"

"Forget it." Gloria lit a fresh cigarette and prowled around the small room.

"Didn't you hear what happened?" Loretta asked her.

"Yeah, I heard what happened. People *say* you can't pick your illnesses and I guess that's true. I don't hold it against you, but I think it's a bad sign."

"It's not my fault!"

"Oh yes it is. It's your fault because you see yourself as Jesus' little dartboard."

Loretta felt too weak for this kind of talk. She closed her eyes and lay a wrist across them, pressing down until she made a beautiful dartboard of purple circles and yellow stripes, all kind of listing to the left.

"Listen to me, Retta! Don't give yourself an easy out."

Loretta started to laugh—it was half laughing, half something else. Gloria was gearing herself up for a big blow and there was no way to avoid it. Loretta, Gloria had already explained, was the victim—as Gloria was herself, as she freely admitted—of multiple oppressive and interpenetrating systems: of fate, of class, of gender, of her ethnic group, and of the times. Because of her education, her sexuality, her religious upbringing, her personal code, and even her poorly trained and undernourished body.

"And," she went on, "the problem isn't simply the system: it's you too. you're too weak and malleable for this age. Everybody has their private theatrical to put on, and they all pick you for the audience—the audience, the actor, the stage, too." Gloria had gotten this from the horse's mouth, she said, lighting another cigarette and pulling *The Gay Science* from her picnic basket to read a quote she had been saving for just this purpose. "Do you know Neetch?" she said. "All right. Listen: 'The ability for acting will have developed most easily in families of the lower classes who had to survive under changing pressures and coercions, in deep dependency, who had to cut their coat according to the cloth, always adapting themselves to new circumstances, who always had to change their mien and posture, until they learned gradually to turn their coat with every wind and thus virtually to BECOME A COAT.'" Gloria asked if she should read it again.

"I heard it," Loretta said. "I'm the coat. I got it."

"*The Gay Science*," Gloria added, holding up the book.

"Yeah," Loretta said.

"Do you get the point?" Gloria asked, then went on. In addition to being fodder for the system, Loretta—and Daniel, too—were also victims in a subtler way. The world refused to support their pathetic cottage industries, letting them sink deep into poverty, the cast-offs of a crumbling middle class. "You don't even have the prerogatives that the educated class used to enjoy," she shouted. "You live like pigs!"

Loretta pretended to be asleep.

"That's the down side," Gloria said, "—and there's not much on the other side, because you do *nothing* to help yourself. No political agenda, no thought, no feminist demolitions. You haven't even tried to barricade yourself behind a wall of money like certain others of your generation. You're not a reader, so you draw no consolation from the struggles of the past. What economy are you *in*, Loretta? What do you get and receive?"

Loretta was listening. "You mean *give* and receive, don't you?"

Gloria considered. "No, I don't. I mean *get* and receive. 'Give and receive' is another discourse."

"I don't want to talk anymore, okay?"

They sat in silence, Loretta with her eyes closed. When she opened them, she saw that Gloria had gone back to Neetch. Loretta watched her. She had never seen the girl's soft, round face so thoroughly at rest: the eyelids were at half mast, the cheeks windless and the mouth a normal shape. Even relaxed, it was a plain face, the face of Aunt Rita, but without the lines and rings of tension. It was a face so elastic that it could convulse with the waves of violent speech, then collapse, once the moment was over, into a smooth, vacuous calm. Loretta wondered if this resilience meant that Gloria's speeches didn't count. Isn't that what an economy meant? Things cost and people have to pay. Maybe Gloria wasn't paying enough.

Now Gloria was watching. "I've mouthed off, Loretta," she said. "I'm not taking anything back, but I could have picked a better time."

Loretta was silent.

"Now I've upset you." Gloria dropped off her chair and knelt on the floor. "Will you forgive me, please?" It was only half in jest. "Loretta?"

"What's in the other bag?" Loretta asked, pointing.

Gloria dropped her head down on Loretta's bed. "I've been dreading this moment," she moaned. She rose and went to fetch a box from the depths of the paper bag and laid it gently on the bedside table. "Guess what this is?" she said. Loretta waited. "It's your wedding present! It finally tracked you down." Loretta looked at the box, then at Gloria. "Laugh," Gloria said. "Laugh! It's funny. Imagine, at a time like this, this crappy thing found you."

Gloria waited for the laugh, but Loretta was more interested in the box. "Okay," Gloria said, "I'm going down to the cafeteria. Margaret has nothing in her house but baby food. Can I bring you back something? Why don't you just lie back and get used to the idea that this," she said, pointing to the box, "is here."

Then she seemed to change her mind. "You don't need this," she said, "with all your other problems." Gloria moved toward the door, grabbed her purse. "I didn't want to bring it. But your aunt said, 'Take it, Gloria, or I'm going to throw it out.' So, I took it. *You* throw it out." Gloria was in the doorway. "I'll be back, Retta." And the door swung shut.

Long after Gloria had gone, Loretta was still looking at the closed white door. Why were people (even Gloria—especially Gloria) so anxious to give you their two cents? Didn't they have better things to think about than Loretta and her stupid problems? That morning Daniel had come to tell her that disease was its own discourse; she just had to figure out the code. "People don't want to know what the disease is telling them, so instead they go after the 'cure.'" He also said that it was probably him she was trying to "eject." Or it might be something more complex, something having to do with the originary family. "Think," he said, "what Freud says about the return of the repressed. You never had the chance to do the mourning or the working through, so your body found a way to send you the message." He paused. "You know, I envy you in a way. Nothing speaks so clearly to me."

Margaret thought this was true—the part about clarity— and said so. "It *might* have been him you were rejecting," she said. She thought about it a minute: "You don't think it was me, do you?"

Another time Daniel had come in to refine his notion. It might be *ressentiment* toward the second family, a feeling that was repressed and then returned in the form of—

"What second family?" she had asked.
"The Gillises," he said. "Who else?"

Loretta turned to the window. It was darker out now, but the fog had lifted and a hem of flame-colored light blazed on the windowsill. People were leaving the hospital: nurses in white, orderlies and maids in blue, all fanning out to the different rows of cars and unlocking their car doors. They were in a hurry. She listened to the different engines starting up. The flood of people slowed and thinned, and soon the parking lot was empty of people and of half the cars. It was too early for visiting hours, so the patients were alone and safe in their hospital. It was peaceful. Before leaving, Gloria had figured out a way to turn off the overhead light, and now the room was filling with a rosy twilight.

She enjoyed this for a while, but then harrassing thoughts returned—just like Daniel said. "The message" had come only forty-eight hours ago, although it felt like months ago. In the middle of the night, she snapped awake in a warm and sticky puddle. When she lifted herself up, she felt it trickling over the side of the bed and down to the floor. She used a towel to mop some of it up, then threw the dripping rag into the bathtub and ran the shower on it. She went to the kitchen for paper towels and dripped a path of blood into that room, then back to the bathroom, where she sat down on the toilet and let her head drop to her knees. The pain was much worse: she cut through a plastic glass with her sharp teeth, and ground her toes on the bathroom tiles. Her hair and nightgown were matted with blood. She took the nightgown off, but used her bloody fingers to wipe away the coats of sweat, so now her body was streaked with blood. It was an awful mess but she was too sick to care. Could she wake Daniel?

She must have passed out next. The firemen came. Someone called them, and Daniel wrapped her in a coat so they wouldn't see, but they took off the coat and wrapped her in something slick and cold, then carried her down the stairs to the ambulance. It was a hectic scene: the firemen were yelling questions and Daniel was trying to answer them—their landlady from downstairs was talking at the top of her lungs (she didn't like them anyway).

Loretta must have collapsed again because the next thing she knew it was morning in this overheated room and Daniel was standing there with a bunch of flowers in his hand. They looked half dead, and so did he. He was sorry, he said. He had taken a sleeping pill and hadn't heard a thing. Loretta said it didn't matter, everything was okay. "I'm sorry," he said again. "I took two sleeping pills. I was completely out. Do you believe me?" Yes, she said, it's okay. "No, it isn't okay," he insisted, "you could have died. Don't you realize that?" He tried to catch her eye, and held her head firmly: "Why didn't you wake me?"

For a while, the graphic shock of "the message" satisfied everybody. Something definite had happened and people focussed on the signs: the blood, the ambulance, the firemen. But as Loretta got better, different questions were asked; people were more relaxed and could take the long view of the thing. What would cause Loretta to lose her baby? Something had to cause it. What did it mean? Loretta didn't feel up to this view yet, so she ignored the questions as best she could, and tried, when she was alone, to think of something else. Like what? It was easier when there was something nice to look at out the window. She ran her mind's eye over Gloria and Gloria's latest "uniform"—the white dress, the shoes, the little starched cap. The uniform reminded her of another one, one that was a little more interesting. The uniform—no, it was better than that— the *costume* Gloria had worn to the wedding at the Gillis home. Loretta remembered it very well—was it because it was a happy day, or just an odd one? It was a maddening occasion. People, herself included, had done everything they could to wreck it. Were all weddings like that? (If so, why did people have them?)

This was not a happy line of thought. Loretta raised herself slightly to look out the dirty window: the street lights had been turned on to blight the twilit landscape. The parking lot, scene of such a beautiful sunset, was now stenciled in harsh loops of pink fluorescence. The night around the lamps was broken by wavy arcs and haloes of salty light.

She tried to concentrate on the costume. The dress was rented from some theatrical house in New York, she remembered that. It was a relic of the 1890s. Black and white stripes. There was a blouse and matching skirt, wide belt, buttoned shoes, whalebone corset and a feathered hat. The stripes were wide and horizontal so she looked a little like a convict, but it was a flattering style for her, full and graceful. Compared to this gaudy pomp, the bride was plain in a buff-colored suit, and the bridegroom plainer in slacks and sportsjacket. Plainest of all was Margaret, who forgot to bring a decent dress and had only a skimpy jersey sheath that had dusted the bottom of her closet for months before she stuffed it in a suitcase. The girls were trying on their dresses the day before the wedding, and Loretta suggested that Margaret hang hers in the bathroom and run a hot shower. When it was clear that the shower wasn't enough, Gloria, arrayed in her beautifully starched clothes, asked if Margaret had ever heard of the concept of the flatiron. "The flatiron! How quaint," Margaret said snidely. So far, Margaret had wasted few words on Gloria, and Gloria had returned the compliment.

They tried on their outfits in Gloria's old bedroom, now a sewing room with the single bed used as a couch. Next to the bed was a basket filled with the makings of a big piece of knitting: balls of hot pink and white yarn, some of it worked into lurid squares and strips. Gloria was digging into the basket and pulled out a handful of crocheted roses. "These are the decorations," she said.

"What decorations?" Margaret asked, and had to ask again, but still received no answer. Loretta was studying the pile of knitting, obviously an afghan or blanket that hadn't yet been laced together. There were afghans all over the house, lying on beds, draped on chairs and folded away in closets and chests: Aunt Rita lived to make them.

"What is this thing?" Margaret was still asking.

Gloria gazed at Loretta with her gleaming eyes. "Recognize it?"

"No."

"Oh yes you do," said Gloria. She pulled out a long pink strip. "This is the extra yarn from that lamp doll she made for the Christmas Bazaar a thousand years ago. Remember that 'article'?"

"What are you talking about?" Margaret asked.

"Never mind," Loretta told her.

Loretta remembered the sight of Margaret wandering through Aunt Rita's house evaluating what she saw, sometimes with a word, sometimes with a look. She passed swift judgment on many of the aunt's prime knickknacks and ornaments, but these things, Loretta noticed, were not so different from the "objets trouvés" Margaret was always hunting down in Soho. Tacky Aunt Rita and stylish Margaret owned a few of the exact same figurines, although Margaret would die before she'd call them that. Both had a hobnailed glass slipper with a blue heel. Aunt Rita kept straight pins in hers, while Margaret's was used for roaches and a few old baby teeth, dried and yellow. Loretta remembered watching while Margaret surveyed the row of knickknacks on top of the fake mantlepiece. She spotted the glass shoe and made a beeline for it: "Where did she get *this?*"

She made other such discoveries, and each time was puzzled; she did not seem to understand that Aunt Rita had gone out looking for pretty things to decorate her house, had selected these very shoes, Turks, ballet dancers and praying hands, and bought them new. Her knickknacks weren't meant as campy statements, they didn't refer to a bygone era and the squares of that era, their pointless products and silly ideas. They *were* those ideas!

Gloria watched Margaret too. She couldn't believe what she was seeing. "What a snob!" was all she could bring herself to say at first, but later she indicated that she thought Loretta's friend was also a fool and a vulgarian. Still, Gloria was fascinated by Margaret—which was why she called attention to the bubblegum-colored afghan, and whatever else might offend the finicky girl's tastes. Gloria even installed herself outside the bathroom door while Margaret was in there inspecting things that only gays would own: the nylon-net slipcover on the toilet seat, for instance, with matching slipcover for the tissue box. And the teacup resting on the toilet tank planted with a rubber datepalm and porcelain Arab. Gloria had a few things of her own she wanted to show Margaret, but Margaret was not interested in the fat cousin, not in her things or in her opinions, and she made this very clear.

Together, Gloria and Margaret, the Gibson Girl-convict and the brown mini, were the stars of the wedding. It was a strange wedding: everybody thought so, but then they had all insisted on having a hand in its design, which was why it was so strange. The celebrant was Father O'Brien, a young priest whom Gloria had cultivated. She made it a practice to introduce herself to the parish priests, the monsignor and his clerics, so that she could be free to visit them and criticize the church's position on abortion, on the poor, on birth control, and to rock their serene apathy with a strong dose of the latest in Liberation Theology. At first they listened, Gloria said. They were polite, but they never had anything much to say for themselves. The oldest parish priest, Father Devlin, was the hardest to convince. He told his young cleric (who told Gloria) that lectures like this, so bull-headed, so one-sided, on such delicate matters, and conducted by a girl wearing pants, were disrespectful of the cloth, and therefore must be discontinued. But Father O'Brien liked Gloria well enough to agree to marry her cousin, a lapsed Catholic living out of state. He was all right, Gloria said.

The young priest surprised the couple by inserting into the ceremony the lyrics for John Lennon's "Imagine." Gloria followed his variation with one of her own: a quote from Mary Shelley and a eulogy for a Peruvian martyr-priest and Marxist. Margaret recited an Anne Sexton poem that had menstrual blood in it, and Daniel and Loretta exchanged their simple vows, Daniel's ending with one of Donne's Holy Sonnets and Loretta's with a passage from *Little Women*, partly as a joke.

People seemed to enjoy the ceremony, even the aunt and uncle. Aunt Rita picked her own reading from the *Little Treasury of Well-Loved Verse*. She liked the famous sonnet from the Portuguese because she always recognized it. Uncle Ted didn't want to read anything. He stood next to Daniel at the altar rail, and Loretta, flanked by Gloria and Margaret, came marching in from the side aisle. "Be good to my girl," Uncle Ted whispered right before he retreated to let the couple stand together. Loretta thought this was nice, but then looked up and saw that Uncle Ted wasn't looking at Daniel at all when he said it: he was looking at her.

Uncle Ted didn't seem to like Daniel. He made no effort to get to know him. Instead he talked a lot to Margaret, and Margaret loved the attention. It was Aunt Rita who liked Daniel, so elegant and handsome and such a talker. "He must be awfully smart," she said to Loretta, after the first family dinner, "with that vocabulary. Sometimes I don't understand a single word he's saying."

When the ceremony was over, the priest sprayed them with holy water and the bridegroom shared his wedding present to himself, a "bomber" packed with Algerian gold, with his bride and her attendants, as he drove them back to the house for the reception. There they met Daniel's family—those, that is, who'd chosen to attend. The father and brother stayed home, they had other commitments, Daniel's mother said. Daniel said it was done purely for its insult value. Mrs. St. Cyr added to the insult, according to Gloria, by wearing a dress just as crummy as Margaret's. "Why did she have to wear a duster to your wedding? Is that all she has in her closet?"

Loretta told Gloria to cool it. No one was getting along. People were drinking and bickering, and Gloria was even more argumentative than usual. Loretta remembered they were standing out on the porch, just the young people, and having a calm discussion about music, movies and the Movement, when Gloria piped up: "No matter where you are in America, no matter what school or what neighborhood, whether you're in college or working in a gas station, you all listen to the same groups and see the same movies! Yet you think you're *so* different—and so radical! You think you're undermining the state—the military!—with your protests. You think the military is worried about you? You're just a bunch of dumb kids, you're just being cool. Your project is no more radical than that."

They thought she was finished, but then she started up again: "You think there's a big difference between your generation and the fifties, but there's no difference. You're just as simple, you're just as programmed as they were. *More* programmed!"

"No one cares what you think, Gloria," Daniel said. "You're out on the margin." (Loretta and Margaret had already noticed that Daniel didn't have as much to say when Gloria was around, but it was Margaret—and for once she was right—who said: "You're both saying the same thing, Daniel. You just won't admit it.")

Daniel was chain-smoking. One time he had two cigarettes lit, and had to put one out. Gloria pointed out that his oral needs would drive him to addiction.

"How do you know?" Margaret demanded. "Are you a junkie?"

There wasn't enough liquor to get high, just enough to make everybody tired and grouchy. Daniel took Loretta aside ("Is there something wrong with you? I've never seen you so out of it." "I'm not out of it," she said, but she was out of it). They snuck into the bathroom so that Daniel could smoke the rest of the bomber. He was sick of having to talk to mental cases like Margaret and Gloria. He didn't know which was worse, the flaming narcissist or the crypto-fascist. Loretta wanted to know which was which, but suddenly there was someone banging on the bathroom door. "Hurry up in there! Give another guy a chance." Who was that? Loretta suggested to Daniel that they go on their honeymoon; I think I'm ready, she said.

But they weren't going on a honeymoon. They didn't have the money and anyway Daniel didn't believe in honeymoons. They were just going back to New York on the train, but they couldn't go back yet. The wedding wasn't over. On the way out, they ran into Gloria, who was gulping down a can of beer. She told them that she had just had it out with Daniel's mother. Daniel started to walk away, but Loretta stopped him.

Gloria said that Mrs. St. Cyr had been looking around for someone to talk to—someone on her level. She was curious: she knew very little about the girl her son was marrying. What was her major in college? (Gloria, when she saw that she had Daniel's attention, began rendering the story in his mother's fluty tones.) "What was the *name* of the college she went to? *You* went to a good college, and you both come from the same family. How do you account for that?"

Gloria then said that, before giving her Account, she gave Mrs. St. Cyr a look that should have shrunk her head, but no, the woman kept on talking: "*Daniel* had extracurricular interests in college, too, but it didn't hurt *his* grades."

Gloria said she pointed out to Mrs. St. Cyr that grades

were irrelevant today, but Mrs. St. Cyr said she didn't mean grades, she meant accomplishments, and went on to list Daniel's genius-level IQ, his National Merit Scholarship, his doctoral program in philosophy. "I don't think they have much in common," she said to Gloria, and Gloria asked her what she had in common with *her* husband.

And that was when Gloria began to give her Account. First she smoothed things over by telling Mrs. St. Cyr that Daniel *was* star material, but that he had been given every chance in life, every privilege, so that, although he did have the "accomplishments," they weren't exactly to his sole credit. That was number one. Number two, she said, was telling the mother to give *herself* some credit. Didn't she know that intelligence travels on the *x* chromosome?

As Gloria went on giving her Account, Mrs. St. Cyr became uneasy. A naive woman, she wasn't a match for someone like Gloria, so confident and so aggressive. Gloria explained that this uncertainty made Mrs. St. Cyr especially receptive, so Gloria planted many ideas about how to treat her daughter-in-law. A subtle girl with a quiet quality, one you have to solicit, to cultivate.

"She took it in," Gloria told the couple. "I told her it was the least she could do. Even our family took the trouble to try to like you, Daniel. And I told your mother our family hates everybody, just like she does. She didn't think that was funny, but too bad."

Daniel waited for Gloria to finish, and for Loretta to finish laughing, and then he started to give *his* Account, but Gloria didn't listen. She had taken Loretta aside: "This family looks down on you," she said. "You're too low-class for the St. Cyrs."

That was not true, Daniel insisted on the train going home, but it *was* true of Gloria. No, Loretta said, he was wrong there. Gloria was not low-class—she was trying to work *outside* of the classes. She was a successful girl, but she didn't want ordinary success. She got all A's in college and did the course work for half a dozen careers—medicine, biology, English and French, politics, journalism, law and even religion, but none of these sustained her for very long. She held a brief against organized professionalism of any kind.

Daniel said it smacked of a preemptive move. "She's afraid she might fail at a career, so she's got an excuse ready."

No, Loretta said, that wasn't it. Gloria felt that coming from a family and class like theirs, she could never be a success. It wasn't even worth trying.

"That's exactly what I'm trying to say," Daniel emphasized.

No, it was different from what he thought. Gloria felt it was a deeper problem, an impossible one to correct. The Gillis-Costellos of the world did not have the right faces, the right features, the right expressions, the right genetic code. They didn't know the codes. They didn't like the right things, and they didn't know where to buy them. It was entirely hopeless because it wasn't anything overt, but you couldn't learn it, and the stupidest person from the privileged class could see it.

"Then why is she so ambitious if it's hopeless?"

Loretta explained that Gloria couldn't have a real career, but could make a career out of subversion: she could make *fun* of the classes.

"Baloney," Daniel said, "you can't," but he was interested, and Loretta continued. She was not trying to justify Gloria, but simply to give her her due: she was a generous girl and had some good ideas.

"Like what?"

She wanted to give the family some financial security if she could.

"How," he said, "is she going to accomplish that?"

First, she wanted to work a few years in the Peace Corps, she wanted to travel, she wanted to get more involved in worldwide leftist groups; she was also deeply committed to feminism and ecology. On the practical side—

"Oh, bullshit," Daniel sneered, "it's *all* practical. She's an activist. I know the type."

On the practical side, she'd like to study law and run for office in a pit like Providence, try to retool the old machine so that the kickbacks and other illegal profits of government might fall into the hands of the deserving.

"Who would that be?"

All the people, Loretta said, who don't get it now.

"That's a 'new' machine exactly like the old machine," Daniel said. "Different cronies, that's all. Doesn't she know that?"

Yes, but she was considering doing it without entering into the profit-making sphere. If times were better, she'd go into the convent. The church needed the overhauling. Not just on the parish level, but at the College level with the cardinals, sexist and ignorant to a man, as she put it.

"She hates men, doesn't she?"

Loretta said she herself had wondered if the "College" was ready to listen to a nun.

"To say the least."

But Gloria had the right ideas about the church. She was always saying how the Latin Mass was the last vestige of a beneficio from Mother Church to her people. It introduced into their lives the only aesthetic element that wasn't corporate sponsored and that they didn't have to pay for.

"True," said Daniel.

He was starting to like Gloria, you could tell. But that was a long time ago. They had long since stopped trying to understand each other.

The ward was quiet. Sometimes it was quieter in the late afternoon than in the middle of the night, when sick people seemed to suffer most. Why was that? All you could hear was the nurse's soft soles squeaking on the waxed floors and a few metal things clinking on the medicine cart. Something smelled bad, like rotting garbage, but now someone was spraying the air with a disinfectant—a sweet and piney smell. It was supposed to cover the garbage but it didn't: you could smell both layers. Now was the time to sleep, but she couldn't sleep. Instead she reached for the box Gloria had left on the beside table. The time had come to deal with the afghan.

It was in an old blue box: "Boston Store." The store had been defunct for twenty years, the building wasn't even there anymore; in its place was an outdoor mall. Aunt Rita kept everything—even an old box like this. Was this her best quality? The archaic box, frail but perfectly preserved, still smelled a little of the department store with its rough pine floors. Loretta remembered the glass display cases, warm to the touch and lit from within by tubes of violet light. And the tearoom, connected to the store by a tunnel, where the shoppers, in their hats and gloves, and a chain of minks around their necks, ate their chicken croquettes.

She opened the box, so soft with age that it was powdery. Inside a folded tissue paper was the afghan, taut and springy. Over the years, it had lost none of its energy or gaudy color. It was still a headache to look at: hot pink and paste white, day-glo pink and cocaine white—or was it simply the color of a package of Hostess Snowballs? The colors now had a little history of their own, a trail of dated ideas and outmoded styles. The years had done it some good. She pulled it out of the box, thinking about the many times she had meant to haul the hateful thing home. Each time she'd arrive at Penn Station, gather her bundles around her, and no afghan. It was still in Rhode Island, another oversight.

She remembered opening it the day before the wedding. The house was packed with guests: the neighbors, relatives and neighbors from the old house—people Loretta hadn't seen in a long time. Each had brought a package wrapped in white or silver paper, big boxes containing "only practical things," someone had said apologetically, "because no one knows your taste"—a fancy 15-button blender, a fondue kit, a hurricane lamp to use as a decoration, silver-rimmed coasters, an electric knife. Among these was the box from the family.

People oohed and aahed when Loretta opened this box and unwrapped the tissue paper. She lifted out the pink and white wooly checkerboard: big floppy roses laced to the white squares, the pink squares left blank. When the afghan was shaken out, the heavy roses flopped and drooped.

They were standing in the dining room, opening presents so that Aunt Rita could display them on the sideboard for the curiosity and satisfaction of the guests who had given them. Loretta held the afghan up in front of her face so that people could see, but also to think of something to say. She might have waited a fraction of a second too long. Aunt Rita turned away to speak to someone else, who was asking how long the afghan took to knit.

"Not long," the aunt said in a loud voice. "I never did rosettes before, so I had to practice those." The voice had a sheen of anger to it.

Loretta thanked her aunt—it was safest to use the simple words—but the aunt didn't seem to hear, so Loretta said it again. Aunt Rita was still talking to the neighbor.

"It's beautiful!" Gloria blurted out.

Aunt Rita wheeled around. "Do you like it, honey?" she asked her daughter.

Gloria was still looking at Loretta. "Don't you like it, Retta?"

"I said I liked it."

Nobody talked. Then, in Aunt Rita's icy tone: "Don't you know that Loretta never shows her feelings. That's her way."

"I *am* showing my feelings," Loretta said, but the neighbor, Mrs. Pollard, Aunt Rita's best friend, was talking again, and Gloria dragged Loretta out of the room. "Don't make it worse," she said.

"Don't make *what* worse?"

"Look," Gloria said, when they reached the bedroom— Loretta was still holding the afghan—"the thing is hideous and you hate it. Why shouldn't you? But she didn't make it just to insult you. She thought you'd like it."

Loretta looked at the afghan.

"It's a fright," Gloria went on. "It's not even made of wool." Gloria started to laugh. "Hey, maybe Margaret will buy it off you. She'd love it. In a year or two, it'll have just the right degree of—"

"Why didn't you help me?"

"I said it was beautiful."

Loretta wondered if she had spoiled her own wedding.

"Look," Gloria said, "I'm sorry I laughed. Think about all the work that went into it. Doesn't that make it easier to swallow? Retta?"

Loretta closed the Boston Store box and lay back on the bed. She felt very weak. The light from the corridor was seeping into her eyes, even though her eyes were closed and swelling with water. Why was this so upsetting to think about? Worse things had happened. She remembered all the times she had made Aunt Rita cry: "You're against me because I'm not your real mother. I know how you feel. That's why you're so hateful acting." And Loretta *was* hateful acting. The time she was filling out a college application and swept the paper off the table and onto the floor, so Aunt Rita, who had just walked in, couldn't see what she was writing. "Everything you do," the aunt had said, "is a slight to me. Do you think I don't notice?"

Loretta was sorry now. She had been sorry for a long time.

But she didn't want to be thinking about other people's pain, because she was in pain herself—and pain was good, it was a distraction, it was an invitation to think about yourself, to be selfish. No wonder so many sad people got sick. Daniel was right: the "illness" was going to speak to her, if she would let it. But it wasn't an illness, it was an early miscarriage, and what was inside her wasn't even quite a baby—it was just a few cells. That's what the doctor had said. The others didn't consider it a baby either. They considered it a symbol. People didn't want to talk about a baby, they wanted to call it cells and forget about it, or call it a symbol and analyze it.

Daniel had said, "I'm sorry, Loretta, but neither of us was really ready for this, so it's just as well, don't you think?" But then he went on to say that it never would have happened if she hadn't, "on some level," wanted it.

"What the hell do you know about it, Daniel?"

He had no answer.

Margaret had cried a little. Gloria dealt with the subject by asking her if there were anything special she wanted to talk about. When Loretta said no, Gloria asked what she would have called it.

"Eddie."

"A great name!" Gloria said. "Who do we know named Eddie?"

"Why should it have to be named after someone we know?"

She had also been thinking about naming it Cantilever Roof. Not out of disrespect. Cantilever was the only baby she knew who was really treated like a baby. And this baby, whether it was called Eddie or Eileen, was going to be treated as well as that cat. Eileen was her mother's name. She wasn't going to tell anybody, but she planned to wait till the very last minute when they carried the baby to the baptismal font, and then, when the priest asked what name it was getting, she was going to say "Eileen." "Eddie," if it was a boy. That was her plan.

Eileen was dead. Dead or not, she deserved to have someone named after her. The loudspeaker clicked on: "Calling Dr. Edwards, Dr. Rice, Dr. Edwards. Calling Dr. Edwards, Dr. Rice, Dr. Edwards." The nurse came in with a batch of cards that had gone to someone else's room by mistake. Loretta pretended to be asleep. The nurse dropped the cards on the bedside table where Gloria had left the whiskey. The nurse picked up the bottle, looked at the label, unscrewed the cap, and sniffed. When she left, Loretta sat up and blew her nose. Then she opened the box, took out the afghan and spread it on top of her bed, crawled underneath it.

She was thinking about the last time she had had a good talk with Eileen. It was a long time ago. She had bunked school one day. She forgot why—something must have happened. She left the schoolyard at recess and started down Academy Avenue. It was a cold fall day. Was it fall or winter when it happened? It was freezing cold, so it was winter. She had never seen such a beautiful day. The air was crackly dry and the light so dazzling that it cut out each of the little stores and houses all jammed together, and filled in their windows and doorways with black. A few cars went by, their cheap paint and chrome glazed by the blinding light. She kept walking; the street was empty. No— there was one guy, she remembered, coming out of Benny's, with a big fat stomach and no jacket on, and walking into the 5 & 10. She didn't like the smell of the 5 & 10 anymore, so she held her nose against the sawdust, the rubber, the oilcloth— someone was behind her, so she turned down the first side street.

She remembered this very well. The street was so boring. No trees, just rows of three-decker houses, with a porch on each floor, one old faded flag flapping from a second story. It was such a beautiful day. Was she thinking about poor Eileen? Not yet. When was it that she had started calling her mother "Eileen"? She and Gloria called her that: Eileen, or sometimes Poor Eileen.

People had told her that this kind of thing was a time bomb, that it would catch up to her, then boom! Her mother would have laughed to hear it. "A time bomb! What jerks people are, always exaggerating." Her mother was a character, she knew how to judge people even though she stayed home all the time and never stepped foot outside except to run an errand. Poor Eileen, she knew a lot, but no one ever asked her her opinion.

Was she talking to Eileen yet? Loretta didn't know. All she knew is she started bawling her eyes out halfway down the street. She used the only decent tissue she had until it was just a sopping mass of threads. She could picture Eileen digging in her apron pocket for something—a napkin, even a dustrag, if that's all she had, saying, "Use it, no one's going to know." What a fool. Eileen never knew what hit her. The saddest song on earth was, "Me and my shadow, strolling down the a—ven-you." She was singing that song, but who was the shadow? It was a beautiful song, but a little sickening, too. There was very little air on the street and when the wind wasn't blowing right in her face, she had a hard time sucking any in. She was tired too, she remembered that. There was no place to rest but the bus stop, so she sat down on the bench. Eileen sat too, and said, "Well, did we miss the bus?" She asked Loretta if it was that silvery thing up the street, or was that her imagination? Loretta looked at the silvery thing, but it never moved, so it couldn't be a bus. She tried to remember what Eileen's hand felt like. She couldn't remember its size or the exact color of the skin. Eileen shouldn't bother looking for that bus, because—she remembered thinking—that bus was never coming.

Loretta stayed on the bench by herself. She didn't have anything else to do. She waited for an hour, at least an hour. It was freezing cold, but she didn't feel it. The lady watching her from the window at 121 Center Street began to feel nervous as time went on, wondering what the girl out there was doing. There were no busses in the afternoon. The dog was yapping and the TV was blaring. She didn't know what to do, she told Loretta, when she finally got Loretta into the house to tell her. "I kept calling you," she said, "but you didn't answer. I thought of calling the police. Then I thought of calling the rectory. *They*'d know what to do. I thought you might be lost. I didn't know what to think."

Loretta asked the lady for a glass of water, then ended up drinking two glasses of water, the second one with ice. The husband decided to drive Loretta back to where she lived. By that time, school had let out and at home the Gillises were all worrying, ready to send someone out looking, or to call the police. They had a million questions to ask, and they asked them.

People always had questions. They would rather ask questions than look at a thing hard and decide for themselves what it was. They wouldn't put themselves to that much trouble. Loretta felt hot and sweaty lying under the afghan and the hospital blanket, but she didn't have the energy to throw these covers off. It was easier, for now, just to lie under them and live with it.

A shadow fell over the bed. Someone was in the doorway. She looked, and without seeing who it was (she couldn't see: her eyes were blinded by the glare and her eyelids were sticking together), she said, "Don't come in."

And the person—whoever it was—stood there a minute, and then went away.

What is Home?

■ ■ ■

*L*ORETTA was attacking Daniel, was also attacking the apartment and the world too, and each time she finished, she would start tearing at herself. Daniel kept offering to call a girlfriend—Margaret, Miss Fallows, or even the awful cousin.

"I don't want to talk to them." "Why?" Loretta didn't answer. The last time Gloria called, Loretta asked about Aunt Rita and Uncle Ted—why didn't *they* call? Gloria said what she always said when Loretta asked this question: "They don't call New York. It's out-of-state." "So?" "They can't risk calling because they might get *him,* and they don't know what to say to him. Even if they get you," she went on, "it's not that easy." "What's not that easy?" "You live in New York. They don't know anyone who lives in New York. Maybe you're eating steaks at Delmonico's, or dancing in the Rainbow Room. Who knows what they think? They don't know you can live here like a couple of rats in a hole." "Don't be absurd." "Don't *you* be absurd. I'm telling you why they don't call you." Loretta asked did they know she had been sick and almost died? Gloria sounded disgusted: "That's why she sent the afghan! She dug it out of the

cedar chest and made me lug it all the way down on the train."
Why didn't they write if they were afraid to call? Gloria exploded: "Have you gone senile? You haven't been home in three years! You hate their guts!" Loretta said it hadn't been that long.

Gloria must have reported home in detail, because Loretta then received a string of Hallmark cards, one with a sick bunny on the cover, his foot in traction. A momma and poppa bunny, pink and blue bunny hats, standing around a fever chart: "Hoppin' you're mended soon," it said. (Aunt Rita had underlined all the words.) Inside was a carrot. "Love, Aunt Rita and Uncle Ted," the scratchy writing said. The envelope was addressed to "Mrs. L. St. Cir." (They were the only ones who called her "Mrs.")

"If you don't want to talk to your friends," Daniel was saying, "and if you won't talk to me, and you don't want to do anything to lift the gloom, and you don't want to go back to school, or get a job, what *are* you going to do with yourself?" He was sitting at the kitchen table making a grocery list. He had already asked if there was something special she'd like him to cook.

Loretta turned away from him. There was nothing to see out the window but two old trees, an old one and a dead one, and the empty warehouse behind them. One of the two trees seemed to be dead, if by "dead" you meant it grew no more leaves in the spring, but was holding on in the leafless state. She said, "Maybe it isn't dead, that tree."

"What tree?"

"*That* tree. It looks dead, but it's hard to tell this time of year."

"It's summer, isn't it?" he said, walking to the window to look at the tree, or at what was visible through the fourth-floor window. It was more likely dead: the branches looked dry and brittle.

"Yes," she said, "but when it rains, the branches get black and oily. Maybe some of the branches are alive."

"The tree is dead," said Daniel. A minute later, he remarked: "How can you question a thing like that? If it's dead, it's dead! Are you denying sense-knowledge now?"

Loretta rolled over on her back to look up at him. "Certainty has never been your specialty either."

"You're right." A minute later, he said, "Do you really think that?"

Daniel was different these days. He was acting younger and less certain—and not just about things he took pride in confusing. He listened more, he worked a little less, he stayed home a lot and tried to be entertaining. He *was* entertaining: he talked a blue streak, read her interesting things from the newspapers and from novels, he played his guitar and sang, he went out and bought a small stereo so that Loretta could listen to music and not be bored. He was entertaining, but Loretta was not interested in entertainment. She was reading a lot of philosophy. Daniel accused her of being idle, but she was doing a lot of reading: Nietzsche, Schopenhauer, Kant and now Sartre. Daniel picked up these books from time to time, and sometimes made a comment, but she didn't pay attention. She was reading for a different reason.

"What?"

"I don't know exactly. I can't put it into words. And I don't *want* to put it into words!"

When Daniel finished the grocery list, he returned to the bed and lifted a strand of her long, limp hair from the pillow. "What can I do for you?" he asked. "Do you want an appointment with someone? You could talk to *my* psychiatrist. He's not going to laugh in your face, I promise you." Daniel got up and paced around. "Don't be insulted by this, Loretta, but I don't think your problem is hopeless. I think other people have been through this kind of thing. What do *they* do? Aren't you interested in finding out?"

She didn't answer.

"Don't you believe that suffering has some value? That's what you used to think. Why aren't you interested in finding out?"

Loretta said she didn't want to talk to any more doctors: she wanted to go home.

Daniel sat down at his table. "You're kidding, aren't you?"

No answer.

"I'm waiting for your reasons," he said sarcastically.

"I don't have any reasons. I just want to go. Are you going to stop me?"

Daniel got up from his table and started pacing again. "I'm not going to answer an insulting question like that." He added, "What do you think you're going to *do* there?"

"Nothing."

"That's what you do *here!*" he said, trying to make a joke of it. He walked to the bed and studied the face—thin face, papery skin. "Do all artists act like this?" he asked. He was trying to be agreeable.

"I'm not an artist."

"It's all right with me," he said, a minute later. "I'm not going to be difficult." He sat down, he got up. "You're not trying to leave me, are you?"

They talked a bit more, argued, then Daniel went off to the grocery store.

After he left, Loretta waited a few minutes, then pulled the phone cord until the red telephone toppled off the desk. She dragged its parts across the floor. She dialed. "Margaret? I want to talk to Gloria. Is Gloria there?"

Margaret didn't want to get off the phone, but Gloria grabbed it out of her hand. Loretta listened to the struggle.

"Thanks for calling," Gloria said. "I wasn't going to call again and have to talk to Mr. Ed."

"I'm not calling to chat, Gloria. I want to ask you a favor."

"What?"

"Call the folks and tell them I'm coming for a visit. Ask them if it's okay, if they can spare the room. Will you do that?"

After a pause (Loretta could hear Margaret asking questions, then trying to get the phone back), Gloria said: "Okay. You want to know what they say?"

Loretta said that she was going to start getting ready. To call only if they said no, or acted weird. "And Gloria?"

"What?"

"Call them right now."

"I'll call them. If you don't hear from me in five minutes, go."

Loretta packed some books, called a cab, then skipped the cab. She walked the half mile to the subway station. "Dear Daniel," the note on the kitchen table said, "I'm not leaving you, but I'm going. I didn't want to wait. Don't call me up there. Write if you want to. I'll be back. LCSC."

It was a long way home. Home was at the end of a long northeastern track, and after Loretta had settled her things on one seat, she sat on the other and looked out the window. This view didn't change. Whatever was built around the railroad tracks stayed there. People weren't interested enough in these weedy strips of land to put up an apartment house or a chain drug store: the dilapidated houses—rowhouses, projects, shacks, three-deckers and saltbox cottages—stayed where they were and got even shabbier. People still strung their laundry on clotheslines: raggedy towels hung with towels, tee shirts next to tee shirts and rows of matched socks. What did they get out of life, these people, that made them want to stay the same, do things the same old way and live beside the railroad tracks? This was a stupid way to put it. They didn't want things to stay the same—they wanted to move, they wanted to drive their laundry to a laundromat or move to a house full of appliances, where everything worked, and if it didn't—throw it out! Nobody wanted to live here and sink into the ground while the trains went whizzing by.

It wasn't all slums. In Connecticut there was a strip of pretty houses between the tracks and the ocean; people who lived there had lawns and some even had woods. Were things the same here? No. Inside these houses, things were different: the old families were gone—the mothers who had planted the flower gardens and the tomato patches and the fathers who had mowed the lawns, hosed the cars and thrown garbage on the mulch piles. The children who raced through the woods were also gone. So who was here? I don't know, yes I do. Here was a couple with no children, who rode the train to Manhattan and worked in a bank, and here was a single man who had a phone in both his cars and who meant to retire early to enjoy his natural shingle house, to marry, and to do in a few years what people used to spend their whole lives doing—with the help of outsiders and specialists trained to speed the process up: doctors to make an aging woman fertile, gardeners to force a neglected pile of dirt to produce in one season, nurserymen to bring in baby trees once the full-grown ones had been cleared, maids and laundresses to wash and iron the baskets of cotton and linen. Where were the time-saving fabrics of yesteryear?—the rayon, dacron, orlon and nylon, the drip-dry, acrylic and permanent press? The shirts and pants, the dresses, blouses and suits you could pull out of the washer, hang on the line, fold up and wear? And where was all the time they saved in ironing?

Sometimes Loretta would spot signs of a family living in one of those nice houses: something hanging out a window, a toy on the lawn, a few pieces of laundry on the clothesline and a car in the garage. But this lived-in house would be followed by a row of empty-looking ones with their glassy pools. Not even a dog or a cat trailing across the wide, well-trimmed lawns. Were these the depressed thoughts, she wondered, of a tired-out woman with no baby, or was this reality? Her own interior felt like a slum—the tenant kicked out and the slumlord home alone, old witch squatting in the empty gingerbread house after the children had been baked and eaten.

"Are you all right, Miss?" the conductor asked.

When he'd moved on, there was nothing but woods on both sides of the car.

So people were moving from old places to new ones, going from the country to the city, or from the city to the suburbs. So what? Even the aunt and uncle had moved: they didn't live in the old house on the old street. During the years when Loretta hadn't visited once—not for a weekend, not for an afternoon, not for an hour—they had moved away and things had changed. They didn't even live in a house. They lived in a bayside condominium, bought with the profits from a smart investment of Uncle Ted's pension and the sale of the old house for four times what it had cost. They brought their old things with them, and then bought some new things. At first it was too crowded: the eight rooms of old things did not fit into the four new rooms, so some of the new things went back to the stores, and lots of the old things were sent to Gloria, who kept track of everything and wouldn't let her mother part with so much as a beat-up metal ashtray on a beanbag. Once they had room to move around, the Gillises were comfortable in their one-floor home with its thin walls and French door facing the bay.

There was even a porch enclosed by a frail wrought-iron fence—room enough for two beach chairs if you kept the backs up straight. The aunt and uncle would gladly sit out there and watch the sun go down, if that sun—blazing across the polluted water and meeting the big cloud of heat rising off the bubbling blacktop (the aunt liked to exaggerate, especially if her thoughts were paraphrased by Gloria)—weren't enough to kill you. They kept the doors and windows curtained and shaded and the air conditioner going full blast.

About ten in the evening, Uncle Ted told Gloria, there was a breeze and you could go out and enjoy it, if the cars—in and out of the parking lot at all hours—didn't blind you with their headlights. Maybe some night in the dead of summer, some holiday when the other residents were up in Maine staying in a condo there—maybe then, he said, it'll be nice to go out and watch the pleasure boats cruising in and out of Providence harbor, or the sailboats gliding down the channel. On a night like that, sitting on the porch with something to see out on the water, it'll be worth it.

"No it won't," Gloria said. The place wasn't even as nice as they tried to make it sound. They were disappointed but they couldn't change their minds and buy back the old house—it cost too much, they'd lose the equity, plus they didn't want to move again. "But most important," Gloria said, "they don't want to admit they were wrong." So they kept their complaints to themselves. They weren't complainers, Aunt Rita liked to say. And even if they were, what good would it do them? Were things going to get better by and by? What would make them better? And who was to say they'd still be alive to enjoy it? (Gloria could get belligerent on this subject. Loretta simply said that when you reach their age, isn't it best just to settle? What's the alternative? This enraged Gloria, who, face like a broken tomato, shouted: "They've been cheated out of their retirement! Can't you see that?")

The cousins had had some terrible fights before and right after the wedding. First they fought about the marriage, then they fought about Loretta's indifference and ingratitude to the family that had raised her. All their discussions would lead inevitably to politics.

"Was she always so dogmatic—Gloria, I mean?" Loretta's old psychiatrist had asked. Loretta, who was hurt by the fights, but who was never going back home to apologize, had been trying to sketch a portrait of the family. She had just finished telling how her uncle was a simple working man, very devoted to his family, a good father, although sometimes a little moody.

"That's pretty dull," the doctor said. "Was he that dull?"

Loretta said he didn't talk much. The aunt did. You heard her opinion on every subject, but you still didn't know . . .

"Her feelings?" the psychiatrist finally said.

Yes, Loretta answered, but even her thoughts you didn't know because all her opinions were defensive. You could sense that her back was pressed against the wall.

"Maybe she didn't have thoughts," the psychiatrist offered. "Why do you seem so sad about this, Mrs. St. Cyr? Does she make you sad?"

No, Loretta said, it was nobody's fault.

"You're making progress," he said, "compared to before." ("Before" was when she was going too slowly with her stories. One day he told her that she had, at most, ten or fifteen years of sessions to come out with what it was she had to say. "I'm not telling you to hurry or to cut anything short. I'm just saying what the human limit might be. At least," he added, for he would always add a kind word or an excuse, "you aren't glib. When you say something, there's no need to say it again. I'll never forget it.") But that day, she had cut a little deeper. "What you've said today," he announced, "is interesting and I've learned a lot, but now we have to stop."

It was good, she thought, looking back on that day, that he had enjoyed a session or two, because it turned out that he didn't have the ten or fifteen years to listen to stories. He died early in the first year of therapy; he had a heart attack. His secretary said his life had been very hard, he was all alone and all he had was his work. His wife was dead now ten years and he still missed her. He had the retarded son who was also recently dead, killed by a drug addict a year after they released him from a mental hospital to take care of himself. Loretta went to the doctor's memorial service. There were a lot of people there. Patients, said the nurse. "They loved him, don't you think?"

Loretta decided to stop seeing a psychiatrist after poor Dr. Fidelman dropped dead, but another doctor took over his patients. He contacted her to say that he had set up two sessions for her, to help her to "handle the separation."

"Your aunt was your rival," said his new doctor.

"I was talking about my uncle," Loretta replied. "My stepfather was someone who—"

"Did he adopt you?" Dr. Major demanded.

"No."

"Well, he wasn't your stepfather then, was he? What did you call him?"

"I called him Uncle Ted."

"QED."

Her uncle, she went on, was someone whose thoughts were hard to figure out, although he wasn't secretive.

"Go back to the rival," the doctor insisted. "Later on, we'll paint the picture of the perfect father."

When they had talked for the two sessions and covered the accident, the new house, the new family, Dr. Major—who had trained in Paris with the French Freudians—said: "So you undermined your aunt's authority and cheated her of the love and respect of her children and her husband, right?"

Child, she said. There was only Gloria.

"The family," he continued, "had been a calm country— no, quieter than a country—a mere map. Everyone was perfectly content. Inert, but content."

Yes, she said.

"And you came along with your deaths and your accidents and the orphanage stories and tore it all to shreds, threatened and alienated everybody, left nothing in place, clawed your way to the top to take up your place as the center of the universe!" He paused. "So, what were we saying?"

I—

"*I'll* talk," he said. "After you killed your parents, long after you had wrecked their lives and turned them into drunks—"

She was shaking her head.

"Don't shake your head, it's true, the truth hurts. And before you ruined your husband's career and aborted your child— No, nod your head 'yes.' And cheated your friends and broke up your mother-in-law's marriage—wait, let me finish," he said, taking his thin pad from under the cushion of the chair where he kept it hidden, "you drove your aunt and uncle from the homestead, destroyed the careers of two prominent New York artists and killed a man of my profession. First, you turned him into an idiot, then you killed him."

Loretta was laughing, but Dr. Major said, "Don't laugh, be serious," as he sat straight in his leather chair and guided them to the end of the hour. "Are those your accomplishments? Say 'yes.'"

"If Gloria were here—" she started to say.

"Say 'yes.'"

"Yes," she said.

"Good," he said. "You can confess next time."

This was more like it. It was New Haven. At New Haven, she got out and watched the trainmen switch engines. They enjoyed their work. Nobody really cared about the trains, they weren't important to industry and business, or even to most travelers, so they were run in the old way, unspoiled by new ideas. These engineers were old-timers, they knew their trains and ran their own kind of trainyard on their own schedule. It was their train and it was their timetable; it was their club car, their tickets and their track. The passengers were a kind of freight. It was fun, even if the stations were shabby and pitiful, the windows thick with dust, the seats grimy, the toilets filthy and the food always the same semi-frozen sandwiches.

Dr. Major had said: "If you leave Daniel, don't come back here. You've signed your own death warrant, and his."

"Why are you talking like this?" she said.

"I'm talking to you," he said, during the third session, "in the only way you understand. Brutality is your language—everyone who knows you knows that. So I'm giving you no quarter. You want to live—leave him. Leave the families, leave the ugly friends, leave, start over. Drop your anchor somewhere else, if you see what I mean."

Loretta said she didn't.

"You do. How else—let me put it this way—are you going to face your tragedies and your guilts, if I don't smack you in the head with every one? We have to dig them out, we have to see them and dig them out. Then you have to grow a new skin."

It's kind of interesting, Loretta said, when Gloria asked about the sessions—and Loretta was still answering her questions. Gloria said the guy sounded like a sicko. Maybe, Loretta said, but that's just his strategy: he turns everything into something bad. He'll try something else after a while, she hoped. But, after the sixth session, she was sick of hearing how rotten everything was and how malicious and stupid and petty all the people were and how, only through her superior wiliness, had she outfoxed them all. She was also tired of his only piece of practical advice: leave the husband. Had Daniel figured out that this was Dr. Major's message? Was that why he seemed so anxious for her to find another doctor—any other doctor?

The trainmen were disconnecting a couple of big hoses after springing the clamp connecting the old engine to the cars; they chatted with the conductors who had wandered up to the front to have a cigarette. "All right, then," one of them said, and Loretta—who had also wandered up there—walked to the door of the first car, the conductor right behind her. As soon as they had stepped aboard and the conductor saluted the platform, the train moved in that subtle way it had, without any jolt or feeling of propulsion, smooth as air. It made Loretta smile and the conductor also smiled. But once the train had gathered speed, it rattled and jogged like any other mechanical thing forced on against inertia, and Loretta settled back in her seat and the conductor went about his business.

Her aunt and uncle were at the station. They never took a train, no one they knew took a train and the aunt was surprised to see that the trains were still running and tax money being spent to build a new station: a gray dome, stone and cement inside and out, a structure featureless and blank.

When Loretta came up the escalator with the small bag and large bag (she had no idea how many books she had packed, but they were heavy), there they were at the top. Gloria must have given them an earful: their faces were tense, their eyes darting around. And *I'm* supposed to be the nut, Loretta thought. Even when they spotted her and Aunt Rita called out and waved, their faces didn't relax: hers was beet red and his was sallow. The strain was hard to look at. She started hearing Dr. Major's voice: "Loretta, even as you breathe in and out, you're bringing these kind, hard-working people ever closer to their death." They too were talking: "You're thin, you don't look well. Have you had some supper? We wanted to take you out for supper. Are you hungry? I bet you aren't even hungry. How's Dan?" Loretta said something in Chinese and Aunt Rita went on: "Did you see Gloria, she called us. You're losing too much weight, Lori, look how skinny you are. Don't carry them, let *him* carry them. Your hair looks nice. Did you lighten it? Oh, she's still pretty. And young-looking. Let's go then. Or are we going to stand around here all night?"

Aunt Rita was all worked up. She cried herself to sleep that night: the apartment walls were just as thin as Gloria had said, or maybe Aunt Rita was crying twice as loud as she used to. In the old days, she sometimes cried herself to sleep two or three times a week. That was one of the reasons—along with snoring, cold feet, sharp toenails, rosary beads, the reading lamp, Ben-Gay and general restlessness—that they came to sleep in separate bedrooms. Aunt Rita slept in the four-poster in the big bedroom and Uncle Ted slept in the guest room on a single bed. There was barely enough space around that bed to make it up in the morning. It was just like sleeping in a coffin, Loretta was thinking, especially with the door closed. They were standing in the doorway of the tiny room, in the middle of a tour of the new condo. "If you wake up in the middle of the night," Aunt Rita said, "you'll know where things are."

Next they moved to the aunt's room, the "master bedroom" without the master, while her aunt rummaged through a built-in dresser for sheets and a blanket. All the rooms were sheathed in storage space: Aunt Rita showed Loretta many closets, cabinets and special drawers, some of them just a couple of inches deep. When her aunt discovered this shallow but continuous envelope of space, she recalled her linens and woolens, silver teaspoons, knick-knacks and china, old clothing packed in cedar and mothballs, to fill these crannies, every one. She handed her niece a stack of pink sheets and pink pillow cases and a flowered blanket. On top of this, she laid a cake of soap shaped like a seashell, a pink washcloth, large towel and small towel.

On top of that, a nightie and housecoat and a pair of slippers packed in a see-through plastic case. "Do you need a tooth-brush?" Loretta said she didn't, but Aunt Rita followed her into the living room with a new toothbrush, a box of powder, a bottle of hand cream and a jar of face cream, a tiny pillow sachet, a paperback novel and the latest *Redbook*, a small box of candy— Whitman's Sampler—and oddly, since it was past 11—and where could Loretta go out here in the suburbs?—a key to the house and one to the car.

"It's nice to have a young person in the house," Aunt Rita said, as Loretta came out of the bathroom wearing the nightie and housecoat. She saw that her clothes had been unpacked and put away and the books neatly stacked on the coffee table. It was the only mention made of Loretta's sudden visit and of the long absence that preceded it. Aunt Rita had changed—no one could miss this: she was being thoughtful, she was going out of her way to be nice.

The three of them settled in the living room, where Loretta was going to sleep on the fold-out couch. Aunt Rita flicked on the set and they watched the end of the eleven o'clock news. "Af-ter the news," Aunt Rita said, "we'll turn it off. You can sleep or read if you want. Or turn it back on, as long as it's not too loud."

It was the local news. A heavy, middle-aged man in a pale blue jacket sat at the anchor desk, a big red hand gripping a single sheet of paper. His face was purplish and he talked out of the corner of his mouth. Loretta remembered him: he had been around forever. During the commercial, Uncle Ted said he lived right there in the complex, but in a bigger apartment on the top floor, one with a roof garden. "When you go down in the morning," he said, "look up and you'll see a couple of trees— that's him."

"Is he married?"

"What kind of question is that?" asked the aunt.

"A younger woman," Uncle Ted went on. "He went and divorced the wife."

Aunt Rita reported what he paid her in alimony.

Loretta's not interested in local dirt," said Uncle Ted.

Loretta asked how Aunt Rita knew what he paid her in alimony.

"The papers," they both said. "They followed the case," the aunt went on. "They sent a reporter to the courthouse, and they printed every word of it."

"It was nobody's business," said Uncle Ted.

"It was interesting," Aunt Rita went on. "People like to read what's happening to people like Jack Jenkins—important people. And just think: he's our neighbor. I said hi to him just the other day."

"Big deal," said Uncle Ted.

"It *was* a big deal. Maybe not to you, but to me it was. Just because you don't like living with celebrities over our heads doesn't mean no one does. I learned a long time ago," (the news was on again: tenement fire on Broad Street, arcs of water shooting up from the sidewalk. The firemen were getting nowhere. "That building will be gone by morning," Uncle Ted remarked) "whether you're listening to me or not, Daddy, to enjoy what there is to enjoy in life. And I'll grant you, in our life, there isn't much."

"Oh, quit blubbering, Rita. Save it for later."

"Who's going to listen to me later? *You* don't listen to me."

Loretta climbed into the couch bed and switched on the reading lamp.

"Aren't you watching the news?" asked her aunt.

"I'm listening to it," Loretta answered, opening her copy of Sartre's *Existential Psychoanaylsis*. She liked reading Sartre; his disgust with life was greater than hers, and more elaborate. She didn't understand every thought behind it, but she found it useful anyway. She could use some of Sartre's ideas on futility and nausea to spark an argument with Dr. Major and help him with the sessions—if she ever went back to any sessions. He couldn't, then, accuse her of ruining Sartre's life or his career, or of hurting a book like this just by reading it. What could he say then? He could say that her reading about disgust was a way of hurting *other* innocent people, including himself, by putting his sentimental notions into question, or by disparaging his education in dialectics, a training inferior to Sartre's, or for having a less radical project, or simply for not living in Paris and sleeping with a lot of girls. He could say: "All the books you read are weapons!" But that wouldn't keep her from reading. It was up to Dr. Major, after all, to fight off Sartre's disgust and her disgust, if he could— if he was *worthy* of Sartre. If his ideas were not as good as those in *Existential Psychoanalysis* or *Being and Nothingness*, which she had also read ("Don't bother with Sartre," Daniel had warned, "he's a lightweight"), and if he didn't live in Paris anymore—this was fun. She was getting the hang of it.

Jack Jenkins was talking about a game he had seen that season: the Friars vs. Canisius College. The referees had gotten into a fight which was then broken up by the mother of one of the players. "It took guts," Jack Jenkins said. "But who has more moxie than a mother, an Irish mother—? Son spent a season on the bench. Waiting for the moment when the coach would call him. Into the game. The center had just been fouled. Then these refs had to argue about whether or not the player was fouled legally. How could you *not* understand. What she felt."

The story took up a good ten minutes of news time, and it was still confusing. There was footage from the game and an interview with the mother, then one with the son—a man who looked a little old to be in college, and spoke as if his lips were glued together—then one with the coach, who was used to television and spoke right up, then one with the referee from Boston, who said very little. The foul was declared legal over this referee's protest, but another player was substituted and the son never played at all. Even the updated story ended on "a sad note." The Boston referee had just entered the Mass General Hospital for liver cancer and the kid, it turned out, shouldn't have been on the bench at all—or even in uniform—because of "continual academic failure."

"No one would have noticed," Uncle Ted was saying, "if the mother hadn't interfered and made a scene. That kid could have sat on the bench for the rest of the season. And even got some court time."

"I think you're wrong," Aunt Rita said.

"He's a good player and now he'll never play," said Uncle Ted.

There was "talk," Jack Jenkins went on, of a suspension or even expulsion for breaking the "intercollegiate athletics' rule," and for lying.

"It's the coach," Uncle Ted said louder, "that's at fault here. And no one's going to call him, not with a winning season last year. And this year too, if he can keep the players from using their fists."

"Don't jump to conclusions," the aunt said.

"Shut up, Rita!"

Jack Jenkins signed off for himself and for the staff at WPRI. The set was flicked off and Aunt Rita, patting Loretta's blanket, "Nightie night," went off to bed. Loretta, who had noticed her uncle's ugly mood—so unlike him, who once put up with anything from anybody—returned to a long and tortuous paragraph that covered two pages, where Sartre said something—how gross life was—and then un-said it. Then he re-said it: how unworthy was the whole human race, how ridiculous its projects—and then refuted it, then said it once again in different terms. This was exciting. He always went too far. He must have thought so too, because the prose was so overheated and complex. With a work like this, you had to concentrate: tear your eyes off one passage and move cautiously to the next, snatch it up, hold onto both— (She wondered: who *was* wrong? Was the player's mother wrong to interfere? Did she know what was at stake, or was she too stupid? And why was Uncle Ted so mad about it? He never played basketball.) It was a perilous thing, to read, and with the next phrase, the first two slipped out of her mind and she had to start over. (It was unforgiveable *and* stupid. Completely avoidable. No wonder he was mad. The stupid, interfering bitch.) Still, there was pleasure in it, even with the frustration. She felt the mental exercise begin to strengthen a mind almost collapsing under its own weight of uneasiness and contradiction. Daniel was right, and Gloria was right: philosophy *would* help. Sartre was also trying to dig his way out of the garbage of life; he was pretty good company, he had no hope at all. She reached the last word of the endless paragraph and ran her eye backwards to see if she could piece it all together. The sentence said backwards what she thought it said forwards: a good sign. She went on, with confidence, to the end of the section, bravely uncoiling its resistant thought. Of course, Sartre *did* live in Paris. What, she was wondering, if Sartre had had some of these thoughts at 54 Canton Street? Would Aunt Rita have let him write such a thing as *Being and Nothingness*? She would have killed him first.

Out of the corner of her eye, she noticed Uncle Ted, still sitting in his chair staring at the TV set, no picture. (Would he have been any help to Jean-Paul? Doubtful.)

"Are you sleepy?" he asked, still looking at the screen.

"Yes," Loretta answered, putting the book down. "Very."

"Did you have a nice trip?"

"Yup," turning off the light.

"That's what you said. You like the train. I don't think you ever told me why."

Loretta opened her mouth to answer, but Uncle Ted was still talking: "You don't have to say anything, Loretta. I'm just glad you're here."

She looked at him. His hair was pale brown, lighter than before because of all the gray. It was thin, too, and she didn't want to have to see how thin it was, or hear him talk either. But he wanted to talk. She picked up her book, folded down the page where she'd left off. He was saying how glad they both were to see her. They'd missed her. This was her home and he hoped she realized it. How was she doing? Was she doing all right? That was a stupid thing to ask because he knew she wasn't doing all right. Would she tell him what happened? He did know some of it. Gloria told them. Loretta started to speak, but he broke in: "I know you're not doing that good. Things like this shouldn't be happening to my old sweetheart. You—"

She interrupted: "Uncle Ted, do you want to hear my answer to your question, or are you going to keep talking yourself?"

"I didn't mean to be boring you, Loretta."

"It's not that," she said, but she didn't finish the thought and there was a long silence.

"That's okay," he said.

Loretta picked up her book and reached for the lightcord. "I didn't mean to say that," she said. She opened her book, but it was hard to read because her hands were shaking.

Uncle Ted got up and left the room. He didn't even turn off his lamp. Loretta heard the flimsy door of his bedroom close shut. She got up and turned off his lamp and then hers. In the darkened room, a beautiful column of moonlight slipped through the drawn drapes and fell across the carpet. She got up again to open the French door and watched as the wind drew out the curtains and worried the column of moonlight. With the curtains opened wide, the couch was plunged in a silvery light. It was like a movie. Beyond the couch and the porch railing were the black waves not quite visible; you couldn't see them but you could hear the wind slapping the water and stirring it, rolling its edges and folding them down again. She lay on the thin mattress and picked up the book. But it was too late to read.

That's all it took, Dr. Major was saying: one sharp word from you to break that poor man's heart. Oh shut up, she told Dr. Major.

Loretta turned on the light and stared at the twin Lazy Boys they had bought, over Gloria's dead body, for the condo. Blame Gloria, why don't you? Dr. M piped up, but she stifled him again. It was Gloria who, on seeing these chairs—Aunt Rita was stretched out flat on hers with the back down and the feet up; Uncle Ted was using his as a simple armchair—had said: "Oh, I get it. You're going to worship your TV box in a couple of big cribs. I like that. Or do you think they're more like stretchers?" She made a point of using the most insulting terms not just because she was tactless, but because she so despised "the uniform pattern of consumption" practiced by the workers in retirement. The proletariat had had better things and better taste when they were young and had no money to squander on mass-produced trash.

"Now," she told Loretta, as she had told them, "they have their plastic money and their checking accounts, the low-interest loans and the factory-financing—but what do they have to show for all this consuming power? Nothing but junk. Things that are ugly, flimsy, more expensive, more breakable, even more artificial. Harder on the eye and rougher on the skin, less individual and more ostentatious." (Okay, Loretta said, I get the idea.) "Vulgar," she went on, "and contemptible." (I know, Loretta said.) "It's fascinating to see how the fascist and the atavistic impulses are merging—and with a rampant technology working day and night, our world has not a trace of civilized life, not even as *they* knew it!" (Yeah.) "The day will come when they'll be using concrete blocks as lounge chairs. They won't need air conditioners because their living units will *be* air conditioners. And they want it!" Gloria boomed. "They've learned to prefer a simulated environment. A tomb—only not as natural, not as peaceful or as final." (It's not that bad,

Loretta offered.) "It's worse. You've been underground for years, you can't even imagine how bad it is." (Loretta asked if Gloria said this stuff right to their faces.) "Sometimes. Why not?" Loretta wondered if Aunt Rita had ever thought of dragging her loud daughter to the bathroom to wash her mouth out with a cake of phoney soap moistened by the infested waters of the reservoir. Probably not: Gloria was a strong and unstoppable talker. Maybe they didn't even understand what she was saying. But *he* understood. Loretta noticed his weird smile as the aunt was giving a tour of the new condo: his lips were curved into a smile, but the rest of his face was tense and embarrassed.

Gloria was right about a lot of things. What she said explained why things had changed so much from the old days, and why it had happened so fast. But it was too dire a view: it went beyond disgust. It ignored the little bit of sordid life that survived even though the chairs were fake leather and the house a concrete cube, and even though the inhabitants were ripped off in every way and by everybody. Gloria's reasoning put a too-definite stamp on the whole collection of dumb things, familiar things that—without that stamp—would have no point or pattern. These dumb things could easily elude a hard explanatory formula; they always had before, that was the whole beauty of it. She thought this without the help of Dr. Major and decided on her own to set Gloria straight. When Loretta couldn't stand to hear another one of the cousin's "reductionist" ideas, as Daniel would refer to them, she said to Gloria: "Your father isn't a helpless pawn of capitalism. His life has more in it than that. He has other problems. Worse problems." Gloria took this in. She said that Loretta was being too literal-minded. In a certain way, the system had created *every one* of his problems. It had created his desires, and then had thwarted them. Then she asked Loretta what problems did she mean?

"Oh, I don't know. He's sad, he's frustrated."

"No he isn't."

"You've just finished saying he *is!*"

"You don't understand what I'm saying," Gloria replied in her smooth way. "You never have had, and you never will have, an abstract mind. Everything to you is people, people, people. You're not going to get anywhere thinking of people. You've got to have *ideas* to work with. What ideas do you have?"

Loretta said she still didn't think Gloria's father was just a labor statistic.

"I didn't SAY that!" Gloria bellowed. Then she voiced her surprise at Loretta's sudden interest in him when she had spent her entire life ignoring all of them. "Where were you all those years when they could have *used* a little of that 'sensitivity'?" she said. "See? You have nothing to say for yourself."

"I always liked you," Loretta said.

"You hated me. You *tolerated* me—sometimes. You were our convict, but that didn't mean you had to like us. You made it very clear you didn't." Gloria waited for a reaction, then went on: "You never paid attention to anyone but yourself, really. Now you've decided to become human, to be their defender. Well, I don't buy it."

Loretta paused, then said: "You're mad because I used the word 'capitalism.' It's just a word, Gloria. I still have no ideas."

"Oh, smart. You sound just like Daniel."

"So?"

"I hate you and I think you stink."

"I think you stink too."

"Don't try to make a joke out of this."

"I'm not."

"And don't be pitying my father. That makes me sick!"

Gloria had her reasons for being suspicious. It wasn't only because Loretta was a political naif. Gloria complained and her mother complained that the father never showed the "least sign" of affection for anyone: he was cold, he was undemonstrative, he never hugged or kissed; or if, once in a blue moon, he did, the kiss was too hard, or there was mockery in it. Instead of a kind word now and then, there was criticism, sarcasm: "That dress is wrinkled, Shorty. You didn't comb the back of that rat's nest. You got a run in your stocking"—to his daughter. His wife was too fat, spent too much money, talked too much, whined and bellyached over trifles, never acted her age. Over the years, they both wanted to know why Loretta didn't come in for her share of the abuse.

But they never found out. Aunt Rita tried to compensate for this inequity by criticizing Loretta more and more. She had her reasons: simple hatred, jealousy, resentment at having to raise the extra child, competitiveness for herself and for Gloria too, although it was pretty clear who had the looks and who had the brains and Uncle Ted was forever saying which was going to go farther in a hard and unfair world. And—Dr. Major whispered—the main reason! The main reason she hated you was—what? *You're* the one he liked. He liked you better!

Loretta was very tired now. Sometime during the night someone had closed the French doors and drawn the drapes. In a dream, a teacher asked Loretta to marry him, but then changed his mind. No, I'd better not, he said, I've already married the perfect woman. Then he asked again. Later, they were standing looking down at smooth cement columns. If you slide down one of these poles, he said, I'll show you where the fire truck is. But she couldn't slide down any of the slippery poles, she had the wrong shoes on. It was graduation day and she walked across the stage and picked up the keynote speech hidden in an envelope. The teacher met her at the stage door. We've gotten all this way, he said, without getting involved. She felt sad to have to lose him after all this time, but there was shopping to do.

Another time in the night, Uncle Ted came out of his room, like he used to, and sat in a chair near the couch bed.

Loretta heard him, but she pretended to be asleep. He had started coming out at night and sitting by her bed when she turned fourteen. Her birthday present was the use of the old sewing room as a bedroom. The machine, the baskets, the chair and the dress form were scattered throughout the house to make room for Loretta's bed and chest. When Loretta moved her things into the new room, Aunt Rita saw that there was some space left, so she put some things back: the big rocker, the lamp, two sewing baskets. She explained several times that she would do knitting, quilting, embroidery, hand-sewing and crocheting in Loretta's room—the machine sewing she could do in her own room, using the kitchen table to cut out patterns. (Aunt Rita didn't do much sewing of any kind any more, now that she needed bifocals to do it. But still, it was a generous offer and Loretta liked it.)

She must have been sleeping there about a month, on a twin bed pushed against the wall with one of the matched chenille bedspreads folded along the foot and a throw rug on the floor, when she woke up and smelled cigarette smoke. There was a tiny red light too. She looked at the light through slitted eyes, then fell back to sleep, but it was gone when she woke up again. She knew it was a dream. But a few nights later, she woke up again and kept her eyes open long enough to see that it was a real cigarette. It moved and turned bright red, then faded. By this time, she could see the puff of smoke, too, and a smoke ring, so—even if she didn't already know who it was—she did then, because Aunt Rita couldn't blow smoke rings.

He didn't say anything. "Uncle Ted?" she said, but he didn't answer. She closed her eyes but couldn't fall back to sleep. She opened them, but she couldn't stay awake either. In the morning, the room stunk of cigarette smoke. She opened the window and by the time breakfast was over, you could hardly smell it. In the course of the day, she forgot, but after supper—when she remembered—she asked Gloria if they could both sleep in the same room again. Loretta said she would help roll the other bed in. Gloria didn't answer. Loretta looked at her thinking face. Then Gloria asked: "Why were you in such a hurry to get away from me? And how come you want to come back now?

"*And,*—" she went on, raising her voice, so that Loretta had to say: "Shh, don't talk so loud! Forget it. I'm sorry I even asked. I take it back."

"No," Gloria said, "I'm *not* forgetting it. And I'm *not* going in with you and you're *not* coming back to my room, unless you tell me why."

Loretta thought of saying she was afraid, but Gloria would never believe it, so she said: "You know how much you like sharing a room and talking at night, so—"

"You're lying," Gloria said. "I can always tell when you're lying."

Loretta looked at her. It was hard to keep from laughing at that goofy face trying to look so serious.

Ten minutes later, Gloria was asking, then begging Loretta to come back: "Why don't you? You *want* to come back!" the little girl keened.

"I changed my mind."

They went over this some more, until Loretta said, "Okay, some nights—if you want—you can roll *your* bed in with *me.* But I'm not coming back."

Next time he came in, she wasn't even sleeping, and she wasn't sleeping when he left. He sat in the sewing chair, but didn't rock. Sometimes when he visited, he talked; sometimes he smoked cigarettes. Most of the time he just sat there in the sewing chair, but once he sat on the foot of the bed, then got up and paced around. He told the story of how he had gone from being an ice man to delivering groceries to working on a fishing boat, and then was drafted. "I don't know what the hell I did with my life," he said. "All I know is, I never did things right."

He said that he had never had the chances people have today, that he really hadn't made any choices for himself. He just ended up the way he was because—because, he didn't really know why. "I never got to find out what I was interested in," he said. "And it's too late now. Maybe I don't *have* interests," he said bitterly.

Loretta thought he did have interests: he played golf, sometimes he went down cellar and worked on something. He built a model car, she remembered that, but Gloria raced it on the driveway and wrecked it, and he never built another one. She was going to say this but waited too long for it to sound natural, plus sometimes people didn't want to hear good things about themselves. It made them mad. One time he told her that he was giving up smoking and opening a bank account of his own with money he had saved from not buying cigarettes. If she needed money some day, he'd have it saved up. His voice sounded weird. Was he crying?

When he first gave up smoking, he chewed gum, then sucked on lifesavers, then he gave those up too and gave up beer and whiskey for a while, and sugary food. "I feel better," he told her. "I look better, don't you think?" He was thinner than he'd ever been and he had never been fat. Gloria made a lot of this. "You two," she said, "are turning into skeletons, while me and Ma are blimps."

Gloria never seemed to know about these secret visits to the new bedroom, but something made her even more curious and pushy. The cousins fought all the time. Maybe she *did* know. It was hard to imagine there'd be anything Gloria didn't know, with her nose for news. But she was odd. If you wanted her to pay attention to something, she wouldn't. Still, she managed to take in a lot and it was possible that even this subject would turn up in one of her cracks or anecdotes, with a political interpretation thrown in, to show she wasn't wasting her time.

But all during the years when things were happening, she was no help at all: she was like a dead thing.

"Are you awake?" Uncle Ted was saying. "It's hard to stay asleep out here. You're not used to hearing the ocean. It's peaceful, isn't it? I knew you'd like it, Lori."

She said she liked it.

"You miss New York, though, don't you?"

"No."

"I thought you loved New York."

"I do."

"He likes New York and you don't—that's what we thought."

Uncle Ted opened the curtains again, and Loretta could see parts of the room turn sharper in the moonlight. Then, if you blinked your eyes, the room was obscured again,, folded in darkness.

"I bet he misses you. I'd miss you. You were always good company."

Loretta was able to see more of the room—some of the pictures on the wall and objects on the mantlepiece—if she focussed harder. She didn't know this room, but she knew the things in it. She asked Uncle Ted if he could see any boats on the water from where he was sitting.

"You don't really want to talk to me, do you? You made that pretty clear."

She concentrated on the sounds: the wall clock ticking in the kitchen and a softer sound, something outside. Was it boats bumping on the water, or knocking against the dock?

"You didn't come home to listen to me," he was saying. "I know that. You had your own reasons. But I missed you, too. You've been gone a long time, Loretta, but I still miss having you around. I could always talk to you. You're an easy person to talk to. You know that, don't you?"

He wanted to talk, but she wasn't encouraging him. She used to encourage him because she felt bad that he had no one else to talk to. She was too young, and didn't always understand what he wanted, although she listened carefully to all his stories. They were adult stories full of disappointment and embarrassment. Loretta got that much out of them, but she couldn't see why he had the life he had—so boring, so ugly and full of aggravation. He didn't know why he had it either. "I'm in a rut, Loretta," he said once, "and I don't know how to get out of it." Loretta tried to say something back, but he didn't hear. "Maybe it's too *late* to get out of it."

He was silent a moment. "Let me tell you something. Listen to this." He told her how he had never been in love with his wife. ("Aunt Rita?" she asked. But who else could it be? It was a stupid question, so she didn't ask any more questions.) He had never been happy with her aunt and he hadn't been happy a single day in his life, except when he was a kid. He didn't realize how happy he was then, just to be young and free, "like you— you're young and free." Then he said that she didn't seem happy either. (Was that true? Could people see it?) He came to the bed, knelt beside it and laid his head down on her stomach. It was heavy and she didn't know what to do but lie there quietly. After a while, he raised his head and whispered, "I'm glad you're not scared of me. There's nothing to be scared of."

She hadn't even thought of being scared until he said it. But then he got up and said good night. After that one visit, he didn't come back for a long time. The longer he stayed away, the weirder it got. He didn't seem like the old Uncle Ted, and it was hard to say his name out loud. When she had to name him for some reason, she said "him." "Who?" Gloria said, when she noticed. "You know." "I *don't* know. Who?" (Aunt Rita told them to stop bickering.) "What's *her* name?" Gloria said belligerently. "Aunt Rita Margaret Gillis," Loretta answered. "Then, what's his name?" "Mr. Ted Gillis. I don't know what his middle name is, so I can't tell you." Gloria said it was "Edward," not "Ted." "Ted" was a nickname. "Say it again!" Gloria hissed, and when there was no answer, she screamed, "Ma! Loretta's calling Daddy a *name!*" Loretta could hear the pulley line screeching, so she dragged Gloria over to the window so she could see her mother was hanging clothes and couldn't hear. "Why can't you say his name?" Gloria demanded, and Loretta wanted to answer her, but she didn't know how.

Loretta lay on the couch bed, her skin soaked in sweat, although there was a breeze blowing through the window. They were right after all: in the dead of night, there was an offshore breeze, cooling and fresh.

"I thought you could do better, Lori," the uncle was saying. Why was he saying this? What right did he have to judge her life, when the only friend he managed to find for himself was a 14-year-old girl, and one who was stuck listening to him? Loretta checked herself, and tried to listen to the rest of what he was saying. Then she said, "You can skip this, Uncle Ted. I don't want your criticisms, I don't need them."

"You never asked us for anything," he said softly.

"I'm not going to criticize you either," she said. "That's what you want, but I don't feel like it. I've got my own life to criticize."

"I would never criticize you," he said.

"Shh," she said. "Go back to bed now."

But he continued to talk, so she said: "Let's not talk any more, okay? Talking doesn't help. We always knew that, Uncle Ted. That's why we were friends."

There was a long silence. The sky was brighter and so was the room: Loretta hoped it was morning.

"You're a smart girl, Loretta. You always were, but you're like me. Your smartness doesn't do you any good."

Why was he talking like this? He was borrowing that know-it-all tone from Gloria, and on him it didn't sound natural. She felt like laughing at the fatuousness of this statement, and at its triteness, but she was not a laugher or a jeerer. "What?" he said, and Loretta realized she was doing some of her thinking out loud. The uncle had leaned over, and Loretta studied his face in the gray light: he was old. What had he done with his time to end up with no accomplishments and no satisfactions? "What did you say?" he asked again.

"Say goodnight," she said, pulling his head down to kiss his cheek. She felt the stubble of his beard on her face and touched the bristles on his head. She felt the skull, too, through its thin covering. And finally when he did go, he closed the door behind him.

Loretta drew the curtains shut and burrowed deep under the sheet and blanket, put the pillow over her head. She couldn't sleep: she was assaulted by anxious, giddy thoughts. Is this, she wondered, what Daniel feels like, and she pictured him alone, sitting under his hot light, his head a hive of swarming thoughts. To quiet the thoughts, she assigned them a hefty counterweight: death, that perfect silence, the clean point, end to all foolishness. But she still couldn't sleep, the hive was still buzzing. Death was the firmest ground: nothing could be firmer. And yet, it felt like there was something under it. Under it—she got up again to open the curtains and to see the carpet of black waves and the gulls floating in a watery circle. Their ground, by contrast, was flux, ceaseless flux and flecks of giddy light. What was under it?

Daniel had once said—it was a different time, things were peaceful—that she was always framing experience in some arty way, so that the logic and feeling were lost in an aesthetic pattern—although, he had added, you could also call it a "phantasmatic" pattern, the product not of an artist, but a dreamer or nut, satisfied to skate over the surfaces of life.

This could be true, Daniel could be right, or—she closed the curtain and turned back to bed—he might have been trying to erode the only firm ground of happiness. And now she knew what the ground was. Death didn't change things: its rigid frame stabilized the beauty and poignancy of every life, and created a sense of accomplishment and satisfaction where there had perhaps been none. It honored the business of life with formality. All the past was dead, was formal, and that was its great attraction. The old life was returned, boxed and finite, with a powerful conclusion to give it shape. She opened the curtains a little, watching as the sun hollowed out a pale face on the water line. So the box was good, the box was a present, but never given back to the original: the box went to someone else.

End of Summer

■ ■ ■

G LORIA had been at Margaret's for several weeks now, idling. Margaret had given her beautiful thick sheets, and a feather tick to soften the couch she was sleeping on. But Gloria wasn't doing much sleeping. When Margaret came out of her room at night to pee or to fix a snack, Gloria was always awake. Sometimes Margaret found her stretched out on the floor next to the couch, her face just visible in the red rays emanating from the nightlight. Margaret tried to start up conversations, but Gloria was mute, although occasionally she'd pad into the kitchen behind Margaret, and sit with her while she ate.

Gloria was depressed—anyone could see it. When Daniel called the apartment to ask Gloria to have a cup of coffee with him, even *he* could see it. Gloria told him that she had no will. He asked what she meant, but before she could answer he said: "I know what you mean." They ordered large espressos and discussed their symptoms, their feelings of grief and rejection.

"I used to think I could control life from my head," Gloria said. "I thought everything was in there, and I was in charge."

"I know what you mean," said Daniel.

"This proves otherwise, doesn't it? Something can happen on the outside too, and nothing you do on the inside helps."

"Yeah," murmured Daniel, his tone thick and slow from all the time alone. He drank some water and told Gloria how depressed *he'd* been. "I can barely get up in the morning."

They brooded over this and other things sitting in a sunlit window of the Turk—Gloria had pushed open the dusty green curtain and let the morning's light seep through. For a while they just sat and watched the people. Then Gloria ordered fresh coffees. "How's Margaret?" Daniel asked eventually, then downed his coffee in one gulp.

"Don't ask me. Everybody always asks about her. She's fine." Gloria ordered herself a fresh coffee. "I *need* this," she said. "I'm completely unplugged. I'm a lump." Daniel smiled. "Well, Margaret's okay anyway. I'm sick of dumping on her all the time. She's basically okay."

Daniel seemed unsurprised. He said he had handed in his fourth chapter, in spite of everything. There was only one part left to write, but he had decided not to go into philosophy after all.

Gloria glared at him over the cup. "Isn't that typical of you! You can't stick to things, Daniel."

Daniel looked at her; he waited. He ordered a Mexican coffee, then he said: "The culture of the ordinary speaks, Gloria. It's coming through loud and clear."

"You know what I mean, Daniel. You can't go through life this way. How old are you—thirty-one? You're too old to be as free as you think you are."

The table had become a field of little coffee cups and tiny spoons, saucers with lemon rinds curling in them. Gloria started to chew a lemon rind. Daniel watched her. "Why don't you get yourself a boyfriend? You need to get laid."

"Me!" snorted Gloria. She spat out the rind and felt around in her mouth for shreds of its sour skin.

The subject, and all the coffee, made Daniel feel giddy.

"You think sex is unimportant because you're living in your head, but it *is* important. You have no animal life."

Gloria threw a lemon rind at Daniel and it landed in his coffee. As he fished it out, the couple at the next table turned to look. "It kills me to say this," Daniel said in a louder voice, "to a commie dog like yourself, but you're in the human race, Gloria, much as you might think otherwise."

"Stay in philosophy," Gloria sneered. "You're *not* in the human race."

At that moment, the waitress came to the table. "Shall we order something else?" asked Gloria, trying to keep from laughing.

"Why not? I have nothing better to do." Daniel corrected himself: "I didn't mean it that way, Gloria. I'm glad to see you. I need to talk to somebody."

Gloria told Margaret about this conversation, and Margaret said: "I think he's right. I think you should get a boyfriend." So Gloria told the story of the time when, without even having to work at it, she had had one. She was living in a cooperative house on campus and a group of people decided to help Cesar Chavez during semester break. They chartered a bus and drove it to the Imperial Valley. Gloria had had her eye on a blond, a midwesterner who cooked for them at the co-op. "More Loretta's type," she told Margaret. "A book of poems in his back pocket and nothing else. No money. But get this—a French bike with all the trimmings."

"I like that type too," said Margaret.

"*Every*body likes that type. Needless to say, he wasn't into me."

"That type likes dark-haired women, the exotic type."

"Like yourself?" Gloria asked snidely.

"No," said Margaret. "But yes, like me, only more so."

Gloria went on: "I lost a lot of weight on that trip. I was infatuated, but also we didn't have the cash to buy food. It was tough. My clothes were falling off me. But it didn't help. It didn't make any difference at all!"

Margaret laughed.

"He didn't give me a second look. But another boy *did*. We met him when we got out there. Half-Mexican, a student at some Mexican college. He was in the valley to help the people, the illegal migrants, and he was never going back to his old life. He was going to stay. Never in my life have I met anyone so pissed off. He was angry every minute of the day."

"Wow!"

"We had our involvement."

"Why do you call it that?" asked Margaret.

"If I say 'affair,' I think I'm in the movies. It was okay."

"Was it?"

"Yeah. We both got something out of it, as long as it lasted. But that's not the most important—I learned a lot."

Margaret waited.

"I'm not a beautiful woman," Gloria said, "and this is considered a disadvantage. But for me it's been an advantage, because it makes me seem more accessible to Third World men. They like *any* white woman—they can't tell the difference. Refinements of bone structure, of complexion, mean very little to them. What I'm saying is, to them we all look alike."

Margaret sighed.

"I'll draw the colored males my own way, and—"

"So what happened with the guy? What was his name?"

"Juan Antonio."

"Wan with a 'J'?"

"Yeah. After a while we got bogged down in petty differences. His English wasn't good and it made him nervous that I talked all the time and he couldn't understand. That bothered him. I was quote-unquote in love, I guess, and it was painful the way that idle people like to say their amours are painful. But I got over it. It wasn't the end of the world." Gloria paused. "It's surprising what'll hurt people's feelings." Margaret was studying her. Gloria talked faster, trying to draw Margaret's attention away from her face and onto the words. "But it'll happen again, it wasn't a total freak of nature—I'm not important enough for nature to make a complete exception for me."

They returned to the subject again, and Gloria liked the attention. Margaret was being nice these days. She hadn't started out that way, and when Gloria first noticed the change she thought that maybe Margaret had found a subtler way to be mean and selfish. But no. When the girl bought herself a treat at the New, for instance, she either ate it behind closed doors or shared it with the hungry and impoverished Gloria. And Margaret no longer liked to say, "Why don't you go home? Loretta doesn't need you anymore—or if she does need you, it isn't *here*." And the one time she forgot and *did* say it, she apologized. She was making a pan of frosted buns and handed one to Gloria. "Take it. I said I'm sorry," Margaret insisted, when Gloria refused to accept the bun or even to see it. Gloria finally took it and Margaret continued: "I don't resent your being here. I know you think I do. Sometimes I even like it. No, I mean it. You can be good company, Gloria. Who else would put up with me day and night for no good reason?"

Gloria took another bun, and so did Margaret. Together, they ate them all and Margaret was set to bake another round when Gloria said to wait: they'd taste better later on, when their stomachs had had a chance to empty and relax.

"How scientific!" squealed Margaret.

There were other signs of change. Margaret was designing and building a set for a workshop production at the Greene Street Rep, and when Gloria, bored and frustrated, unwilling or unable to go back home, offered to help, Margaret went along with it. They bickered and squabbled on the job, but the set was built, and it wasn't destroyed or upstaged by the director. "A success!" Margaret exulted to Gloria, after attending opening night to make sure she wasn't being tricked again. "That was not Retta's fault," said Gloria. Margaret said she knew that, but added that it always helped to work with someone strong and practical, like Gloria.

"Mr. Aschenbach likes you, too," Margaret added to the praises now coming Gloria's way.

Maybe he did, but Gloria still didn't feel very liked: she knew her faults—she didn't listen, she wasn't sympathetic, she made jokes out of sacred cows, she was a know-it-all and she put politics first. Plus she was a fat slob.

"No you're not!" said Margaret, but Gloria could tell that she was lying.

One night, around 3 a.m., Margaret woke up hungry and found Gloria once again on the floor. Her eyes were closed, but she wasn't asleep, Margaret could tell. "Excuse me," Margaret whispered. Then she invited Gloria to share an angel food cake she had bought that afternoon and was now going to frost with a special frosting. Gloria could watch.

Gloria said she wasn't hungry, but she followed Margaret into the kitchen anyway, zigzagging past the boxes and appliances. "No one eats angel food cake anymore," she said glumly, settling herself in her regular spot on one of the kitchen stools. Margaret opened her tattered *Boston School Cooking Book* with its filthy ribbon markers. "Well, it *is* an old-fashioned cake," she admitted, "but I'm making an old-fashioned frosting. Have you heard of Fannie Farmer's seven-minute frosting, Gloria?"

Gloria said that everybody's mother had a Fannie, and Margaret laughed.

When she had cooked the frosting and spread a snowy pad over her cake, she made coffee. "Don't just sit there," she said. "Talk to me!"

Gloria cleared a place for herself at the table and asked Margaret when she thought Loretta would come back to New York.

"I don't know." Margaret first poured the satiny brew into two yellow demitasse cups, then repoured it into white bone china. "See?" she said, pointing first to the delicate ivory cake and then to the thin cups with their ebony pools. "I can't resist this kind of perfection. But let's eat." Margaret cut a wedge of the cake and served it to the underfed, and thinner, Gloria. "Why don't you pay attention to your own life," she said, "instead of worrying about her?" When she had cut the cake, she poured milk into a white pitcher, then hunted through the kitchen drawers for her silver sugar tongs.

"I have other things in my life," Gloria said defensively.

Margaret pinched a sugar cube and dropped it in Gloria's coffee, then pinched another for herself. "More?" she asked.

Gloria looked puzzled. Margaret was ready to drop the extra cube in her cup, but Gloria put up a hand to stop her.

"By the way, what is she going to do with herself now?" Margaret asked, depositing the cube in her own cup.

Gloria said she didn't know.

"You know what I think? I think she should leave the asshole."

Gloria laughed.

"She needs a fresh start," Margaret said. "And you do too. You're too old to be following her around like a shadow."

Gloria sipped her coffee.

"Where are you going with your life? Do you have any plans of your own?" demanded Margaret, cutting two more slices of cake. Gloria tasted her first piece: "Delicious, Margaret." "I asked you a question! You're a brilliant woman, Gloria. If I had your brain, I'd *do* something—law school, medical school, anything! You could get in. No one's going to reject intelligence like you have.

"I'm talking to you!" shouted Margaret. "Do you want to

live like this for the rest of your life?" Gloria finished her cake and put her plate in the sink, then sat down on the stool again. "If you don't like the professions, you could go into the arts— you have some talent. Or business, even better." Gloria folded her hands together and put them on the table. She leaned over—but Margaret wasn't finished. "I don't want to hear excuses, Gloria."

"Margaret," Gloria said in a patronizing tone, "do you know the kind of person you're dealing with? Have you noticed anything in all the time I've been here?"

"What kind of 'person' am I dealing with?" said Margaret in her snottiest tone; then she shifted key. "You're going to tell me how naive I am, right? Or if you don't come right out and say it, you're going to imply it." She got up and cleared away her own plate, and ran water over the sticky dishes.

Gloria was sitting still. She was listening but also concentrating on the sensations of digesting so much sweet cake. Her deprived body was suddenly electrified by the sugar bundles flushing through her bloodstream; things were sparkling and fizzing; her skin felt tight and hot. It was like a mild shock treatment. In her euphoria, she planned to give poor Margaret a break, but Margaret was too angry to hear it. "I know what you are," she said accusingly. "Daniel told me you're a leftist malcontent."

"Is that what he said?" Gloria asked with a slight smile.

"You're an anarchist and a wobbly—whatever that is. You want to smash the state."

"Did he say that? I love the words. Too quaint."

"I don't want to talk to you any more, Gloria. You never take what I say seriously."

Gloria told Margaret that it wasn't what *she* was saying, it was what *Daniel* was saying. "Let's stay away from this particular subject, okay? This is not a consensual area for us. It's not part of our discourse. Is that fair?"

But Margaret pressed on and Gloria ended up shouting, "I

am going to do something! I've already done things. There are
times when I've thwarted the system just by being alive!"

"Sure," said Margaret snidely.

"I haven't institutionalized my protest yet, okay, but that
doesn't prove anything. In fact, it's a mistake to go too fast. I've
seen too many people make that mistake and I've learned from
it. You have to stand your ground, yet remain flexible until the
right moment arises. See?"

Margaret said she didn't.

"No one has ever reckoned the true power of an empty center," she went on, "in a system where everyone is a force, criminal or otherwise. Nietzsche was such a center. Do you see what
I'm getting at?" She paused. "Do you?" She began again. "There's
ample time for me to play my hand. True intelligence—which
you say you admire in me—is knowing when the active principle
should be privileged. In other words, most people, in order to
believe they exist, have to see themselves *doing* something. *I* remember *exactly* who I am from day to day. *I* can flex my muscles
without moving them."

"Stop bragging for a minute," Margaret said, "and let *me*
talk for a change. Someone looking at you, Gloria, without
hearing your bullshit, wouldn't think you were so hot. You
don't have a job, you don't have money. You don't own a single
decent thing. And yet you think you're wonderful. How can
that be?"

Gloria sighed: "I have a headache now and it might be too
late for you."

"Sure. Every time I have something to say, you get sick.
Why can't you listen to me like I always listen to you?"

Gloria was mute.

"You like talking, but you hate to listen. Some empty
center."

Gloria conceded Margaret's point, and they went on. They
moved the discussion, eventually, to more fruitful ground—the

ground of Alfred and "relationships." Gloria asked what had happened with Alfred. At first Margaret didn't want to say: Gloria had no real experience with men, so the conversation would be too one-sided. Gloria was obliged to draw Margaret out: she was curious, none of it bored her. She induced Margaret to go back to the beginning, to the boyfriends before Alfred and to the specifics of these encounters: the dates, phone calls, dresses, conversations, break-ups. Gloria found it all interesting.

Margaret said it was more than interesting. There was a pattern. Hadn't Gloria noticed? These boys were nothings, or they were abusers. If they had the least talent, or anything at all in their favor—looks, money, even a nice car—they were abusers. If they didn't, Margaret dumped them first.

Margaret burrowed into her past, back to her high school experiences, to the boys she knew then—losers, nothings—and finally back to life at home, to Dad and Mr. Eikenberg, and to another lover her mother had before Mr. Eikenberg and during her marriage to Dad. Her mother, Margaret explained, had set the pattern, by letting those various men treat her like dirt. The men were interesting, but not so interesting that they didn't need a woman to bully just to make themselves feel *more* interesting.

"All right!" said Gloria.

After telling her extra stories, Margaret applied the same interpretation—what Gloria explained was a variant of "the game of even and odd": the man was on top, or Margaret was. Things never got any further, but simply reversed in the eternal pattern of mutually constitutive opposites. So there was no sense to it at all. It was pure dynamic.

"That's right," Margaret said.

"You've learned something," Gloria said.

"You think so?"

"Yeah. Now you're *ready* for Hegel."

"Really?" Margaret said, beaming with pride.

"I mean it. You're ready to understand the dialectic. Dialectic will explain the necessity and the mechanics of this cold repetition. Then you'll come to consciousness, and you won't have to go on putting up with shit—or dishing it out."

At first Margaret felt elated by this and she started copying out lists of books, recommended by Gloria, to prepare her for the course in dialectics. Then her wrist got tired and she had a headache from the sugar, and was sorry that she had told this stranger, this odd girl, so much about her personal life. Gloria's mood darkened, too: she felt restless and ravenously hungry. Margaret announced that she could not stay up another minute, and Gloria followed her back weaving her way to the makeshift bed. It was almost five and the window shade was fringed in a sickeningly pale light. Gloria lay on her couch, then sat back up again. She turned on the lamp—she would not sleep one minute tonight—and began casing the pathetic library arranged on Margaret's shelf. There was only one decent book there: *Mysteries*, but she had already read that. She made a mental note (pulling out a tattered paperback, *How to Get Organized*, with one dogeared page in the preface) to call Loretta in the morning, no matter what.

Every few days, Daniel got a note from Loretta, written on her aunt's flowered notepaper, small sheets and the space available for writing made even smaller by the gold-lined border and the peonies stamped across the right-hand corner. Loretta would start her writing mid-page, using the rose-colored ballpoint pen kept in the box of envelopes and papers; the ink was red. The whole effect was somehow very youthful. She liked writing the notes, but her account would never go beyond the day's news: say, that she and Aunt Rita had gone to the mall just down the highway from the condo. They drove. Loretta had already tried to walk. First you had to cross the four-lane highway, then more roads within the parking lot itself, made dangerous by fleets of cars whose drivers didn't expect to see a pedestrian, and who speeded up when they did.

They went to the mall to buy things for a pool party thrown by the condo management and advertised in the mail room, the laundry room and the parking garage, in every hallway, elevator and stairwell. The management provided nothing but the pool and the pool furniture, which was chained to the ground, and a few fireworks. Every guest had to bring his own food, drinks, place settings, grills and coolers.

They spent, she wrote, two hours at the party: they swam, ate barbecued chicken and potato salad, a fruit compote of grapes, pineapple, carrot shreds and marshmallows and drank Cold Duck and decaffeinated no-cal sodas. They didn't talk to a soul and skipped the fireworks. "We watched TV instead. The fireworks lasted ten minutes. Aunt Rita had to close the French doors and curtains and turn up the air conditioner to drown them out."

Loretta's new activities, together with the reading of philosophy, filled the days better than building sets and reading cookbooks. One minute her mind was sunk in peaceful torpor, then it would be jolted awake by the intrusion of alien thoughts all knotted up in a system. This, she was sure, was how a certain class of people handled the ordeal of living. Philosophy was a little like booze or an exercise bike.

Her favorite activity, during this reading period, was something she and Aunt Rita did on Thursdays. They drove out to West Warwick to an old folk's home, a place for bingo games and other supervised activities, including a hot breakfast and lunch. The elderly neighbors who couldn't drive or make it on foot were picked up by a mini-bus. Some of them couldn't even manage the bus, so volunteers like Aunt Rita would deliver their lunches by car. This delivery took up most of the day, and Loretta had written Daniel several letters describing the process in detail:

In each of the shabby houses or apartments, a big TV was always playing, its volume driven up as high as possible, usually with no one watching. The parlors, dark except for the gaudy TV images, were overheated and smelled worse than any hospital because of food that had been overcooked and left to stand and rot or be reheated, and because of all the dust and grime trapped in the slipcovers and heavy drapes, and because of other things you couldn't quite name. In these rooms there were junky old things and hideous new things: Infants of Prague with velvet robes and gilt crowns, recent color photographs of wedding couples and fat babies, signed photographs of John F. Kennedy and pictures of the pope, snake and rubber plants in dusty macrame holders. The shut-ins, even when they weren't "touched in the head," as Aunt Rita put it, were vague and distracted; sometimes friendly and outgoing, other times annoyed and sulky. Most of them were all alone, and lonely. For company, they had the voices from their TV sets, Aunt Rita for a few minutes on Thursday, and the tables and bookshelves crammed with family photographs. No wonder they were loony.

Daniel answered this, and each of her letters, with one of his own. He urged her to send him something a little less detached and descriptive than what she'd been sending. He was not criticizing the letters—they were interesting—but she was not writing like a wife to an estranged husband; she was writing like a prison pen-pal to the outside. Loretta thought that was funny, but it was too bad that he felt the way he did and that he thought of himself as "estranged" from her. She didn't know if that was true.

He complained that she always signed off with her initials.

Why? It was so impersonal. "I love your name," he wrote: "Write your name!" She replied that she didn't feel full enough to write her name. "I feel abbreviated, but it's not painful like it sounds." So Daniel started signing off with "D" and then he began his letters with "Dear L," then just "L." She wrote back: "It seems right, don't you think? That's as much as we know about each other." When he read that—and he assumed it was true if she said it—he wept. He had thought the *D*'s and the *L*'s were a sign of perfect understanding. He added that he had no choice but to trust her impressions, since he had no control, at the moment, over anything.

From his next letter, he seemed to be feeling better. In fact, he had regained his sense of humor and chided her for using all four of her initials: "That's a lot of personality, don't you think? What do you think you are, a corporation?'" She signed her next letter "F.B.O.E." He signed a letter "S.P.C.A." When she signed "W.C.T.U.", he wrote back that, in truth, her initials should be "A.W.O.L."

She ignored the hint and went on with her story about the senior center. Visiting the shut-ins was only part of the day. When Aunt Rita and Loretta first arrived at the center, they helped with the serving, dishing the food into individual aluminum trays and packing them into picnic baskets. They dipped ladles into the vats of watery brown beans, spooned peas and carrots, poured gravy over chicken legs, cut out squares of meat loaf and lasagna and filled in each tray's dessert compartment with a dollop of pudding or applesauce. One lady, Lilian McVey, a neighbor, came every day and organized the serving. She was old herself and had just a month earlier been in for surgery to have her second breast cut starting with the armpit. Lillian had taken a liking to Aunt Rita and would begin to talk as soon as the woman came into the kitchen with her quiet niece, and kept talking until they set out with the baskets. She told Aunt Rita everything. At first Loretta didn't want to hear this woman's stories—they were too depressing. However, as the three of them took turns ladling food from the steam trays, packing the baskets and hauling them out to the car, Loretta found herself listening.

Lilian, who had worked in a suit factory since she was fourteen, had recently retired. She had spent her life sewing linings into men's suitpants, five, sometimes six days a week, never sick a day, never took a day off, gave her three girls church weddings, took care of her old mother, even brought the mother home to live with her and her ailing husband. The mother lived to be ninety-two, enjoyed perfect health and died one sunny day last year, sitting in front of the TV set, after eating a good lunch. She wasn't bragging, Lilian said: these were the facts.

Now, in her first year of retirement, the old lady was volunteering five days a week at the center. It hurt to move that left arm and shoulder, but she insisted on dishing out food and helping with baskets until Aunt Rita had to yell at her to stop. And now that she wasn't working in a filthy factory, she could wear the white blouses she'd been saving all those years: thin nylon blouses, puffed sleeves, some so old they were yellow. Under them she wore a silky slip or camisole, but you could still see the bandages wrapped over one shoulder and around the ribs.

Her husband was also dying, but from an inoperable tumor. The cancer, she explained, demonstrating with her good arm, goes from his throat all the way down his windpipe, and he had a tumor in his lung too, even though he had had the lung operation, and there was only one left. "The poor bastard is so tired," said Lilian, stopping work for a moment, "it's pitiful." She then spooned out a steaming bowlful of the hot, collapsed beans swimming in their thick red gravy and handed it to the aunt. "Here Darlin', these are good. Eat 'em up." She turned to Loretta, silent behind her: "You should have a bowl too, Skin-and-Bones." But no one forced food on Loretta. Aunt Rita had warned them all to leave the girl alone, not to pester her with food. Loretta marveled at her aunt's new tact, but accepted it as part of the woman's blossoming so late in life: there were many signs of it, mostly good.

The husband was in pain, Lilian went on, tired and out of breath, but this wasn't the bad part. "The bad part," she said to Aunt Rita, "is they won't give him the chemo. He tells them, 'Try the chemo. How can it hurt?' but they won't do it. They say it's no use."

She had finished with the beans and was serving chicken. "He's mad at them. He keeps saying, 'They gave up on me. How can you keep on going, Lil, when they give up on you? Tell me that!' The poor guy can hardly stand up, he's so weak. He even cried once. Forty-five years of marriage, I've never seen that man cry. It must have killed him to do it in front of a woman. But he's been better since. It cleared the air. I told him to put it out of his mind now, to look on the bright side.

"His sister's staying with us now, but she's feeling punk too. Glaucoma, and broke a hip last winter. She's still on the walker! We had to get a visiting nurse in one day last week. We were all laid up and pitiful. Grace tripped on the rug and fell with the walker on top of her. Bill tried pulling her up, but that knocked *him* out, and we had to call the rescue because he couldn't get his breath. The dog was barking, and Grace was blubbering because she couldn't get up, and Bill wheezing and choking. You couldn't help but laugh, it was the most pathetic thing I've ever seen."

And what happened next? Aunt Rita asked. (Only Loretta was laughing.)

"Oh, someone came in for the day, a Miss Cutler. She straightened us all out. She put me to bed—I'd been out of the hospital only two days, and I was taking care of *them!* She got him on the respirator and then the rescue came and took them both to the hospital for a few days. They checked for breaks and fractures. Poor Grace—her bones are like eggshells. Mine are thin, too, but if I fall, I break one, maybe two. Grace falls, she breaks them all!"

Lilian had finished filling the trays and stood there grinning, a spatula in one hand and a spoon in the other. "She had broken some she didn't even know about. They told me they found real old ones that had healed on their own. Imagine that! And she's only five years older than me.

"I tell Bill, cancer or no, he's lucky his bones are strong. All those years laboring couldn't have hurt. It's too bad, the cancer. He'd live to eighty, easy. His father lived to eighty-five, buried the wife. Now *that's* unusual. His father died sitting up in a chair watching 'Jeopardy'—just like my mother.

"As it is," she said, putting down spoon and spatula and drying her hands on a towel, "the doctors tell me—him they don't tell, but he knows—that he won't live to see Christmas. Or if he does, it'll be his last."

While the lady talked, some of the seniors, playing cards or pool, crocheting doilies and drinking Postum or Kool-Aid, sitting by the window or looking at the calendar, had crept up to the kitchen doors to listen. Lilian was so absorbed in her story and her work that she didn't notice, but when she had finished, she turned and there were the old, curious faces. Aunt Rita tried to shoo them away: "Clara, take Clyde here and play him a game of checkers, why don't you?" Clyde was pushed away in his wheelchair, but the rest stayed. They had questions they wanted to ask Mrs. McVey: there were parts they didn't understand, and other parts that they could clarify; they had stories of their own they wanted to tell: this was their subject!

When Aunt Rita started ordering them back to their card tables and chairs at the far end of the room, Lilian McVey told her to leave them be, what harm were they doing? A story worse than their own might give them a lift.

And it did—Loretta could see that it did. The center was crackling with conversation, giddiness and a weird kind of tension. She looked to Aunt Rita to see if *she* understood, but although Aunt Rita had matured a little, and on her own, she still didn't know why such a story gave them a lift. Loretta knew why, but she didn't tell. This was exactly the kind of thing people had to figure out on their own. If you told them, they wouldn't believe it.

The aunt was studying Loretta's face with an odd expression, a timid expression that Loretta had never seen before. Then, she smiled; it was a smile like Eileen's, fake-looking because of the emotion it was trying to mask. There was a lot to be learned about this smile, but Aunt Rita, unfortunately, was the last person on earth to tell stories. She kept her stories, hoarding them: at sixty years old, she was still a mystery to everybody.

But it was time to pack the car with baskets, and then Loretta and her aunt were on their way. In the car and during the deliveries, Loretta kept her eye on Rita: the aunt was at her ease with all the ancient loonies; she didn't seem to notice how bad their houses smelled or how ugly they looked. She gave the olds their dinners, she talked to them in a friendly way and then drove off. There seemed to be nothing left over when she was finished: no feeling, no thought.

When they got home, Aunt Rita was tired and she took a nap. Later on, Uncle Ted served them drinks on the porch, where they waited for a breeze. It had been hot and humid for days. The bay was still, rusty-looking in the glare. "We're stupefied," Loretta wrote, "so I'll stop here and write tomorrow." She had used up several sheets of the flowered stationary on this one letter. There was only one sheet left.

He would read these letters walking up the four flights from the mailbox. He could picture life day by day in the four-room condo and on the highways around it. He could imagine the effects of this life on a neurasthenic like Loretta, frail and alienated. She was making it sound funny, but it wasn't really funny. What was funny about it? It had a bleak quality, and was even more depressing at a distance, but she didn't seem to realize that, or she would have spared him. Still, he made himself read every word. The recent letters were about the heat and mugginess affecting everybody's mind. They affected his mind too; he was having horrible dreams and the only thing getting him through the days was reading Sartre—better than he had thought, although certainly limited—and the occasional conversations with Gloria or Margaret, or with both of them. Lately, Margaret and Gloria were busy, they were doing theater together and had joined some women's group. They were easily annoyed by his talk, and they showed it. So he saw less of them, read more, slept more, borrowed cat food from Larry because he never remembered to shop; he was tired all the time, yet plagued by insomnia, so he was taking three or sometimes four sleeping pills a night, and when they finally worked—*if* they finally worked—he would sleep all through the next day.

He carried the new letter into the apartment and put it into the candybox where he kept all her summer letters. The apartment floor was littered with paper and books, but the handwritten letters were neatly folded into their envelopes and stored in the box on his worktable. Under the box was a stack of drawings Loretta had made before she went to the hospital. He had numbered the drawings and studied each one carefully. He had the time; he was experiencing his time, every expanding and contracting minute of it, as pain. Pretty soon, he thought, he would be picked clean as a bone by the penance of this abandonment. Whatever she did, he felt he deserved it. No being was more worthless than himself. He curled up in the bed under a sheet and felt the cat's body tucked up against him.

Loretta had been gone five weeks and the summer, in everybody's opinion, had lasted too long. It was still too hot, although much of the waxy green color of the foliage had turned rusty and gold—"the bright pendants of death and decay," Daniel wrote in his journal. Soon, though, the cool dry winds of last fall and of the fall before would come back, circulate along the sidewalks, and by then—he hoped—she'd be back. She had said so in an early letter, but in every letter since he had looked for a date, and none was ever given. It seemed even hotter and stickier in New York than in that stale New England suburb, but every day he looked for a shift in the wind, and the sign (no wind, there's no wind, he thought, on days when he got no letter, but often two would then come stuck together the next day) of fall.

One night in early October, the temperature dropped thirty degrees along the New England coast, and the concrete hide of the condo was iridescent in the dawn. Uncle Ted had gotten up early and was patrolling the tiny beach in front of the apartment. The rays of red sunshine splintered over the dark waves and fanned up the condo's rough surface, picking out the bits of grain, glass and sand. The hurricane wall, too, was alive with sparkling points. He paced up and down the short beach: one end was blocked by a jetty; on the other side the beach simply disappeared, the sandy strip narrowing until the waves tumbled against tiers of seaweedy rock. It was the first time he really felt that he was living next to the sea, *on* the sea even. Dazzled by the sun at the horizon line, he had walked a little way into the water and his shoes and socks were wet, but he hardly noticed.

The aunt rolled over in her double bed when the cold wind sucked the shade against the screen and the square of light above her head curled up and disappeared. She was dreaming of a cat she'd had as a little girl, Maxie its name was, a tabby with white boots, asleep on the back porch rug and a baseball traveling through space to smash the hall window. Eileen did it, meaning her sister. And where was Eileen? Hiding in the house somewhere or sleeping in her crib. You always blamed me, she yelled, and I don't do nothing wrong.

Loretta, immobile, face pushed into the pillow, was in a cone of darkness, dreaming of finding a nest or a cave and fitting herself into it, part by part. And here was her mother pulling her out limb by limb. Sometimes the limbs stayed on, sometimes they snapped right off. Once she had been pulled out, her mother climbed in.

The aunt and niece awoke when they heard him frying eggs in the little kitchen, just a niche carved out of the living room and sheltered by a breakfast bar around which Aunt Rita was already marching to get to where she could interfere with the cooking. When the first hot ball of angry words was shot, Loretta was out of bed and in the back bedroom, searching the bottom of her suitcase for the train schedule. Lots of trains were going south to New York, Philadelphia, Washington, Savannah and Miami. She picked the Penn Phoenix because it was going all the way. She was going to live somewhere else, another part of the country—or right on the edge of the country, near the ocean or in some other distant, lovely, place where you could look out the window and not see another window, or hear these voices—always voices—spitting and boiling in frustration. She emptied the contents of her drawers into the suitcase, and hearing the sudden commotion, her aunt and uncle flew into the room. "I'm going," she said.

Poor Daniel, meanwhile, was waiting, although he was asleep. A call was about to come, but his phone was off the hook and his sleep unmolested for the time being. He was stretched corner to corner across the flimsy bed, rolled in the blanket with an arm across his face. Books strewn on the floor and a chairful of clothes, dirty dishes on the counter with the armies of roaches and ants evacuated after a night of fruitful raids, and a mountain of daily newspapers and magazines under the window.

It was 8:40 a.m. Someone was knocking, now pounding on Daniel's door. Peewee was sitting on the bed, looking. Daniel lay still, burrowing his way along a cable, inside the cable where it was dark and pestilential, although filling up with perfume and clear marbles of bubble bath, soft as they touched him, as they pressed him here and there, but didn't hurt. This was something better, and he could breathe until they started to invade his nose and mouth.

It was Margaret and Gloria who were awakened by the phone call from Larry. Margaret talked to him and then woke up Gloria. They got up, dressed, drank coffee, paced around the apartment, but they were still afraid. They marched crosstown in sweater and jacket, stunned, and Gloria felt the cool of the morning and pondered how much heat must gather during the day from all the swarming bodies, cars and trucks. Neither ventured out until afternoon, so the morning was fresh territory. On the Village streets there was much industry they had never seen before—fruitmen and garbagemen, factory workers, street cleaners, and truckers hauling things into the city for the city's long and needy day. Margaret told Gloria that she would never sleep late again. "What difference would *that* have made?" Gloria snapped back. Margaret continued to talk, nerved up by the uncertainty, the earliness and the fresh air. Sometimes she stopped talking and would start to cry. Gloria was quiet—she was thinking. If Loretta would come back, she could go home. It was unbearable here. None of these people had any skin, let alone any system, to protect them from the encroachments of

life: she had to get away from them. She'd stay for a while, see
what happened. Something would happen. Things wouldn't
stay the same now.

Loretta did not receive the phone call. Uncle Ted was driving her to the station—not to the one in the city, but to the
village station near the ocean. They drove along a country road
lined by scrub forests and very old stone walls, some turf farms,
a few farmhouses and cottages. The two were silent in the car
and—midmorning on a weekday—there were no other cars on
the road. The landscape was not dramatic: it was mostly flat
with stands of oak or pine on rocky ground. The sun was slicing
through the tall, dry-leaved trees and baking the stacks of pine
needles and oak leaves fallen to the ground. It smelled a little
rotten, the way fall can smell, when things are still alive, but
overripe and starting to decay.

"This is your favorite season, isn't it?" asked Uncle Ted,
and she nodded—not wanting to start a conversation that
promised to be as awkward as the one before—when Uncle Ted
suddenly braked. A squirrel–was it a squirrel or a rabbit?—
jumped out in front of the car. He flung an arm across the seat to
keep the passenger—safely buckled—from flying through the
windshield, an automatic gesture from the days when there
were no seatbelts. The hand hit her in the neck and left a mark
there. "Are you okay?"

And then, suddenly, the sun had gone in and you could feel
the wet rawness of the season through the glass; the leaves were
changing and a few maple trees burned through the dull landscape with a red or yellow luster. She was thinking about
Daniel. She hadn't heard from him in a couple of days, and had
the oddest sensation. She felt he was almost present, but not in
the usual way: as if he were speaking, but not in his familiar
language.

And it was later, when they had arrived and Uncle Ted was

waving from the platform, that she felt him beside her again in the empty seat, laying his heavy head on her shoulder, speaking to her—not speaking, but whispering in that feathery, whistling tone that poor Eileen had used that beautiful winter day when they had met again and sat together in the peacefulness of the day.

About the Author

JEAN MCGARRY grew up in Providence, Rhode Island, around the time of Vatican II, and thus is old enough to have experienced, firsthand, a Solemn High Mass, sung in Latin by three priests in full sacerdotal regalia; yet she is also young enough to have watched the church, and other neighborhood institutions, flounder and go out of style. After twenty years of Catholic school, McGarry graduated from Harvard, spent some years as a reporter and musician, and later studied fiction writing at The Johns Hopkins University, where she now teaches. McGarry has published two books of fiction, *Airs of Providence* and *The Very Rich Hours*, and has had stories published in the *New Yorker*, the *North American Review*, *Southern Review*, and other literary journals. She has received fellowships from the National Endowment for the Arts and from the Bread Loaf Writers' Conference. Her first book won the 1985 *Southern Review* LSU Short Fiction Prize, although it wasn't about the South. When not writing fiction, McGarry sometimes writes prose poetry and was awarded a Pushcart Prize for "World With a Hard K." Her prose poems have appeared in many magazines, including *Sulfur*, *Temblor*, and the *New Orleans Review*.